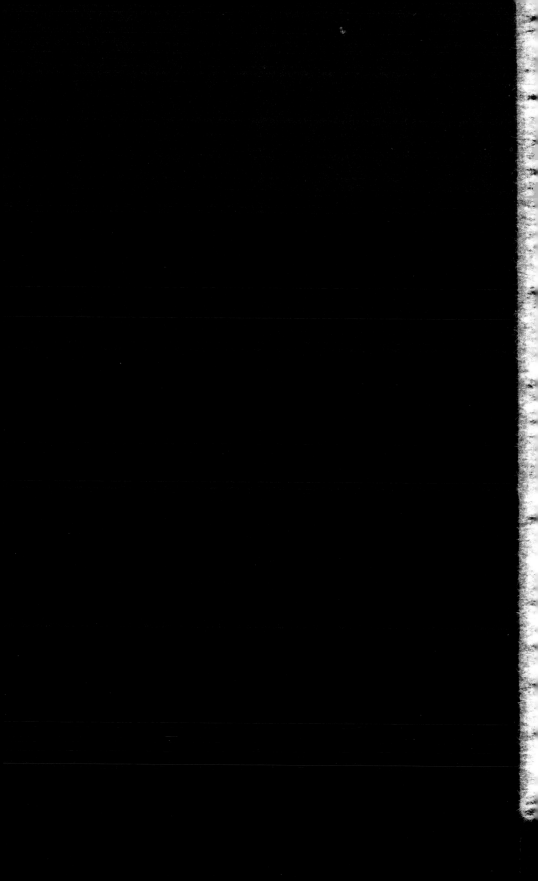

OUR LADY OF ALICE BHATTI

ALSO BY MOHAMMED HANIF

A Case of Exploding Mangoes

MOHAMMED HANIF

OUR LADY OF ALICE BHATTI

JONATHAN CAPE
LONDON

Published by Jonathan Cape 2011

2 4 6 8 10 9 7 5 3 1

Copyright © Mohammed Hanif 2011

Mohammed Hanif has asserted his right under the Copyright, Designs
and Patents Act 1988 to be identified as the author of this work

First published in Great Britain in 2011 by
Jonathan Cape
Random House, 20 Vauxhall Bridge Road,
London SW1V 2SA

www.vintage-books.co.uk

Addresses for companies within The Random House Group Limited can be found at:
www.randomhouse.co.uk/offices.htm

The Random House Group Limited Reg. No. 954009

A CIP catalogue record for this book
is available from the British Library

ISBN 9780224082051 (HARDBACK)
ISBN 9780224094085 (TRADE PAPERBACK)

The Random House Group Limited supports The Forest Stewardship Council (FSC®),
the leading international forest certification organisation. Our books carrying the
FSC label are printed on FSC® certified paper. FSC is the only forest certification
scheme endorsed by the leading environmental organisations, including Greenpeace.
Our paper procurement policy can be found at
www.randomhouse.co.uk/environment

Typeset in Sabon by Palimpsest Book Production Limited,
Falkirk, Stirlingshire
Printed and bound in Great Britain by
Clays Ltd, St Ives PLC

For Hassan Dars
1968–2011

هر ماتُهو ۾ چور نچي ٿو
هرماتُهو ۾ مور نچي ٿو

In every man dances a thief
In every man dances a peacock

ONE

LESS THAN THREE MINUTES in front of the interview panel and Alice Bhatti knows in her heart that she is not likely to get the job advertised as Replacement Junior Nurse, Grade 4. A sharp tingling in the back of her neck warns her that not getting the job might not even be the worst thing that could happen here. No questions have been asked yet, but she knows that all the preparation – her starched white uniform, the new file, a faint smudge of mud-brown lipstick, breathing exercises she has done to control her jumpy heart, even the banana she ate on the bus to stop her stomach from rumbling – all seems like wasted investment, halal money down the haram drain, as her father Joseph Bhatti had put it. 'These Muslas will make you clean their shit and then complain that you stink,' he had said. 'And our own brothers at the Sacred? They will educate you and then ask you why you stink.'

She has been in this room before but is dreading the prospect of sitting down on a chair and talking. She has always stood here and taken her orders: *Have you cleaned the floor, Alice? Why have you not cleaned the floor? Who do you think will clean that blood on the floor, Alice? Your father?*

The room is a monument to pharmaceutical merchandising: the orange wall clock from GlaxoSmithKline, the calendar with blonde models in various stages of migraine from Pfizer Pain Management Systems, the box of pink tissues promising Dry Days, Dry Nights. The ornamented gold-framed verse from the Quran exhorting the virtues of cleanliness carries the logo of Ciba-Geigy: a housefly in its death throes.

Alice Bhatti wonders if she can put in a request to be interviewed while standing. She shifts on her feet and tries to become

I

invisible by clutching the file to her chest. The file contains nothing except a copy of her job application. She doesn't get the opportunity to ask anything as the interview panel is too busy debating the cost-benefit ratio for patients on pacemakers. They are at the end of a heated argument and everyone wants to get the last word in. She doesn't really understand what they are talking about, only wonders why she was called in if all they were going to talk about was electricity generators, ventilators, running costs and heartless relatives of the deceased arriving from Toronto or Dubai, brandishing their grief to save some dollars or dirhams, refusing to pay up, holding ambulance drivers hostage, demanding compensation.

She has an odd sensation of overhearing a conversation that she is *meant* to overhear. She thinks maybe this conversation is part of the recruitment exercise; she'll be asked her views later and she should pay attention. The head of the orthopaedic unit only brings up words like 'professionalism' and 'Canadian immigration' when he is angry. Ortho Sir is very angry by now. 'I am a professional.' He pulls out a pink tissue from the Dry Nights box and pats the bald patch on his head. The grey diamond-shaped mark on his forehead is a testament to his five-times-a-day prayer routine, but his designer goatee belongs in some kafir fantasy. 'My job is to cure people, to cure them at the worst of times. I don't decide when someone is going to die. He does.' He raises his forefinger towards the ceiling. Alice Bhatti looks at the ceiling fan in confusion: *Put Your Faith in Philips*, it says.

If the relatives of the deceased are in Dubai and Toronto, she wonders, then what is the deceased doing in this death hole otherwise known as the Sacred Heart Hospital for All Ailments. *Rights of admission reserved*, it says in three languages on the signboard at the entrance. *Enter at your peril*, someone has scrawled under it, summing up the customers' sentiments. *Leave your firearms and faith at the gate*, says another sign under a small wooden cross, slightly askew and not painted in a long time, in the hope that people will forget that it's a Catholic establishment. This is not the kind of gate where anybody leaves anything, this is not the kind of place where people forget where you come from.

Senior Sister Hina Alvi sits on the interview panel with a paan tucked in the right side of her mouth, her tongue occasionally licking the crimson juice before it can become a dribble. This well-timed anticipatory lick will remain her main contribution to the proceedings. Alice Bhatti doesn't need an advanced nursing degree to know that Sister Hina doesn't like her. The only consolation is that there isn't much that Sister Hina Alvi does like. Alice smiles at her in the futile hope of winning her over. Nothing. She looks at her terrifying poise, the imperceptible movement of her jaw, the crimson lips, and her eyes that seem to be taking part in the discussion, and realises that Senior Sister Alvi's feelings towards her are slightly stronger than indifference: she hasn't yet decided whether this Alice woman even exists or not. Dr Jamus Pereira, the chief medical officer of the hospital, is Alice Bhatti's only hope on this panel; he is the CMO for no reason other than the fact that he inherited the Sacred from his father, and he inherited it because of his inability to say no. But who can say no to a dying father who is pressing the family bible into your hands?

He sits with his fist under his chin and seems to be wondering how long before Ortho Sir will start healing multiple fractures with the power of his principled stance.

Alice looks at him and realises that if Dr Jamus Pereira is your best hope in this world, you'd better abandon all hope.

'And what do you want?' Ortho Sir looks at her as if she is a child trying to interrupt a grown-up conversation.

'A and E vacancy.' Dr Pereira speaks before Alice Bhatti can turn and run. 'Please have a seat, Alice.'

Normally Alice finds Dr Pereira's politeness irritating – *Sir, if you don't mind, I would like to inform you that the gentleman you accompanied to this hospital at the time of his admission has breathed his last.* She always thinks his struggle to bring order to this world through the practice of good manners is a bit pointless. But she likes every word of it now. She likes the fact that he has called her Alice. It implies acceptance, professional fellowship, even intimacy, an innocent type of intimacy. She likes the way he has uttered the word 'seat'.

She also realises that when you start feeling gratitude to people for asking you to sit down, you are obviously not at the top of your game.

'How many candidates have we got?' Ortho Sir looks at his watch impatiently. He is on a break from being a humble professional. This usually happens when underlings are around. In private he can make his superiors feel like little gods. When he is brazen and publicly rude, the network of veins on his bald head swells up and you can see them turning green with anguish, like an alien realising it's not going home for a long time. That the earth has run out of the fuel that his spaceship relies on.

'Only the lonely,' Dr Pereira says, looking optimistically at both his colleagues. Senior Sister Alvi curls her lip in a smile that seems to suggest that she knows the con, has heard the joke before, but is too far above all of this to bother.

'Then why do we have to go through this?' Ortho Sir pushes the file away and looks at Alice Bhatti.

Alice Bhatti looks at a lizard on the wall, desperately willing it to move, as if its movement will affect the movement of her stars.

'Procedures,' says Dr Pereira. 'And if my colleagues here have objections, we don't have to, we can advertise externally. But there are not many qualified candidates with experience. Privates snap them up. Or they go to Dubai or Toronto.' There was a time when he could assert his authority and claim that the hospital was built by *my* father and named after *our* Holy Mother so why should anybody have a problem hiring a nurse who happens to be Catholic? Now he must stay polite and humble in all his little battles.

'All the good ones go to Dubai and Toronto.' Ortho Sir is mild now – and mean, having fully exposed the inherent inefficiency of the system. He has just received his Canadian visa and it has given him more confidence than those twenty-five years of setting bones in an operating theatre, even more than his two trips to Mecca. Spiritually, he always reminds his colleagues, he feels much more settled now; he quotes from the Hadith, which says something about knowledge and having to go to China. Nobody reminds him that Toronto is not in China. Not yet.

Senior Sister Hina Alvi looks at them with contempt, as if they have stepped over some invisible boundary of good taste, as if words like 'procedure', 'vacancy' and 'candidate' are vulgar and shouldn't be used in front of ladies. She does all of this with a little twitch of her upper lip and a pat on her steel hair.

Senior Sister Hina Alvi has thirty-five years of bedside experience, she has worked through riots and massacres and saved the life of a foreign minister's wife. She knows about these things. Alice Bhatti is always surprised how Senior Sister can get the world to obey her with the movement of an eyebrow.

Alice Bhatti first sits on the edge of the chair, feels dizzy, then fears that the chair might slip from under her and she will end up sprawled on the floor with her legs splayed in the air. She moves back in the chair, the chair squeaks and she puts the file in her lap, then picks it up and clasps it to her chest. Then realising that she is making a spectacle of herself, she puts it back in her lap and thrusts her hands under her thighs, to stop them from trembling.

'So are you Alice or are you Bhatti?' Sir Ortho believes that this country can only progress if people start spelling out their middle names, tucking in their shirts and paying his full fees in advance.

'Both. That is my name.' Alice Bhatti feels silly having to explain her name. There might be things in the application she has embellished, but her name is not one of them.

'I am surprised that you are trying to hide basic information. Your full name is Alice Joseph Bhatti. Are you ashamed of your father's name? Now Bhatti is a respectable clan from Punjab and I am sure the Josephs are a respectable lot from wherever they are from. Let me tell you something: my father was a schoolteacher and went to teach in a school on his bicycle for thirty-five years. Same route. Same bicycle. Am I ashamed of him now? No, that bicycle is parked in my garage, along with my Camry. So that my kids can see it and learn. Do I hide it from the world? No.'

Dr Pereira's administrative intervention comes in the form of a polite cough, the clearing of an already clear throat and his fingers playing a half-remembered jazz beat on the table. He was practising his drums with the Hawks Bay Kittens the night his father called him and before breathing his last handed him the Sacred Heart Hospital for All Ailments. 'The application form doesn't have provision for middle names, and Bhattis are pretty much everywhere, in every religion, so if we can start the—'

'So, Miss Alice Joseph Bhatti, why should we give you this job?' Ortho Sir asks her without looking up and starts scribbling furiously in his file. The bicycle-riding-schoolteacher's son has come this far in life because he knows when to move on.

Senior Sister Hina Alvi looks at her with a beatific smile, as if already forgiving her for all the mistakes she'll make in the rest of her brief and miraculous career. Dr Pereira sends her silent messages: *Praise Our Lord Yassoo, now don't let me down, child, not in front of these Muslas.* Short, to-the-point interventionist prayers are Dr Pereira's other management tool besides good manners.

This is simple. Alice Bhatti knows the answer. She has rehearsed it in front of the mirror. But now she needs water. Her heart beats in her parched throat. A strange croak comes out of her mouth, a voice that surprises her, the voice of a baby frog complaining about being too small for this world. She notices, for the first time in her life, that the lizard has four feet.

'I have qualifications . . .' She realises that she has forgotten the rest of her answer. She decides to carry on recklessly, like a pedestrian caught in the middle of a fast lane who decides that if they close their eyes and rush forward they will end up safe on the other side. It all comes out in a jumble. Accident assessment. Paediatric management. First-aid course: FA second division. Serving patients and humanity. Taking care of the sick and dying. Experience in TB ward before it was closed down. Personal setbacks. Difficult patient-and-doctor relationships. Maternity ward internship. Flexiworking.

Having spoken for one whole minute without fainting, Alice Bhatti takes a deep breath and realises that she has just blurted out everything she was supposed to say over the course of the entire interview.

An ambulance siren sings in the distance, and the ceiling fan suddenly picks up speed. Her dupatta flares in a gust of wind and the faces of the three people sitting in front of her blur into a crowd, a crowd that is headed for a pre-planned lynching somewhere else but decides to first warm up on a stray dog. The ambulance siren comes very close and Alice remembers a dream she had the previous night. She is in an ambulance, the ambulance is a ball of fire, it's rushing *away* from the Sacred. She had been puzzled in her dream. An ambulance on fire she can understand. What was she doing in the ambulance? Why was her face covered in ice cubes? Why was the ambulance rushing away from the hospital?

'According to the modern principles of nursing and the patient-carer relationship . . .'

'Did you say you worked in Accidents?' Sir Ortho cuts her short, then pats the alien on his head. 'Oh. Of course. Sure you worked in Accidents. Didn't we have a little accident there? How could I forget?' Alice Bhatti cannot believe that Ortho Sir would remember her face. She remembers his face, though. She

7

remembers a bucket and a mop and a river of blood on the floor. She remembers him tripping over her mop.

It seemed half the city had shot itself in the stomach and spilled its guts over the A&E floor during the shift that she worked as a replacement paramedic.

'Since when does mopping floors count as A and E experience?' Ortho Sir mime-mops a floor with his hands. 'Pereira sahib, if today I work here as a sweeper and tomorrow turn up with an FRCS degree hanging around my neck, will you hire me as Head of Orthopaedics?'

Dr Pereira, a third-generation physician, shakes his head, not in denial but in despair. He is too polite to point out that not all Christians are sweepers. He also fears the retort: 'But all sweepers are Christians.' If Alice Bhatti didn't want this job so badly, if she hadn't stretched the gap between her nursing-school years and her first house job to cover the fourteen months that she spent in the Borstal Jail for Women and Children, she could have told him what her mother had told many a man in her life: if I shove that mop up your arse, you will walk around like a peacock. Instead she ignores Ortho Sir and glances at the boy sitting in the corner, scribbling away, a peon pretending to be a poet, taking notes as if he is taking down minutes in a board meeting, as if he understands anything. As if he could write a straight sentence. She doesn't really mind the scribbling – after all, that is his job – but she doesn't want Noor to be here. Not today.

Later, people will say that they shouldn't have given her this job – any job – that they should have imposed strict patient–carer separation, that she should have stuck to her own and married in her own religion (there are obviously those who will say that she was not the marrying type to begin with), that she should not have carried that Gillette razor in her uniform pocket. Some will say that marriages made at sea always end up in disappointment, others will just mutter that there is something called modesty and will argue for a redesign of the paramedics' uniform. Someone else will say that this hospital has been around for 107 years and its main purpose is to save lives, not suck cocks in VIP rooms. Tongues will wag and pens will do their moral forensics, but that will come much later.

Here, seated in front of the interview panel, Alice looks at the lizard and is surprised to notice that its front feet have five toes. Fourteen months of staring at lizards on the Borstal walls, Alice Bhatti berates herself, and I never noticed they have five toes. It'll be a miracle if I get this job.

Senior Sister Hina Alvi chimes in with her betel-nut-soaked voice. 'Dears, we have to use work-experience girls sometimes. Otherwise how would we manage?'

She manages to give both words – 'girls' and 'experience' – a whole new context.

Ortho Sir moves forward in his chair, clasps his hands, and fixes his eyes on the file in front of him. The alien on his head seems to have decided to make this planet his home.

'Postnatal care?' His eyes are level with Alice Bhatti's breasts. 'Inverted nipples. How do you deal with them? Should you deal with them? Have you any personal experiences to share?' Ortho Sir rolls his tongue around his gums as if there might be nipples stuck between his teeth.

Lewd gestures, whispered suggestions, uninvited hands on her bottom are all part of Alice Bhatti's daily existence. She has a whole doctrine perfected over the years to deal with all of that, but there is something about this parched tongue tracing circles around the receding grey gums that makes her shudder. It is in this moment that Alice Bhatti realises that even if she gets this job, she might end up castrating someone. Or at least gouging a pair of eyes. Or slashing a tongue. Or pulling up those gums with pliers to cover the shame of the naked teeth.

She looks up at the lizard again. It has moved but it isn't going anywhere. It stays stuck to the wall like an emblem that has forgotten its purpose.

Alice Bhatti had woken up that morning to the sound of Joseph Bhatti sawing a large wooden beam he had brought home last night. That was the only thing he had brought home all month, and he was now busy cutting it into a cross as big as an electric pole. She had woken up thinking she'd better get this job.

But she hadn't woken up thinking of a tongue going around, licking imaginary nipples. Has she missed something about the gesture? Is she overreacting?

As she walks out of the room at the end of the interview, she stops by the boy, Noor, who is still scribbling. He lifts his eyes to acknowledge her presence for the first time. 'Is your mother dead yet?' she asks with the indifference of someone who has just flunked a job interview. Then she lowers her voice to a whisper. 'There is a police van outside. I hope they are not here for you.'

TWO

'If there is one thing I have learnt about our hospitals it is this: when these doctors get drunk, they suddenly remember their principles, their stupid oath . . . what is it called? That Hippo-something.' Inspector Malangi puts an arm around Teddy Butt's shoulders. 'Even doctors who work in this slaughterhouse. You would think the mornings are a safe bet. But look at us now. We are being fed medical ethics for breakfast.' His hand traces the immense bulging shoulder that won Teddy Butt the title of Junior Mr Faisalabad three years ago.

Like most people in local governance, Inspector Malangi knows that an arm around someone's shoulder is the first step towards law enforcement. His battered blue police Hilux is parked close to the steps that lead to the A&E of the Sacred, a handcuffed man lies face down in the cabin, and three members of his team with rusting Kalashnikovs slung on their shoulders are leaning against the vehicle. Inspector Malangi seems unsure of all that he has learnt in thirty-six years of policing this city. With his walrus moustache and sunken eyes he could pass as a high-school headmaster, but with three stars on the shoulder of his black cotton shirt, his low-slung police belt and an ancient Beretta in his side holster, nobody is likely to mistake him for anyone except the head of the G Squad trying to finish his shift and go home. The Beretta is only decorative, though. He has drawn it sometimes and fired it close to people's ears when they were not paying attention. But otherwise every time he has had to use a weapon himself he has felt that he has failed at his job.

He walks towards the rows of concrete flowerpots, leaning on Teddy's shoulder as if trying to physically convey to him the burdens of his duty. 'You may not wear this uniform.' He fingers the epaulette on his black police shirt. 'But now you are a member of this family. You may think, what kind of family am I stuck with? But then everyone says that about their family. You may not love your family, but as far as I know, this is the only family you have got.' The concrete flowerpots are full of dried-up twigs and discarded medicine bottles and the occasional sprouting syringe. The whole abandoned gardening effort looks like somebody's good intentions got corrupted on the way. Inspector Malangi breaks a twig and starts poking his ear with such concentration it seems he is digging for an answer deep inside.

Teddy Butt is attentive and solid on his feet. When Inspector Malangi puts an arm around your shoulder this early in the morning and declares you a family member, you have to feel and behave like a loyal family member.

'So I have got a criminal but no crime that I can prove right now. Or at least that's what that whatsisname medico-legal Malick thinks. Did anyone tell him what happened in Garden East? When he is sober, you can get him to sign his own mother's post-mortem report. The bastard never looks at anything before signing, but half a bottle of Murree Millennium in his stomach and he is telling me I need some evidence, that suspicions of sabotage and intents of mass murder can't be proved in a medical lab. I have got Abu Zar in handcuffs but I can't keep him because a drunk Choohra doctor suddenly decides that he is not going to play God any more. What does he want me to do? Shoot myself in the head and then ask for a certificate that this fellow has hurt me in the line of duty? For three months we have been looking for the man responsible for the Garden East attack and I know it's him.' Inspector Malangi gestures towards the back of the van, and the man there moans like a dying animal.

Teddy Butt looks towards the tiny office adjacent to the Accidents and Emergencies department. A battered ambulance is parked outside, with its driver asleep with his head on the steering wheel. The board outside the medico-legal's office reads, *No arms or ammunition allowed inside the duty doctor's office*. Teddy stares at the tiny shack as if sizing up an enemy bunker.

'Why don't we book him for drinking?' he says. He likes saying 'we'. It makes him feel as if he is the one putting handcuffs on a renegade doctor who will not cooperate with the law this early in the morning. It makes him feel an integral part of the family.

'Yes, we can book him for half a dozen things. Do you even know how much a bottle of Millennium costs? How can he afford Millennium on his salary? Probably steals and sells kidneys. OK, Teddy, say we book him for that, what if his replacement doesn't drink but still has principles? Look, his shift ends in half an hour. And then you'll have to deal with Auntie Hina Alvi and, trust me, she has more principles than I have pubic hair. She has probably got a cock too. That woman scares me.'

Teddy Butt is not sure if he is supposed to laugh, so he chuckles as if clearing his throat. He is new to the squad, an honorary member, and is still learning the rules. He squeezes his empty hand into a fist and starts lifting imaginary dumbbells. He does this in cases of extreme darkness. When he did it last, he had gone to meet Inspector Malangi hoping to find work as an informer. He had taken a box of sweets with him but had found himself in a lock-up with half a dozen starving addicts in extreme withdrawal.

The Gentlemen's Squad is a group of like-minded police officers, not really an entity commissioned by any law-enforcing authority. The name of the unit doesn't exist on any official register, on letterheads or websites. There are no annual audits or medals for bravery; it does not hold press conferences to unveil the criminals it catches or kills, or more often catches and then kills. It is a group of gentlemen who, not given to any flights of literary imagination, have decided to call themselves the Gentlemen's Squad. It is a crew of reformed rapists (*I have got three grown-up daughters now, you know*), torturers (*it's a science, not an art*), sharpshooters (*monkeys really, as we spend half our lives perched on rooftops and trees*) and generally the kind of investigators who can recognise a criminal by looking at the way he blows his nose or turns a street corner. They have survived together for such a long time because they believe in giving each other space, they come together for a good cause like they have today, and then disperse to pursue their own personal lives.

'You know I don't like taking work home. The kids are preparing for their exams,' says Inspector Malangi. 'At my age I have to sit with them and do maths revision. Why don't you help out and get us something broken that'll look good to the medico-legal so that we can have this hero to ourselves for a few days? And then I'll get him to confess to Garden East and all the others that he has been planning.' Inspector Malangi pulls out a rusted Kalashnikov with a solid wooden butt, empties its magazine, then on second thoughts removes the magazine, puts it in his pocket and throws the rifle at Teddy. 'Something small will do. Just get me a thumb. Let's throw a bone to the dog and go home.'

Teddy Butt knows that this is not a suggestion, not even an order, just an expectation, how a father would expect to be addressed as father or abba or daddy by his sons.

'Here I go and here I come back.' Teddy snaps his forefinger and thumb before running off, not realising that this might be the last time he'll be able to snap his fingers, to produce that reassuring, consider-it-done sound.

Teddy runs past some patients sleeping on the steps, curses a sweeper who is raising clouds of dust in the corridor and finds Noor where he expected to find him, at his mother Zainab's bedside, massaging her feet gently and with dedication, as if a good foot massage was the only cure for the three types of cancer that Zainab is suffering from. Teddy gets his vitamins from Noor; sometimes before his competitions he gets a free IV drip to give his body that extra sheen that judges seem to love. Teddy believes that since Noor has learnt the art of making friends in jails, he would do anything for a friend.

Noor sees Teddy running towards him with a gun, tucks his mother's feet under the blanket and meets him at the door. Teddy knows that Noor doesn't like to conduct their transactions in front of his mother, so he speaks in an urgent whisper. 'I need a thumb, and I need it now.' He shoves the gun into Noors hands, as if handing over a receipt for a faulty purchase and demanding a refund. They both start walking down the corridor that leads to the back of the A&E, stepping over at least three people sleeping on the floor, stirring in their dreams.

'It's too early in the day. I am sitting in on an interview. I am on a short break, just came out to have a look at Zainab. I have to write lots of notes,' Noor mumbles, in the hope that he won't be asked to do something time-consuming. Or nasty.

'It's all your friend's fault. Inspector Malangi has got this guy Abu Zar in the back of the van. Very dangerous. But he is insisting that he hasn't done anything. You don't know these people; it'll take us at least a few days before we can make him talk. But your Dr Malick won't give us a certificate saying that this man injured one of us. Imagine, Dr Malick wants proof. When he gets drunk, he becomes all principled.' Noor stops to wheel a stretcher out of the way, but Teddy keeps talking, as if giving the context, pinning the blame, underlining the flaws in the system will somehow reduce the pain, or at least justify it, make it worth his while.

'Where are his principles when he is signing blank post-mortem reports? Inspector Malangi comes to ask for a piece of paper and suddenly he remembers his principles? Should we let an attacker go just because he hasn't attacked us yet? We can nail Dr Malick for that Millennium bottle in his office. Do you even know how much a bottle of Millennium costs? We can nail him for how he gets the money for that bottle. What does he sell, a kidney for a litre bottle? We have got death certificates where he has written "cause of death – renal failure" when the renal has been shot to bits, when the renal doesn't even exist any more. It's because of him that I need a thumb and I need it now. Because after his shift we'll have to deal with your Auntie Hina Alvi, and she has more principles than a man has hair. We can nail her too, but right now I need a thumb.' Teddy laughs a hollow laugh. Noor stays sullen.

They reach an electricity pole and stop. They both know what to do next. Noor is in a hurry to get back to give Zainab her medication and then rush to the interview. Teddy has his family's expectations to fulfil. They look up simultaneously towards the top of the pole, where a number of kites, perched on the electric wires, are waking up from their slumber and looking down at them suspiciously. Then both Noor and Teddy glance around to check if anyone is watching them. To their mutual dismay, nobody is.

'Will it hurt a lot?' Teddy asks, as if it has just occurred to him that what they are about to do is something that might involve some physical discomfort. Noor sighs, as if he can't understand why people keep asking the same question. He lives in a world where people want their share of pain measured, labelled, packaged, with its ingredients identified in plain language. They want it to come with an expiry date and a guarantee that there is this and no more.

He sees people crying before pain hits them. Will it hurt, they ask, how much will it hurt? They want a scale of this pain, they want it packaged in small doses. They ask, Will it hurt this much? as they mime a scale with their forefinger and thumb, and then widen it and ask if it will hurt this much or this much. And, like a professional, Noor always lies, because he knows that the anticipation of pain is slightly worse than pain itself, always shrugs his shoulders, pats their backs and says, 'Don't worry, sir, you won't feel a thing.'

'You won't feel a thing,' says Noor, tapping the electricity pole. 'For the first moment. Then your fuse will blow. All lights will go out. It'll hurt like nothing has hurt before.'

'Don't scare me, just do your job,' says Teddy, gripping the pole with his right hand. Then he changes his mind and puts his left hand around the pole, thumb pointing towards Noor, who is holding the gun by its barrel, wielding it like a cricket bat.

The electricity pole is splattered with leaflets and stickers and bits of graffiti. *The Coalition for the Protection of Honour of the Mothers of the Faithful*, reads the poster with a chador covering a faceless woman. *Liberty or Death*, demands a little sticker under a red hatchet and the proposed map of a state where liberty or death will prevail for eternity. Three slogans in different colours proclaim Dr Pereira to be a dog, a donkey and a Christian preacher.

Noor tests the rifle in the air like a batsman getting the measure of the swing he should expect.

'I used to play drums but I never made it to the band,' Teddy says mournfully, as if his thumb is about to be punished for not being an adequate drum player.

Noor rests the gun on the ground and mumbles, 'If you come back later, I could just give you someone's X-ray with a foot fracture or something.'

'No, Inspector Malangi specifically asked for a thumb. Let's not waste time. He has his children's exams coming up.'

Noor takes a last look at Teddy's hand around the electricity pole and notices that his forearm is hairless and has beads of perspiration running over it. It's a bodybuilder's forearm. Noor shuts his eyes, grips the muzzle firmly and swings the rifle with full force. The wood hits the pole and he hears a dull sound like a school bell announcing a break. The kites on the wires flap their wings and lift off. One of them shrieks as if to tell them to take their silly game somewhere else.

17

Teddy is relieved, but only for a fraction of a second, before he sees his thumb, alive and intact, a bit bloodless and white but still all there.

'I am the one who needs to shut his eyes. You need to aim. With your eyes open. Come on now,' Teddy says, shutting his eyes tight and gripping the pole with full force as if trying to uproot it.

It's only when Noor hears the bone crunch against the metal and sees blood splattering on the posters that promise a thousand-year war to protect the honour of the mothers of the faithful, with Teddy screaming and dancing on one leg and shouting unspeakable filth about Noor's own mother, that Noor realises that he should have administered a local anaesthetic. He has a cupboard full of that stuff in the supplies store.

Teddy doesn't look back to thank him, doesn't even remember to take the rifle back from him, but runs, cradling the remains of his thumb like a hunting dog dashing back to his master, carrying back the catch in triumph with the hope of a reward for a job well done.

THREE

If anybody had seen Noor the day he arrived at the gates of the Sacred, they wouldn't believe that he was the same boy who now sat in the Chief Medical Officer's room taking notes, acting all babu-like. He was only fourteen years old, pale and skinny as a stick, and nobody thought that he would be allowed into the building, especially as he had one arm around an old woman who wore cheap sunglasses and looked like someone who had just embarked on a career in panhandling. They wouldn't believe he was the same boy who now helped out the law enforcers one moment, then went to sit in a meeting and take copious notes another. When he had arrived, he knew only two words of English. Excuse. Me. And those were the two words that gave him a new start in life.

The day Noor arrived at the gates of the Sacred, he had to hold up his trousers with one hand and put the other one around the shoulders of his mother Zainab, who, after years spent in the relative quiet of the Borstal, was getting a migraine from the traffic noise. The two words of English that he knew, he tried on everyone. This irritated people. They looked at him with contempt. Multilingual beggars were still beggars; even worse, they were beggars with pretensions. Nobody paid them any attention. Beggars were trying new tricks every day, pretending to be white-collar workers fallen on bad times, with a smattering of chaste Urdu to soften hearts that had hardened in the face of the bottomless greed of half-naked children and droopy, blind old women.

Nobody could have imagined then that by the time he was seventeen he would be practically running the Sacred. When he said farewell to his friends in the Borstal, it would not have crossed their minds that one day he would be sitting in the same room as senior doctors, decorated paramedics, double FRCS holders, taking notes for important job interviews. That he would be keeping records of admissions and discharges, donations and expenditures. Yet it was the same boy who, three years ago, had been standing outside the gate of the Sacred Heart, holding his mother's hand, shifting from one foot to the other, reassuring her that he had got the right address, tugging his loose trousers, his farewell present from the Borstal Jail for Women and Children. Excuse me, sir. Excuse me, madam. He had repeated the words like a password that would grant him access to a world where people constantly excused each other. He was quite puzzled about the writing on the wall, which claimed that Dr Pereira, the man whose address he had been given when leaving the Borstal, was a dog. Why was a doctor a dog? Noor had thought he could read basic stuff, but he wasn't sure any more. Maybe the words had different meaning beyond the walls of the Borstal.

Dr Pereira's approaching car slowed down; he rolled down the window to shoo the beggars away, as he believed they brought the Sacred a bad name. Then he heard that sickly but clean-cut boy gently shepherding a woman shouting 'Excuse me, sir. Excuse me, madam,' to no one in particular. Dr Pereira could tell a well-mannered boy when he saw one, and the older woman holding his hand seemed to be in a lot of pain. Dr Pereira motioned them to get in the car. A beggar who excused himself before making his begging pitch was already making an effort to leave all that behind, Dr Pereira believed. A beggar with good manners deserved a chance to be asked a question or two.

Noor first settled his mother in the back seat, then climbed confidently into the front as if he had been waiting there for a lift. His confidence came from the fact that having spent his childhood behind the closed gates of the Borstal, he would have liked to barge through any door that opened for him. Walking into a room and behaving as if the room belonged to him was something that Noor had already learnt, at a time when other boys his age were only hanging from the windowsills looking in. He was sure that his secret code would work.

And now he sits in the room where Dr Pereira and his colleagues are arguing whether candidate Alice Bhatti has the strength of character to withstand the pressures of a busy public hospital. Noor might be sitting in a corner, but he is sitting on a chair. He will have to go and fetch tea in a while, but right now he is sitting on a chair taking notes, dutifully recording the minutes of the job interview. He knows that his words in the register will be the only record of this meeting. He leaves out Ortho Sir's stories, Hina Alvi's smile and Dr Pereira's despair, and since he is not required to record what he does in his breaks, there will be no mention of his little encounter with Teddy Butt around an electricity pole. A record of a meeting is not everything that happens in a meeting; sometimes it's better to leave things unwritten. Dr Pereira has encouraged him to make his own choices. Dr Pereira says that sacred texts as well as profane novels don't record *everything*.

Like most things in life, the result of this job interview depends on many things. Some of these things have happened long before the interview. Noor had tried to advise Alice Bhatti about the potential problems in the interview. 'Whatever you say, don't get angry. And don't mention Borstal.' And Alice Bhatti had shouted back in a mock-angry schoolteacher's voice, 'What Borstal, you little bastard?' Noor was scared for a moment, then he shouted back, 'Good. Now try saying that with a smile.'

He is relieved that Alice has managed to control her free-floating anger in the interview and that her time spent in the Borstal hasn't come up. It isn't as if she stole from her patients or cheated in her exams. She only almost killed a famous surgeon and did time for it. Noor knows that Alice is the kind of person who'll return a favour by saying fuck you too. He also knows that her fatal flaw is not her family background, but her total inability to say simple things like 'excuse me' and 'thank you'.

The notes that Noor takes sitting in the corner of the room, a fat register on his thighs, will not really be looked at. Noor is not a factor and his notes will definitely not be a factor in the decision to give Alice the job. It's a good thing that nobody asks him if he knows Alice, and if so where they met for the first time. Even at the age of seventeen, Noor knows that the appearance of the words Borstal Jail for Women and Children on anybody's CV will not increase their chances in a job interview.

Noor is a record-keeper, a steno, a secretary for those who are not budgeted to have a proper secretary. He is a scribbler by day, Zainab's son by night, and Dr Pereira's pet around the clock. After all, it's Dr Pereira who has plucked him and his mother from outside the gates of the Sacred, ignoring hundreds of patients waiting under the Old Doctor, a two-hundred-year-old peepul tree that was believed to provide medical care before they built a hospital and now just provides shade and firewood. It was Dr Pereira who gave them a bed, a job, a chance for Zainab to spend her last days in peace and for Noor to learn the skills that one needed to lead a fulfilled life. Noor is Dr Pereira's ticket to salvation. When he sees the boy hunched over his register, scribbling, Dr Pereira's heart swells with pride, he feels the hand of Lord Yassoo on his shoulder, His voice whispering Latin nothings in his ear.

Although Dr Pereira started him on his education right at the beginning, Noor wasn't completely unlettered before he arrived at the Sacred.

He learnt the alphabet in the Borstal after resisting for a whole year. They were very good about certain things in the Borstal. They tried to teach you to wash your hands and they made you learn to read the alphabet and some easier bits from the Quran. They also tried to bugger you at every possible

22

opportunity, but Noor figured out early on that the privileges that were promised after you conceded were temporary. You might get a vanilla ice cream or you might get taken out to a big mosque for Friday prayers, but there were never any guarantees. They could always beat you up and then accuse you of being a habitual homosexual. It wasn't as if you could go to the jail superintendent and complain that promises had been broken. Also, if you let one of them bugger you and said no to the others, the others felt offended. They felt that they were being discriminated against. People might put up with discrimination in the outside world, but in the Borstal they expressed their hurt by leaving burning cigarettes on your mattress at night, or sometimes they just took away your mattress while you were in the bathroom. In the outside world it might sound like a small deprivation and people might say that no mattress is much better than a burning mattress, but there were no replacements and you ended up sleeping on the cement floor for the rest of your term. There is nothing scarier than a sixteen-year-old in the Borstal who feels he has been discriminated against. Noor made it clear from the start that he was not that type, that he didn't like vanilla ice cream and had no particular interest in visiting the big mosque for Friday prayers. In fact, the first year he refused to learn a single letter of the alphabet, as he was certain in his eight-year-old's mind that there was a direct link between A, B, C and someone's hand creeping up your shorts.

Now Noor is learning to write properly. At the Sacred, he started by filling out admission forms, people's names and their dates of birth, their dates of admission. Patients were baffled when he asked them to spell out their names, because many couldn't spell their names or any other words. Nobody had ever asked them to spell anything. Most of them didn't know that their name was made up of letters they should have learnt. Noor asked for their identity cards, or any other bit of paper that might have their name written on it.

Noor wants to get their names right. He wants to get everything right. And here is his first big interview, and he is worried whether Alice is going to get this job or not. He is obviously on her side, because she is the reason he ended up coming from the Borstal to the Sacred: she scribbled the address for him and insisted that he go there and ask for Dr Pereira. But sometimes she says things like what is the difference between a doctor and a donkey? Sometimes she says it in a room full of doctors. When Alice got out of the Borstal, he managed to wrangle an emergency shift for her and she turned up in her civilian clothes and an oversized white coat. Beneath that frayed and stained white coat she could have been a housemaid, newly homeless, or a prostitute fallen on bad times. He felt as if a poor, uncouth relative had walked in when he was trying to impress his new bosses. More than anything else he is worried about getting the minutes of this meeting right. Long after Alice has left the room he is still scribbling away.

Dr Pereira looks towards him and nods ever so slightly, a signal for him to find an excuse and leave the room. 'Should I get some tea?' Noor asks, then closes his register carefully, puts it on his chair and leaves. As soon as he shuts the door, he starts to run and skip. Inside the room he is a brooding, attentive lackey; outside in the corridors of the Sacred he practises a bit of careless living, which, despite his precocious burden, he knows that as a seventeen-year-old he is entitled to.

When people see Noor, their first reaction is, look at that poor little boy, what a pity, working when he should be playing, but they can keep their pity to themselves because Noor considers himself a man of this world. More than even the harsh nights at the Borstal, he remembers waiting outside the gates of the Sacred. He and Zainab stood at the gate for two full days, and although it wasn't the kind of gate where anyone was stopped, the guard wouldn't let them in because they looked like a pair of vagrants, the kind of people who would try to walk through every gate they saw. Someone threw them a half-rotten orange. A beggar walked by and advised them that it was an unlucky spot for starting this kind of work.

People could have called him a poor little boy then because he was the only child of Zainab, and had nobody in the world except some kind friends who were still in jail, who had altered an old pair of trousers for him, stuffed ten one-rupee notes in his pocket and promised to look him up when he became an officer in a big bank. But now Noor is not a poor little boy. He is a ward boy. His name is not on the employees' list but he has more responsibilities than any paramedic with a full-time, pensionable job. His services are acknowledged. Zainab may not be in the best of health, but she has her own bed, adjustable, it goes up and down; it has a pillow, a blanket, sheets that get changed every few weeks; a curtain separates her from the other miserable wretches on the ward. There are hundreds of patients who are envious, who are eyeing that bed. All the people under the Old Doctor are practically on the waiting list.

It has taken him three years to achieve his place in life, but Noor is a man now. He puts food on the table even though there is no table. He fills up the registers in the hospital. On the night of the Garden East attacks, when all the doctors and sisters had their hands full, he took out a bullet from the shoulder of a victim. He hasn't read *Gray's Anatomy*, but there is nothing in that fat book that he hasn't seen strewn on the floor of A&E. 'We stitched up one hundred and forty-three people that night,' he boasts to anyone who is interested in those kinds of statistics. They also charged the relatives of the deceased five hundred rupees each for not carrying out post-mortems. Dr John Malick, the medico-legal officer at the Sacred, had his gloved hands drenched in blood and his white coat's pockets brimming full with five-hundred-rupee notes. 'Look, we live in a city where you can get someone cut up for a thousand rupees. What is wrong with charging them half that money for *not* cutting them up? Do they want a post-mortem? No. Are they interested in the cause of death? No. Does it really matter to them if their lungs gave up first or their heart went pachuk? For them the cause of death is death; they died because death arrived in Garden East and they happened to be buying vegetables there. So buying vegetables is as valid a cause of death as any.' Noor obviously never got any share of that money, just a bun kebab and a can of Pepsi and a big box of diazepam for his mother. He managed to get Alice Bhatti on the shift, though. They needed help, and when he told Dr Malick that he knew this nurse who was between jobs, Malick just nodded and moved on to the next casualty. 'A shift here and a shift there,' Noor whispered excitedly in Alice Bhatti's ear. 'And before they know it, you'll have a full-time job here.' They were surrounded by eight gunnysacks full of body parts that couldn't be identified and placed with any of the deceased.

The morning outpatients are beginning to mill around, occupying prime positions right in front of the barred windows, under the signboards that warn that spitting, chewing paan, attacking paramedical staff and talking politics are punishable offences. Some have spent the night adjacent to the window and are still yawning under their worn-out shawls. The patients and their families under the Old Doctor have broken some branches from the tree and started breakfast fires. They look like a ragtag army that has lost its way and is running low on supplies, the kind of army that can't make up its mind whether it has besieged a castle and is waiting for reinforcements to launch the final assault or just waiting for an ambush to relieve the men of their misery. Something will definitely need to be done about these fires. Noor makes a mental note. He is also the self-appointed health and safety adviser to Dr Pereira.

He notices that the police van is still parked outside the A&E building. A small police party stands around looking glum, as if waiting for bad news. Teddy Butt is sitting in the back of the van, his thumb in an oversized bandage. He looks drowsy and doesn't respond when Noor waves to him.

The medico-legal Dr John Malick has finished his night shift but seems reluctant to go home. He stands outside his office looking at the sun, which is struggling to break through the morning smog. He seems to be complaining to the sun for coming out too early. It is as if he has lots of things to do that can only be done at night, things that will have to wait for his next night shift. Dr Malick is the kind of doctor who actually believes in healing himself. He usually makes this face when his duty hours end before he can finish his nightly bottle of Millennium.

'Has your jailbird got the job?' Malick shouts to Noor, trying to stifle a yawn.

'She's got it,' Noor shouts back. 'A temporary one. You didn't hear it from me. And please take care of my friend Teddy. He has hurt himself again.'

'Congratulations. All the jailbirds are going to end up here,' Dr Malick shouts back.

FOUR

ALICE BHATTI GOES ON her first visit to Charya Ward alone, but returns an hour and a half later kicking and screaming in Teddy's arms. No one warns her what awaits her in that forgotten loony bin, no easing-in time, no guided tours, and no orientation course. A slow Monday in A&E, and Sister Hina Alvi thrusts a clipboard in her hands, papers frayed at the edges as if somebody has been chewing on them. Sister Hina Alvi is broad and philosophical in her brief, even sympathetic, which is a surprise, because she usually blames the patients for their own plight. 'They eat too much, drink too much, lust too much, can't stay indoors when they hear gunshots out on the road; they are attracted to bomb blast sites like flies to . . .' She usually finds a rotting seasonal fruit to complete her analysis of the state of the national health. But today she seems in a generous mood. 'These boys in Charya Ward are suffering from what everyone suffers from: life. They just take it a bit more seriously, sensitive types who think too much, care too much, who refuse to laugh at bad jokes. Same rules apply. No touching, no personal information. They can be a bit talkative and lovey-shovey. And although you look like somebody who doesn't need any more love,' Sister Hina Alvi looks Alice up and down as if trying to decide the right dose of love for her, 'people can be greedy. Even if you need it badly, you are not likely to find it there. Just remember it's called a nuthouse and there's a reason for that.' She opens her handbag, takes out a heart-shaped crimson pouch and starts preparing a paan. 'But as far as I am concerned, the whole country is a nuthouse. Have you read Toba Tek Singh? Nobody reads around here any more. Manto wrote about the nutters in a charya ward and then ended

28

up in one himself. His own family put him there.' She counts out three silver-coated betel nuts and places them on a leaf, rolls it and puts it in her mouth.

Alice notices that Sister Hina Alvi never offers anyone else one of her paans. She might spend the whole day surrounded by patients and doctors but she is solitary in her pleasures, always glowing with some personal insight, content in a world that makes sense only to her and happy in the knowledge that she doesn't need validation from anyone. 'I don't know if you have done any psy-care, but there is only one rule you need to remember: you have to tell them that everything is normal. They might have buggered their own sister and then buried her alive, but you must tell them that it's normal. They obviously did it because some god told them to do it. Of course I don't think it's normal for them to do it or for their god to ask them to do it. But in that ward you have to pretend everything is normal. That's all you need to know about psychiatric care.' Sister Hina Alvi takes out a lime-green handkerchief from her purse, wipes it gently around her lips, and then examines it for stains. 'Do you smoke?'

Alice, who pretended to smoke an occasional biri in the Borstal, just to win the respect of her fellow inmates, is startled by the question. 'No,' she says. 'I tried it at school and it made me nauseous.'

Sister Hina Alvi gives her a benevolent smile, as if they share a secret now and agree that it should stay between them. 'Every girl does something. I really worry about those who say they don't do anything. I worry about the ones who actually don't do anything. Usually they end up with something worse than cancer.'

Alice Bhatti has an odd feeling that she is back in the Borstal being accused of not being woman enough. If only she could strip and show Sister Hina Alvi the knife wound on her shoulder or tell her about the time she kicked in the groin a Borstal warden who was in the habit of throwing their pens on the ground and then making them pick them up so that she could take a peek down the front of their shirts. Maybe some other time.

Alice Bhatti glances at the clipboard. It holds a standard-issue form with standard-issue names. Nothing there to reveal that these people live on the other side: six Mohammeds, three Ahmeds, two Alis. 'Whom do I hand over to after the shift?' she asks cheerfully, as if really looking forward to the beginning and the end of her shift. Sister Hina Alvi takes out a set of keys and gives her two chunky ones. 'Lock up the door, then lock the key in this drawer, and keep this one with you,' she says, patting the drawer. 'I need to go to the waxing person. If you ever decide to get waxed, let me know. There is a first-time discount with my girl.' She winks, gives Alice a bright smile and walks off, swinging her bag, the queen of a sick charya world.

Alice goes out after Sister Hina Alvi, but then retraces her steps and stands in the doorway examining the list. It is blank except for the medication column. Everyone, it seems, is on a single dose of lithium sulphate 10mg. At least they treat them all equal, she thinks.

She stops by Noor's station, where he is hunched over a register, scribbling away as usual. 'Who are we dispatching today?' she asks. He looks up and gives her a busy smile. Whenever Alice sees Noor, she sees a boy in torn shorts trying to sell cigarette butts to women in the Borstal, then running back to Zainab with half a banana or a piece of toast with a little butter on it, and then them both sitting in a corner and going through a 'no, you eat, I already ate' routine.

'Psy ward,' says Alice Bhatti, fanning herself with the clipboard. 'I think I am supposed to collect some lithium sulphate from you.'

'Don't worry,' says Noor, burying his head in the ledger. 'I'll send it with a sweeper. We always do that. That's no place for a decent woman like yourself.'

30

Alice Bhatti can't decide whether Noor is pulling her leg or trying to teach her things about the Sacred she doesn't yet know.

'I am on duty, young Doctor Sahib. Sister Hina Alvi has briefed me all about it.'

'I don't think Sister Hina Alvi expects you to actually go inside the ward,' Noor says in a grave voice, almost admonishing her. 'Unless she wants to teach you a lesson. If I were you, I wouldn't go there alone.' Alice Bhatti is suddenly irritated with this kid who is always acting like he owns the place. An errand boy will always be an errand boy even when he is pretending that the world revolves around him.

'I don't sit around writing rubbish in notebooks all day. I deal with real patients.' She taps her clipboard. 'And these people are not dead yet.'

She leaves the room, ignoring Noor's feeble protests: 'I mean you shouldn't go there alone. I am saying take someone with you.'

'And who would that be?' She turns around and shouts at him before walking off.

On her way to Charya Ward, Alice notices a well-dressed woman holding an umbrella over a wheelie stretcher, covering her nose with her dupatta and looking into space as if pretending she is not in a corridor of the Sacred but in some fancy garden trying to spot migratory birds. She looks like a woman who might once have been rich, at least rich enough not to have ended up here, the kind of woman who is used to being served, the kind of woman who might have taught her servants to pour tea from the right and not from the left. The old man on the stretcher, with three plastic tubes of different colours coming out of his various orifices, is in a deep slumber. Under his cracked oxygen mask, a little froth is bubbling at his chapped lips. The woman is embarrassed to be here, and her shame seems to have marked an invisible circle around the stretcher; people walking in the corridor look at her umbrella, smell her disdain and step away.

Alice doesn't notice the barrier that the woman has erected

31

around herself and the person on the stretcher. She walks up to her. 'Can I help?' she asks. 'Why are you holding that umbrella?' The woman looks at her in horror, as if she had never expected to be spoken to in these corridors. Then Alice follows her gaze towards the ceiling and sees a wet patch that looks like a map of a country in transition. It drips a fat, milky water drop at regular intervals. 'Ah, that,' Alice says. 'Just the baby ward toilet overflowing. Nothing to worry about. I have already reported it.' She takes hold of the stretcher and starts to push it. 'We can just move him.'

'No.' The woman screams, covers her mouth with her dupatta and then breaks into civilised little sobs. 'Thanks. Don't want him to wake up and see that we have brought him here. We are just taking him home. I can't stand it here. This place smells of death.'

Alice shrugs her shoulders and walks on. This whole place, she thinks to herself, is a big Charya Ward. Then she remembers that Sister Hina Alvi has told her exactly the same thing. She smiles to herself and keeps walking.

As she nears Charya Ward, she realises that the usual smells – disinfectants, spirits, dried blood, stale food – have started to disappear. She can see potted plants, pots chipped and plants dead, and moss growing in the cracks on the walls. An arrow painted on the wall points towards the ward, with the words *The Centre for Mental and Psychological Diseases* written in English and Urdu. A half-faded notice under it reminds visitors not to give the inhabitants any cigarettes or drugs or food and to take responsibility for all their possessions. Alice Bhatti walks the walk of someone who thinks they can overcome their fear by taking measured steps. She passes through a swing door, the nursing station inside is empty and covered in dust. Not only have no medical staff been here in recent days, even the sweepers have stopped visiting. Someone has scrawled 'I ♥ My Psychology' on the dust-covered station. A side door stands half open. The room is damp and musty and it takes her a while to recognise the smell. It is the smell of a barbershop in summer. The Rexene-covered padding on the wall has been chewed up and scratched, and only occasional streaks of foam rubber remain, which makes it look like the walls have developed a skin rash. She sees what appears to be a bird's nest in one corner and steps towards it. As she bends down to have a closer look, she recoils and rushes out of the room. She has seen some grotesque things in her life, but a nest the size of a football made of grey human hair with a live rat at its centre is not one of those things. The little rat, its red eyes ablaze with suspicion, scurries across the floor.

'This way, Sister.' A shaved head peers out of the double door. An old man puts a finger on his thin lips and beckons her. 'Surprise them,' he whispers. 'Reveal yourself.'

Alice Bhatti looks at her keys and tries to hide her nervousness behind a polite smile. She wields her clipboard like a shield, and gives the old man a benevolent nod, like heads of state bestow on ushers before moving on to guards of honour.

As the door swings open, they all stand in a line, a dozen of them, not in an orderly sort of line but in three files, with hands folded at crotches, heads bowed. They look at Alice and then look beyond her, and when they don't see anyone following her, they disperse as if they had taken her for someone important and now, having realised that she is an ordinary nurse, all alone, feel disappointed but relieved.

'We knew you were coming. We were told.' A shrivelled old man goes into a corner, takes his pants off and starts shouting at the top of his voice: *Dard aur, dawa aur, dard aur, dawa aur.*

Another one goes over to him, slaps him and shouts, 'No mother tongue here. Did you bring your mother with you? Then why are you complaining in your mother tongue?'

'They told us you'd come,' says a tall man with a bushy moustache and a turquoise handkerchief tied around his neck. 'They told us three months ago, but now you have come. You are late. But you are here now.'

33

Then he goes down on his knees and prostrates himself in front of her as if he is in a mosque. Alice Bhatti has seen people do this in the Sacred's open-air prayer area, and the gesture has always seemed a bit ridiculous to her. Raising your arse to the sky has never seemed to her the best way to express your devotion. But that is probably the best some people can do. There are those who walk on their knees in Nazareth. To each their own, she believes, not that you can talk about these things in public and hope to live. Even to express your bafflement is to invoke the wrath of God's henchmen. She feels the man's tongue licking at her toes, and tries to move back. The man grips her ankles and pulls. She flies into the air, the clipboard in her hand hits the ceiling. Her first thought is that if she doesn't get that chart back, Sister Hina Alvi will be very very angry with her. Missing documents make Sister Hina Alvi angrier than patients defecating in the Sacred corridors. She should have held on to the clipboard, whatever else might have happened.

Alice feels she is airborne for a long time, and then she lands in the waiting arms of two men, who shout 'Howzat!' like deranged cricketers.

They lift her up in the air. She feels exalted. And scared. 'Lord. Yassoo. Yassoo. Save me.'

'Welcome,' they say. And she feels she is on a bed of hands and being carried by twelve men who seem to have emerged from various levels of hell. It's like she is a part of some private celebration as they shout, *'Ya Alice! Ya Bhatti!'* A new arrival shouts, 'Death to America,' but finds himself out of sync and falls into their rhythm, like casual marchers do at a protest. There is something drone-like but pacifying about their gibberish. There is comfort in knowing that these people actually need her help. Dawdling in the air, supported by twelve men, for a moment she feels like an animal from a species not yet discovered by scientists.

They put her on a bed that has no sheets, and the Molty Foam label on it has been slashed to reveal mud-brown sponge underneath. It looks like the skin of a diseased dog. They hover over her and whisper: 'She knows how we live and how we die. She knows. She knows.' She sees one man hitting himself repeatedly on the chest with her stethoscope, another item of hospital property that she should have held on to.

'Don't do that,' shouts the old man in the corner with his pants around his ankles, both hands covering his privates. Half his dentures are broken to accommodate a swollen tongue that stirs like a sleepy animal trying to wriggle out of a cage. 'You'll hurt yourself,' his voice booms in the room. 'Do you want to hurt yourself? You are not allowed to hurt yourself. Hurting yourself is against the law.'

Alice Bhatti sees Teddy entering the room, his Junior Mr Faisalabad arms frozen to his sides, his eyes squinting. With the arms of his T-shirt ripped to show off his heavy shoulders, he looks like a window display in an expensive butcher's shop. The thumb on his left hand is covered in a soiled bandage.

Here comes the chief charya, she thinks.

She has seen him hanging around A&E. She knows that he is some kind of pimp for the police and medico-legal. She has always ignored him. She thinks she knows who has sent him on this rescue mission.

'Leave her alone!' he shouts. It doesn't come out as an order, though. It is more like a hoarse, tiny shriek, as if someone has stapled his vocal cords together. Alice Bhatti has read many stories about women being hacked and burnt or simply disappearing in the corridors of the Sacred, and now Sister Hina Alvi has told her that she should consider everything in this place normal. Alice has a feeling that although she can fight and cajole these twelve loonies, this towering hulk with a funny voice is going to be her real nemesis.

'She has been sent for us,' the man with the turquoise handkerchief shouts at Teddy. They all huddle behind her. 'You can't take her away. She'll be sent back. You'll see that she'll come back for us.'

35

'Unauthorised personnel are not allowed in the ward,' Alice screams, as Teddy scoops her up. 'I still need to give them lithium sulphate.' As she is carried out of the ward, cradled in Teddy's arms, Alice Bhatti is still gripped by the fear of not having done the job she was assigned to do. She tries to scratch his eyes out. She kicks and screams, hitting him with clenched fists, then trying to claw his face. She spouts the kind of filth that has been heard in these corridors before but only from its residents, never from the medical staff. Teddy Butt walks unfazed, jerking his head left and right to avoid her punches; they look like a boy and his father in a mock boxing match. Through it all Teddy grimaces and whistles a happy song: *We are one under this flag. We are one. We are one . . .*

Teddy is surprised that she is so light, so bony. He has carried men before, but they are heavy, even the young ones. They also squirm a lot, always begging to be let go. He feels he can carry her and walk the earth. He feels she has been sent to cure his festering thumb. Maybe to cure all the other wounds he is likely to suffer in his career. But we need to put some flesh on those bones, he thinks. He wants to nurture her. He feels he has been allowed back into a school of happiness from which he was expelled a long time ago.

FIVE

NOOR GOES TO CHECK on Zainab in the middle of a shift and finds a swarm of flies hovering around her face, two feasting on a little dribble in the corner of her mouth. He takes the hand fan from her side table and shoos them away. He soaks an old bandage in a bowl of spirit and wipes the area around Zainab's lips, her chin, and her wrinkled neck. Her forehead is cold and her grey eyelashes that normally flutter during her sleep are absolutely still. He turns back after depositing the wipe in a dustbin to find that Zainab's mouth is slightly open and one of the flies has returned and is sitting on her upper lip. He tries to flick it away without touching Zainab's face, but the fly crawls into her mouth and Zainab's lips close. Noor stands there panicking and wondering if he should squeeze her nostrils to force her lips open so that the fly can come out. Above the thin lips and wrinkled cheeks her nose is young, wide and shiny, as if transplanted as an afterthought. As Noor's hand touches Zainab's nose, her lips part and the fly comes spinning out. Zainab's eyes open and the whites do a little dance, as if laughing at Noor and asking him, *What were you thinking? Did you think that I was dead?*

Noor covers her face with a piece of white gauze, sprays Finis around her bed and goes away, slightly embarrassed but elated at the same time. When she pulls a trick like that, he feels a childish joy and forgets about the three types of cancer racing to gobble up her vitals.

'So what is it really like? What happens when people die?' Noor asks Alice Bhatti, who after finishing her shift has changed into

37

a loose maxi and is lying down on a wheelie stretcher, her forearm covering her eyes. A half-torn poster on the wall behind the stretcher says: *Bhai, your blood will bring a revolution.* Someone has scrawled under it with a marker: *And that revolution will bring more blood.* Someone has added *Insha'Allah* in an attempt to introduce divine intervention into the proceedings. Some more down-to-earth soul has tried to give this revolution a direction, and drawn an arrow underneath and scribbled, *Bhai, the Blood Bank is in Block C.*

'I have done shifts in the maternity ward. I think I have some idea. I think it's exactly like childbirth.' Alice Bhatti removes her forearm from her face but doesn't open her eyes. 'It just starts and you push and push and then it leaves your body ruptured and exhausted and dead so you don't really know if you are just exhausted or dead. You are surrounded by all these people who are saying all kinds of prayers, prayers to save their own lives, prayers to make it easy for you, prayers to get a nice little house for themselves in paradise while expecting you to push harder and harder. You Muslas have a prayer for everything. It's like they are groping in the dark, hoping to get hold of something for you. It's like you are in a race that you must finish. It doesn't matter if you win or lose.'

Noor listens and watches Alice Bhatti's arm, which is white and fleshy above the elbow and dark and scrawny below it. He wants to touch both parts to find out if they feel different.

'Why can't they live a bit longer? I mean not for ever, nobody lives for ever, but if they are given the right medicines, if they are given the right diet, they should have a few more months at least.' Noor is looking away when he asks this. His query is genuine, he has thought about it for days, but he is thrown by the fact that Alice has taken off her bra along with her uniform.

Noor is feeling at home and horny at the same time, comfortable and confused. He used to wonder whether his body had been overtaken by the devil that Dr Pereira kept warning him about, whether this tingling in his loins was the work of the evil one. Now he knows it's called growing up. Teddy has told him that if a man goes nine seconds without thinking about a woman, chances are that he is not really a man. Teddy claimed he saw it on TV.

'Even when you are eating or peeing?' a bewildered Noor had asked.

'I think they mean that you can think of a woman's body parts, not the whole woman. Her mouth or her hair maybe,' said Teddy.

'Yes, I know what they mean. In fact nine seconds is too long a gap. I think about them all the time,' Noor had replied.

Alice turns towards him and props herself on her elbow. 'Don't be a child.' Her right breast rolls and falls over her left. In all the time that Noor has thought about them, he has never imagined her breasts cuddling themselves, like two abandoned puppies confusing each other for their mother.

'It's different for different people,' she says, her expression that of an experienced surgeon trying to choose the right scalpel. 'It's a real fucker for TB patients. It's like a fine silk shawl being dragged through a thorn bush. It leaves their soul in shreds.' The layer of Tibet talcum powder in her armpit is streaked with sweat. She stops twisting a lock of hair with her forefinger and puts the finger on Noor's chest. She draws a careful circle. 'Heart. People with heart problems are lucky. It just stops then tries to start again and then they are dead.' She falls backwards on the stretcher, her neck lolls back, her breasts shift into their original position.

To Noor she looks the opposite of death. For about nine seconds he doesn't think of a woman or any of her body parts.

Now he sits beside her, and the wheelie stretcher under them sways and screeches as she turns over towards him again. Noor's behind is pressed against the abandoned puppies.

'And when you find out that it's about to happen, what do you do? What do you tell them?'

She shrugs her shoulders with her eyes closed. 'I turn off the

39

IV or oxygen or blood or whatever it is that they are on. Why waste it on someone who is already dead?'

'You never talk to them? Don't you ask them about their last wish, note down their last words for their families?'

She opens her eyes and looks at Noor as if he has suggested a sexual act that she has never heard of.

'Do you know how much I get paid in this hospital?'

Noor feels ashamed of himself. He feels as if he has just accused her of not doing her duty properly.

'It's not as if they are going to write me into their will.' She sighs. 'Sometimes I read the kalima, if they look the type or if they ask for it. Sometimes if they are in a stupor I read it anyway, because I know that if they could talk and believe that they were about to die, they would ask for it.'

'You know the kalima?' Noor asks her. The fact that this Catholic girl who hates all Muslims and most of their Catholic cousins could be reciting the kalima to the almost dead depresses him.

'Silly boy, there are lots of things that I know and you don't. You'll learn.'

Alice turns onto her other side. Now Noor is back to back with her and he can feel her quivering spine. She lies still and waits. Noor knows she wants to be asked something. Sometimes she wants to tell him something. But she wants to be asked first.

'You are hiding something from me,' Noor says. This has happened with Zainab too, lots of times. He has to guess and ask her the right question. Women talk differently. Boys tell anybody anything; in fact mostly they do things so that they can tell somebody. Even if people don't want to hear. But women want to be asked. Properly. He has learnt that in the Borstal.

Alice turns her face and looks at Noor, slightly startled, as if he has addressed her by another name.

'I can look at someone's face and tell.'

'I can too.' Noor tries to cheer her up. 'Ortho Sir would rather be an imam in Toronto and convert all Canadians. Dr Pereira wants to write a book about his life but is too shy and hopes someone else will write it. He actually thinks he is training me for the purpose. Sister Hina Alvi thinks she can run this country better than the Bhuttos. And who knows, she probably can. At least she knows when to keep her mouth shut.'

Alice Bhatti is not interested in Noor's talents. She needs to tell him something.

'I can look at somebody's face and tell how they are going to die.'

'Easy if you have their medical records in front of you.' Noor has a strange feeling that he must not find out whatever it is that she is trying to tell him. Sometimes it's good not to know things. 'If a diabetic's sugar level is point six plus and BP lower than one twenty, I can tell his relatives that he'll collapse in the bathroom because of heart failure.'

Alice Bhatti puts both her hands on the edge of the stretcher and bends down. Noor can see a layer of talcum powder between her breasts as well. He's not thinking of women or their body parts. It doesn't do anything for him. Suddenly he feels no desire. He feels like a child who is about to be told a secret about grown-ups that he doesn't really want to know.

'No. Not patients. People. Ordinary people on the streets. I just know. I look at their face and then I see their dead face and I know how they will die.'

'Like your father? Didn't Mr Bhatti cure people by reciting something? You showed me in the Borstal with a candle and a glass of water.'

'Yes, he had only one trick. For stomach ulcers . . . but sadly not many people had stomach ulcers in French Colony. It's a rich man's disease.'

'You could do better. You could start a business. Send us your photo and we'll tell you how you are going to die. You could make lots of money. You can have your own Friday column in a newspaper. You can have your own segment on Telefun.'

'I can't tell from photos,' Alice Bhatti says. 'I have seen hundreds of pictures of Yassoo all my life, but I still can't tell how he died.'

Noor makes a last effort to save himself from her knowledge of death. He removes himself from the stretcher, walks around it, stands in front of her and mimes a hammer hitting a nail into a cross. Streaks of sweat are now running across the talcum-powder patch. She seems tired of having seen so many dead faces.

'I told you I can't tell from photos. I can't tell about babies and young boys, because they always die suddenly.'

'Have you looked in the mirror?' Noor knows, has known all along, that this is the question he is supposed to ask. He knows that he could have asked about himself, but he has already been dismissed as a young boy, and young boys die suddenly, reason not important, and reasons can change at the last moment anyway.

She stands up and crosses her arms over her chest and squeezes them as if trying to steel herself against this cruel world.

'Yes, I look in the mirror. I don't see anything.'

Noor is relieved. He can't imagine Alice Bhatti dead. With her flushed cheeks, and the scar on her chin glowing, she looks like everything that is not death. 'Doctors can't always heal themselves,' he says. 'Your Yassoo couldn't have resurrected himself. Moses couldn't have baked all that manna by himself.' He could have gone on in his attempt to change the subject and narrate the world history of unintended consequences, but he looks at her pale face and stops.

Her voice comes out different. Scared.

'It's not a miracle. It's a bad dream. Actually I can see something in the mirror. But I don't recognise it. It's not me, it's not even a human face. It's a ghoul. I get frightened.'

'Don't be frightened of your own reflection. We all have bad moments in front of the mirror,' says Noor. 'You should probably get married. I have heard that a good husband is the only cure for bad dreams. You know why? Because then you are sleeping *with* your bad dream.'

SIX

THE DAY JOSEPH BHATTI is required to go to court for his daughter's bail hearing, he goes looking for a lawyer. He hasn't got any money on him, but he has done his homework and brought his satchel that contains the tools of his craft. He stands outside the lawyer's office and reads a hand-painted sign on a piece of cardboard. It seems the lawyer can't afford to employ an assistant or even a signboard painter. The piece of cardboard on the door reads: *S.M. Qadri, MA, LLB, civil, criminal, property, divorce, cut-price oath commissioner.*

Mr MA LLB is sitting in his chair contemplating a full glass of milk.

'Stomach ulcers?' Joseph Bhatti asks without greeting him. 'You have tried everything.'

The lawyer shakes his head mournfully. 'I have tried everything. Allopathic, homeopathic, hakims, black magic type things even: white pigeon's blood mixed with young lizard's tail ash. Disgusting stuff. Probably illegal, too.'

Joseph Bhatti listens patiently, then pulls up a chair and sits down. 'Milk. Yes, it works. For a little while maybe. But not everyone likes milk.'

The lawyer clutches the glass of milk as if about to throw it in Joseph Bhatti's face, then gently pushes it aside. 'The only thing that works. But only two hours. And it tastes like castor oil. Have you ever tasted castor oil? My mouth tastes of castor oil all day. I don't know for what sins I am being punished. I spend half my life trying not to throw up.'

Joseph Bhatti notices a calendar on the wall behind the lawyer. The calendar has a camel silhouetted against a desert sunset and some Arabic calligraphy. Joseph Bhatti has heard from someone that there is not a single camel in the Musla book, and yet they can't seem to get them out of their minds. What has Musla God got to do with camels? Why are they stuck on this ugly beast? What's wrong with horses? What's wrong with horses with wings? Hell, what's wrong with trains? Why all this hooves and humps pornography? Do they really think their creator lives in a desert and travels on this ugly, vicious animal? There was a time in Joseph Bhatti's life when he could have stood at a street corner and made a speech about camels, but these days you never know. Especially with people who like calendars with tastefully photographed camels.

He takes his glass tumbler, his candle and matchbox from his satchel and lines them up on the table, as if about to perform a little magic show for the lawyer.

The lawyer looks at the tools of his trade doubtfully and says, 'Will it hurt?'

'Not if you get my daughter Alice Bhatti out on bail. She is appearing in Session Court Four this afternoon. Cooked-up charges of assaulting and causing grievous bodily harm. Try and stay still, it might tickle a bit.'

The table is cleared, the lawyer takes off his shirt and lies down. Joseph lights the candle, puts it in the lawyer's navel, and stares at it and slowly counts to ten. Then he puts the glass jar on the candle, and as the flame goes out and the jar is filled with swirls of milky-white smoke, he shuts his eyes and starts to recite Sura Asar. *By the declining day, man is in a state of loss . . .*

The lawyer looks at him in panic, as if he has been conned into joining a dangerous cult. He is a street lawyer and he has seen all kinds of perverts in his business, but a Christian Choohra reciting the Holy Quran with the zeal of a novice mullah, he has never seen. He is not even sure if it's legal.

In a free market, it's not always the best person who reaches the top, but if someone manages to, people find out. Stop

45

anyone hunched over a blocked drain in this part of the city and ask them who is the best. They won't name a company, or their uncle, or the chief janitor in the Municipal Corporation; they'll say Joseph Bhatti of French Colony. Even in French Colony, not many are born with the instinct to smell a sewer and tell what's blocking it. He is retired now, but they still call him when they can't figure out what's stuck in the bowels of a gutter. He still goes out during downpours and works voluntarily, because rains are rare in this part and they bring their own unique challenges. Suddenly you are not just making people's lives easier, you are saving lives.

The kind of rains they get here would delight Noah.

Like in every other profession, Joseph Bhatti had risen to the top through passion, dedication and natural talent, all of which were very rare in his line of work. God needed prophets, he tells his co-workers, so that they could take care of your refuse, otherwise humanity would have drowned in it. But it's not his deft touch with a blocked drain that impresses the church. Reverend Philip suspects him of being a closet Musla. What kind of Catholic goes around curing stomach ailments by reciting verses from the Quran and lighting candles?

French Colony has a history of producing not just sound sanitary professionals, but also idiot saints every few years. One day you are down in the gutters and smell like a leftover from some plague, and the next moment you are a healer and a prophet with people nailing jasmine garlands to your door. You've got a queue of people outside your shack who want you to heal their measles, you double people's savings, predict the correct cricket scores and soon your reputation spreads to the outskirts of French Colony, which brings in the non-believers who are in financial or love trouble and an occasional flash car, and soon Father Philip starts inserting jibes in his sermon about sorcerers who are leading people away from Lord Yassoo's path.

Joseph Bhatti has never made any claims. People only believe one thing about this man with a full head of shiny grey hair and a jet-black moustache: that he has a ninety per cent record of curing stomach ulcers by chanting some Musla prayers. Nothing more. Nothing less. He can't secure you an Italian visa, he can't bring your spurned lover back, he can't make a venomous boss give you a bonus. He is hopeless when it comes to college exams, he has no advice for warring sisters-in-law or hopeless young men competing for the favours of the same whore. When people with any ailment that is not a stomach ulcer approach him he shakes his head, looks towards the sky and asks: 'When was the last time it rained in this city?' And when they remind him that it was only last year he says: 'I had nothing to do with that. I didn't order that rain to fall. I am not a magician, I am a Choohra. I just recite His words but I can't hold Him to His words. To tell you the truth, I don't even understand His words. I just light a candle and cover it with a glass jar and mumble His words. He is the one who cures.'

When Joseph Bhatti sees Alice at her bail hearing in the session court, he sees something of himself in her. Alice Bhatti carries her handcuffs lightly, as if she is wearing glass bangles. She treats the policewomen as if they were her personal bodyguards, and she looks at the judge as if to say, how can a man so fat, so ugly, wearing such a dandruff-covered black robe sit in judgement on her?

Joseph Bhatti looks around the court to see if there are any acquaintances present for the hearing. Since the case doesn't involve any claims of religious discrimination, any acts of blasphemy or disputed church lands, nobody from Lord's Lawyers or any of the human rights organisations has showed up. Alice Bhatti avoids eye contact with him. He feels a twinge of failure, a bit like going to see an old sweeper friend only to find out that he has set up a laundry shop full of spotless white washing machines, put up a neon sign and hired other sweepers to sweep the floor. Or running into others who have tried to find an opening in the church food chain, donned robes and are on their way to becoming a bishop of somewhere or serving their Lord in some picturesque Italian village. He has seen the postcards they send, and it seems to him that maybe Yassoo wasn't the eternal saviour of all mankind but a visa officer. People from the Bhatti clan have also caught the bug. He has seen their sons and daughters become cooks in four-star hotels, doctors, guitar players, even professors. He has seen them take on Musla names, move out of French Colony and become members of some other species. He has never shown any such ambition. 'I am not proud of what I do. I am not ashamed of what I do. This is who I am,' he often told Alice when she started nursing school. He did save up for Alice, he did send her to school, but he never dreamed of an old age where he would sit at home and live off her income. And he definitely never dreamed of sitting in a court hearing his daughter being charged with attempted murder. Mostly he has been an absentee father, almost embarrassed to come home to a daughter who tries to behave like a son and – like all sons – falls short.

The court clerk announces the State vs Alice Bhatti: Alice Bhatti *hazir ho*. Alice walks into the dock with her head held high, handcuffs clinking, staring purposefully at the judge as if saying: you?

There, Joseph Bhatti tells himself with a certain pride. That's my daughter. 'Your daughter is very pretty,' whispers the lawyer in his ear. And then Joseph feels sad: that's all his daughter is good at, looking pretty and bashing up octogenarian professionals. As if being beautiful gives her the right to behave badly. What kind of father feels pride at his daughter strutting around in a law court facing charges of disorderly behaviour and causing grievous bodily harm with intent to murder?

Joseph Bhatti has himself faced such accusations most of his life. What kind of sweeper goes out and cleans the city on his days off? What kind of Christian never turns up for Sunday service? What kind of Bhatti goes around healing stomach ulcers by lighting candles and reciting Musla verses? When his back was straight and his opium intake regular and pure, he would thump his chest and say: 'This kind of man. Joseph Bhatti Choohra. We were here before the Christians came, before the Muslas came. Even before the Hindus came. I am not just the son of this soil. I am the soil. Yes, I am Joseph Bhatti Choohra.'

It's only when Alice Bhatti is about to be led away and S.M. Qadri whispers a long-winded explanation in his ear and proclaims that the law is the eternal whore for those who can pay for its upkeep that Joseph Bhatti realises that Alice has been found guilty and sentenced to eighteen months in prison.

When the judge leaves his chair and everyone present in the court rises, Joseph Bhatti keeps sitting in petty defiance, keeps looking at Alice, hoping that she'll look towards him, maybe wave a hand, acknowledge the fact that he came, that he brought a lawyer with him. Alice does turn around, but only to stare at the judge, then she spits on the floor of the court and rushes out, two fat policewomen trying to keep pace with her.

Alice comes home four months early, not because of Reverend Philip's intervention as people assumed, but because all women prisoners get their term reduced by four months when someone important dies. Joseph makes her an omelette and puts it in front of her as if she had gone for a sleepover at a friend's house and has come back complaining of the bad food she was fed there.

'I found a baby in the main drain at the Ideal Housing Society,' he says, pushing a piece of cold toast towards her. Alice is not used to discussing his work with her. She is not used to talking about his work to anyone. In the Borstal her standard reply to any question about her father was: he works for the Municipal Corporation. And then she would ask them, 'What does your father do? Doesn't he work for the Corporation too?' As if not working for the Corporation was like being homeless.

'It was in a plastic shopping bag, just this big.' He stretches his palm, moves his other hand along his forearm, trying to get the size of the baby in the plastic shopping bag right. 'Wasn't much bigger than a kitten.'

'Boy or girl?'

'Girl. I think it's a sign.'

Alice pushes her plate aside. She feels she is still in the Borstal, taking bullshit because she has to, but knowing when to stop. 'Sign of what? I think it's a sign that there is no place a woman can go and deliver a baby, that there is no place for her even when her water is breaking. It's a sign that human life can be flushed down the toilet. It's a sign that nobody gives a fuck about signs.' In her head she scolds herself: she shouldn't have used the F-word. But in the Borstal you couldn't speak a whole sentence without saying the F-word and hope to be heard.

Alice can't fathom Joseph's new love for signs, symbols, mixed-up theology picked from random sermons, because he had always maintained the swagger of a Choohra, an untouchable with attitude, not the demeanour of a washed, devout Sunday Catholic. When Dr Pereira, in his days of community work, tried to get him off the opium, he said, 'If I am going to be called a bhangi all my life, I might as well have some bhang.' And after Dr Pereira left, he launched into a rant against him. 'Look at him lecturing us; we are the children of this land, we have lived here for thousands of years and they are just Goan kachra that drifted here on the waves of the Arabian Sea. Now they'll teach us how to be Yassoo's children when they are embarrassed by the fact that we are supposed to be brothers in faith. They'll teach us good manners. What are they? Our nannies? You know what they think? They think we are shit-cleaners. Yes, we are shit-cleaners, but what are they? Shit.'

Joseph Bhatti suddenly remembers that he is talking to Alice, his daughter who has just come home after fourteen months in the Borstal. He feels he should tell her about his life, give her some parental advice. 'I did your Pereira Sahib's house for a few weeks. To pay back for all the help that he gave us, all the petitions he filed. And they fed me in their Choohra dishes and then washed their hands as if I was spreading leprosy. They hovered around me at a distance thinking that if I touched something it would get contaminated. I'd rather clean up sewers. When I walk the streets, the streets belong to me. Have you noticed that when I walk the streets with my bamboo, they cross over to avoid my shadow? What are they scared of? Getting contaminated by their own refuse?'

'I don't know about others, but Dr Pereira is a decent person. He was my only defence witness. He even bailed me out the first time.'

'I know, they are good at that. Dressing up and turning up for events. Courts. Meetings. Prayers. Funerals.' Alice Bhatti knows by now that when Joseph Bhatti says 'they', he doesn't just mean Dr Pereira and his fellow doctors; he means anyone who has become a clerk in local government, or a receptionist at a foreign embassy, or a guest relations officer in a hotel; any woman who has set up a Montessori school in her living room, everyone who doesn't work for the Corporation. And even in the Corporation, if you have risen to become a supervisor, you have joined them.

'And then they turn up at church on Sundays wearing their suits and their devotion, as if Yassoo is not the saviour of all mankind but an usher who has got their names on the guest list, who'll escort them to the roped area in the VIP enclosure, as if he was born and died and was resurrected for the sole purpose that he can whisk them through the formalities and take them into paradise.'

Alice Bhatti starts collecting the plates and speaks without looking up. 'I am applying for a job, at the Sacred. I need money to buy a uniform. I'll return it to you when I get my first pay cheque.' She doesn't expect a straight answer. She actually expects no answer. If he has the money he'll leave it on the kitchen table; if he doesn't, he won't. He won't talk about it. He is as likely to talk about money as she is likely to tell him how she dealt with her periods in the Borstal.

He gets up and starts to go out, then stops at the door and looks back. 'Choohras were here before everything. Choohras were here before the Sacred was built, before Yassoo was resurrected, before Muslas came on their horses, even before Hindus decided they were too exalted to clean up their own shit. And when all of this is finished, Choohras will still be here.'

'Yes,' says Alice Bhatti, the fresh graduate from the Borstal. People can learn various crafts in jail: to pick pockets, to wield a knife, how to use your knee in a fight, to plant flowers in pots made out of cardboard or hook up with someone and hatch a plan to kidnap a film star, or to write poetry. Alice has learnt only one thing: to keep quiet and speak only when absolutely necessary. 'Yes, when everything is finished, Choohras will still be here. And cockroaches too.'

SEVEN

THE OUT PATIENTS DEPARTMENT corridor is cleared of motor-bikes, bicycles and anything else with wheels; there are no food trolleys, wheelchairs, stretchers. Even mops and buckets are piled along the wall, as if the Sacred is closing down for the summer. A gleaming double-cabin Surf, so new it seems to have just rolled off a Toyota assembly line, is parked in the corridor. Those who saw it bump and screech its way up the staircase, negotiating the steep ramp meant for emergencies, are still whispering to each other in admiration and awe. 'No, no, it's not 3400 cc, I bet it's 4200 cc. Yes, I know it's a four-by-four but it didn't even have to engage that to climb up.'

The number plate bears no numbers. In red lightning bolts it says *Devil of the Desert*. Everyone seems to understand what that means. Habitual sticklers for parking rules, especially grumpy ambulance drivers, approach it gingerly, planning to lecture the owners about parking etiquette. But at the back of the cabin, in the open half of the vehicle, are seated four men in uniform. It's not the uniform of any state institution or a recognisable security agency, just black cotton shalwar suits and crimson berets with a random number of stripes on their shoulders. Their Kalashnikovs are pointed vaguely outward, the muzzles lazily tracking any passer-by, even when the gunmen are looking the other way. There is only one person in the front, a driver sporting the same uniform but with more stripes, one arm dangling outside, holding a revolver and flicking its safety catch off and on out of sheer boredom. He seems like the kind of person who, if bored for too long, could start a small massacre.

Patients milling about the ward are not scared by this little militia; they are resigned to the fact that someone has arrived with a shiny new object and obviously the owner has every right to protect his investment. They had seen the owner step out of the vehicle: Rolex, Ray-Bans, Bally, Montblanc; he walked like someone wearing a million rupees' worth of accessories in a place where half a pint of O-positive costs two hundred rupees. It's only the grumpy ambulance drivers who have a problem internalising the notion that it's not just a vehicle with a whimsical number plate; it's movable property. It can't be parked just anywhere. They are missing the whole point. It needs to be protected, but it also provides protection. The vehicle occupies a space and then makes it its own, like a ferocious dog marking its territory.

'Your bedside manner has really improved,' Sister Hina Alvi tells Alice that morning, unexpectedly tousling her hair and then withdrawing into her professional reserve. 'But there is always room for improvement, so I am assigning you a room where you can really improve. VIP Two. Night shift. Don't think you are doing me a favour. I am doing you a favour. Fatima Jinnah spent a night there.'

Alice feels a bit baffled, first at her own ignorance about the history of this place, then at the fact that this knowledge is not likely to help her in any way in performing her duties. She does wonder how Sister Hina Alvi gets all that time to read history books. Doesn't she have a family to take care of? It must take her a couple of hours every day just to do that hair.

'Have you read her letters to her brother?' Sister Hina Alvi asks her and continues without waiting for an answer. 'Did you know that Fatima was a dentist, a trained dentist? But she sacrificed her whole life for this country. And how do we remember her? As an old spinster. Someone gives you their whole life and what do you call them: mother of the nation. Now if her brother is the father of the nation, how can she be the mother of the nation? They could have called her *sister* of the nation, but no. Because then people might have mistaken her for a nurse, one of us. It's a nation of perverts, I tell you.'

Alice agrees. Sister Hina Alvi might be a control freak, but at least she has a sense of history.

If the patient is so very important, what are they doing in the Sacred? Alice wonders. Why not Agha Khan Hospital, if they can't go to Singapore or Bangalore, where hospitals are like holiday homes, complete with kitchens and swimming pools.

'She is old money.' Sister Hina Alvi looks at Alice in a now-what-would-you-know-about-that kind of way. Her voice conjures up polished wooden floors, walls full of commissioned portraits, family names adopted from central Asian villages and combination lockers stacked with cash and secrets. 'Her father died here, her children were born here,' she says. 'She is not one of those new importer-exporter types who boast about their grandfathers dying in Cromwell Hospital. She has roots. And those roots are here.'

Alice Bhatti has a vision of the Old Doctor in the courtyard, its trunk made up of gleaming Hilux metal, its branches twisted Kalashnikov barrels, little birds in black uniforms and dark sunglasses and oversized berets hopping on its branches. Sister Hina Alvi sees a smile spread on her face and reminds her.

'You are on death watch, not on a picnic.' She puts the glasses on the bridge of her nose and spreads the newspaper in front of her.

Life has taught Alice Bhatti that every little step forward in life is preceded by a ritual humiliation. Every little happiness asks for a down payment. Too many humiliations and a journey that goes in circles means that her fate is permanently in the red. She accepts that role. 'I'll do my best.'

'Her name is Begum Qazalbash, but she likes to be addressed as Qaz. Convent education, a very self-made lady in a family where even the sixth generation of men don't have to do anything to make a living.' Sister Hina Alvi speaks without taking her eyes off the newspaper.

Alice Bhatti doesn't pay particular attention to the Surfer or its number plate. She has seen enough nicknames, poetic flourishes, family titles, fictional cities and urban legends passing themselves off as vehicle licence plates. She is not amused by somebody's high-school idea of looking important. Devil indeed, she thinks. Why don't they pray to their Devil of the Desert for their Begum of Qaz.

As she enters the corridor that leads to VIP 2, she sees a little gathering of men, a small army wearing black shalwar suits, sitting amid a jumble of Kalashnikovs, eating a meal from stainless-steel plates. They are passing around a naan the size of a tablecloth and are in the midst of a passionate conversation about the comparative merits of the country's best jails. Somebody suggests that Machh might be the most difficult to get out of but that it is the only one with running water in its bathrooms. 'More showers than I have taken in my entire life.'

'What showers?' Another guard speaks through a mouthful of food. 'You were probably jerking off your death-row friends. Didn't they call you Helping Hands?' The Machh jail man giggles and slaps the joker with a piece of bread.

Alice Bhatti stands looming over them and wonders how to negotiate this lunch party when one of them, an elderly man whose henna-coloured moustache somehow complements the mistrust in his eyes, notices her.

'Let her pass.' He moves the plates aside.

'Someone needs to search her,' the death-row slut shouts. They stop eating but keep sitting with their heads down. As if the only thing they haven't learnt in jail is to figure out when a woman stops becoming a threat.

'How do we search her?' someone asks. 'Can't you see she is a woman?'

'A sister,' someone else chimes in, licking the gravy from his moustache with his red tongue.

The plates are moved aside, the bread rolled, and eight pairs of eyes follow Sister Alice's feet like those of caged animals who have just learned to respect their new captor.

The double door closes behind Sister Alice with a discreet, expensive VIP click. A blast from the heavy-duty air conditioner hits her in the face and she smells roses. Later she will count eight bouquets of different sizes. There is the strong smell of coffee cake and green tea. She takes in the patient, a fat old woman with pink cheeks and silver-grey hair, the kind who is always described as a grand old lady, defying disease, her upper half covered in a two-coloured shatoosh shawl. Alice was once told by a transfer prisoner in the Borstal that these shawls cost as much as a two-bedroom house. A sandwich nibbled delicately at the edges sits on the bedside table on a huge china plate.

Two men, their ages indistinguishable and relationship unclear – they could have been thirty or fifty, brothers or uncle and nephew – are sitting in the lounge area, taking little sips from their cups and playing a quiet game of poker. The place is set for three people but the third position is empty, and they take turns playing for the absent player. Some old-money family tradition, she thinks. They look at Alice and nod with indifferent politeness. Their faces are puffy; too many late nights and fading illusions of power. The rustle of a fresh thousand-rupee note is the only sound in the room. Death watch indeed, Alice Bhatti thinks.

She looks at the bedside chart, fiddles with the IV, looks under the bed for a pan. The attendants play with quiet intensity, as if following an old family ritual, as if their mother's life, or auspicious end, depends on the result of this game of cards. CNN plays on a small television. Wolf Blitzer promises to be back in a minute. Fashion models from a developing African country wearing bras made of coconut shells and elephant bones walk down a ramp. Alice Bhatti sits down on the bedside chair and wonders about this woman's life. Her vitals are fine but there is impending renal failure. Periodic

57

blood transfusions will keep her alive but she'll have to go in the end. She has probably had the kind of life that induces people at funerals to shake their heads approvingly and say, 'What a fulfilled life', in tones of mock envy usually reserved for lavish weddings and fanciful birthday parties. Two fat sons at the table, an army of guards outside and a naughtily named vehicle is enough proof of a life well lived. But there is probably more: vaults full of jewels and immaculate wills drawn up by family lawyers. A paid obituary will appear in the papers with a long list of mourners at the end, a list so distinguished that the newspaper will refuse to charge for the advert.

Wolf Blitzer, as he had promised, comes back asking in a voice full of television despair: 'Can we really cut a good deal with the bad guys? Which way is it going to go?'

Alice Bhatti notices that the younger man, the clean-shaven one, is restless now. He is not even concentrating on his cards and he pushes his stack of notes absent-mindedly towards his senior partner. He is imagining me naked, Alice thinks. It never ceases to amaze her that men, even those on death watch, all think the same thing. One eye on the dying mother, the other on the paramedic's tits. She is relieved that at least it doesn't matter whether you are doing your duty in the filthy general ward or in a VIP room, some of the rules are the same. She feels at home for the first time. She allows herself a little smile.

Sister Hina Alvi had explained to her in one of her lectures: 'They are grieving, they want to cling to someone, they want to cling to life. They want to be comforted. And your job, indeed your challenge, is to comfort them without canoodling them. Some mix up the two and bring a bad name to our profession. That's why when your average man hears the word "Sister", he gets an erection.'

The younger one clears his throat and says, 'Can we have some cake, please?' Alice is amused at the fact that these people can't tell the difference between a nurse and their personal maid. Old families treat everyone like a servant. She puts on a smile, slices a thick wedge, puts it on a plate and plonks it on the table. As she turns to go, Junior stops her. 'Pick up a card, please.' Alice hesitates for a moment, then bends down and picks up a card from the deck. In that instant she can feel Junior's gaze piercing through to her cleavage. She hands him the card and in turn he picks up a thousand-rupee note from the table and waves it in front of her. 'Here, you have won.' Alice doesn't mind accepting little gifts from her patients and their carers, but nobody has ever offered her a thousand-rupee note. 'I am not allowed to play cards while on duty,' she says, and turns to go back to her seat. Then she looks back and says, 'But thank you.' She doesn't want to offend them.

She sits on the chair and is wondering if she should ask them to change the channel when Junior points towards the TV and asks, 'OK if I turn up the volume?' Alice gives a confused nod. He gets up, finds the remote and turns up the volume. Wolf Blitzer is still not sure which way it's going to go but has moved on to the bad deals that all the good guys have been getting.

Junior comes and stands close to Alice, so close that his crotch is practically in her face. The smell of sweet perfume is so overwhelming that she has to hold her breath in order to stop herself from sneezing. She tries to stand up. He pins her down with one hand and pulls out a revolver from under his shirt, then stands there with a blank face as if he has forgotten what he was planning to do. 'Suck,' he says in a low voice, as if asking for another slice of cake, waving his revolver towards his crotch.

Alice Bhatti realises that all her struggles and dreams will die in this VIP room. She wonders if Sister Hina Alvi or Dr Pereira know anything about this family tradition. She fears that if she resists she'll end up back in the Borstal. This time for life, probably. 'What?' she says, still not quite able to believe the suggestion. His shalwar is around his ankles now and a flaccid piece of cold meat grazes her cheek. She feels a wave of nausea rising from the pit of her stomach and clenches her throat muscles. She doesn't want to throw up in front of a patient. The barrel of the pistol hits her face and a bit of vomit spurts out of her mouth.

'Do you really have to?' Senior speaks in an exhausted voice from his chair.

This gives Junior another idea, and he says to Senior, 'I can't. Not in front of you.'

'OK. I'll go for a walk,' Senior says in a voice full of protective concern. 'But for God's sake don't wake up Qaz.'

As the door clicks shut, Alice is slapped again, hard. She still thinks she hasn't done anything to deserve this, but she has made up her mind to go through with it. There is, however, nothing to suck at. Her tormentor is still flaccid. He seems intent on doing something that his body has no desire to do. With her eyes shut, Alice reaches out, takes it in her left hand, and pumps her fist a few times. As soon as it stiffens, Junior's hand gripping her shoulder goes limp, as if the rush of blood to his groin has made him weak and light-headed. With one hand still on his penis, Alice reaches with the other into her coat pocket and only looks up when she hears him scream. She is careful and steps out of the way of the tiny shower of blood that has erupted from his penis.

Junior tries to straighten his revolver first, then drops it on the floor and begins to weep. Sister Alice puts the razor blade in the fold of a paper napkin, then puts it in a little plastic bag, seals it and chucks it in the waste bin.

'Go to Accidents. And no need to be shy, they get lots of this sort of thing during their night shift.' Before leaving the room, she turns around and says, 'And stop screaming. You'll wake Begum Qaz.'

EIGHT

TEDDY HAS BROUGHT A Mauser to his declaration of love. He has brought a story about the disappearing moon as well, but he is not sure where to start. The story is romantic in an old-fashioned kind of way; the Mauser has three bullets in it. He is hoping that the Mauser and the story about the moon will somehow come together to produce the kind of love song that makes old acquaintances run away together.

Before resorting to gunpoint poetry, Teddy Butt tries the traditional route to romancing a medical professional; he pretends to be sick and then, like a truly hopeless lover, starts believing that he *is* sick, recognises all the little symptoms – sudden fevers, heart palpitations, lingering migraine, even mild depression. He cries while watching a documentary about a snow leopard stranded on a melting glacier.

He lurks around the Out Patients Department on a Sunday afternoon, when Sister Alice Bhatti is alone. She pretends to be busy counting syringes, boiling needles, polishing grimy surfaces, and only turns around when he coughs politely, like you are supposed to when entering a respectable household so that women have the time to cover themselves. Alice Bhatti doesn't understand this polite-cough protocol and stares at him as if telling him, see, this is what smoking does to your lungs.

Teddy Butt is too vain to bring up anything like stomach troubles or a skin rash, both conditions he frequently suffers from. Boldabolics play havoc with his digestion. His bodybuilder's weekly regime of waxing his body hair has left certain parts of him looking like abstract kilim designs. For his first consultation with Alice, he has thought up something more romantic.

'I can't sleep.'

He says this sitting on a rickety little stool as Sister Alice takes notes in a khaki register. 'For how long have you not been able to sleep?' With any other patient Alice would have reached for the wrist to take the pulse, would have listened to the chest with a stethoscope, but with Teddy she knows that he is not *that* kind of patient.

'Since I have seen you' is what Teddy wants to say, but he hasn't rehearsed it, he is not ready yet.

'I actually do go to sleep. But then I have dreams and I wake up,' he says, and feels relieved at having delivered a full sentence without falling off the stool.

Alice Bhatti wants to tell him to go to the OPD in Charya Ward; that is where they deal in dreams. The whole place is a bad dream. But she knows that he wants to be *her* patient and Senior Sister Hina Alvi has taught her that when a patient walks in with intent, you listen to them, even if you know they are making up their symptoms. She presses on with her diagnosis.

She can also see the outline of a muzzle in the crotch of his yellow Adidas trousers. He looks like a freak with two cocks.

'What kind of dreams?'

Teddy has only ever had one dream, the one with a river and a kaftan-wearing God in it. The dream always ends badly as a drowning Teddy discovers that he can't walk on water even in his dream. God stands at the edge of a silvery, completely walkable river and shakes His head in disappointment, as if saying, it's your dream, what do you expect me to do? But somehow in this potentially romantic setting, bringing up God and His kaftan and His disapproval seems inappropriate. 'I see a river in my dream.' He conveniently leaves God out.

'A river?' Alice Bhatti taps the pen on the register without writing anything.

Teddy feels he is being told that his dream is not sick enough.

'It's a river of blood. Red.'

Alice looks at him with interest. This Teddy boy might be a police tout, but he has a poetic side to him, she thinks.

'Any boats in that river of yours?' she asks with an encouraging smile, as if urging him to go on sharing more of his dream with her, to go ahead and dream for her. Teddy accepts the challenge. 'It has bodies floating in it, and severed heads, bobbing up and down.' He realises that his dream doesn't sound very romantic. 'And some flowers also.'

'Do you recognise any of these people in the river? In your dream, I mean.' Teddy shuts his eyes as if trying hard to recognise a face from the river. He was hoping that somehow his midnight yearning for Alice and his insomnia would walk hand in hand and form a rhyming, soaring declaration of love that would reverberate through the corridors of the hospital. Instead he is stuck with embellishing details of a bad dream.

'I can't really stop your dreams, but I can give you something that will ensure that you sleep well. And if you sleep well then you might start having better dreams.' She scribbles a prescription for Lexotanil, then puts it aside. 'Actually I might have some here. An hour before you sleep. Never on an empty stomach. And no warm milk at night. Sometimes indigestion can give you bad dreams.'

Alice gives him a brief smile. 'You might want to change that bandage on your thumb. I hope you didn't hurt it in a dream.' Then she turns around and goes back to counting her syringes. She does it with such studied concentration that it seems the health of the nation depends on getting this count right.

Teddy Butt stumbles into the OPD the following morning, bleary-eyed, moving slowly. His voice seems to be coming from underwater. There is a sleepy calm about him. Even the muzzle of the gun in his trousers seems flaccid. 'I didn't have any dreams. What did you give me? What did you mix in that pill?' His words are accusatory but his tone is grateful.

'I didn't mix anything. It was a Glaxo original, supposed to help you sleep. Do you want more?' Alice reaches into her drawer and stops. She notices that he is wearing a little cross on a gold chain around his neck. She shows the slight, spontaneous irritation that natives feel when tourists try and dress up like them. 'What's that thing you are wearing?'

'Just a locket,' Teddy Butt says. 'A friend from Dubai got it for me.' The man whose neck Teddy snatched it from was indeed visiting from Dubai. One ear and the side of his face were blown off in an unfortunate accident during an interrogation. The man from Dubai had almost strangled Teddy with his handcuffs before Inspector Malangi put his Beretta near his left ear, shouted at Teddy, 'Knee on the left, bhai. Your left, not mine,' and shot him. The chain with the cross was the reward Inspector Malangi gave him for keeping the man pinned down at that difficult moment. Teddy hadn't killed the man; he was only holding him down. It was his job. If he hadn't done it, someone else would have. If he hadn't done this job, he would definitely have had to do some other job. And who knows what he might be required to do in that new job? He runs his forefinger along his chain and presses the cross into his chest with the satisfaction of someone who is lucky enough not to have the worst job in the city. He had felt the man's breath on his knee when he tried to bite him before getting shot.

For a moment he thinks whether he can source a matching necklace for her.

'It's a cross, not a locket,' says Alice. 'Why would a man want to wear jewellery anyway?' She scribbles another prescription for Lexotanil on her pad and turns away.

Teddy Butt is flummoxed and walks off without answering, without asking anything. He goes to his room in Al-Aman apartments and sleeps the whole day. He doesn't have any dreams, but after he wakes up and starts doing weights, he watches a fascinating documentary about Komodo dragons that hypnotise their prey before going for the underside of their throat.

Teddy decides that he is going to tell Alice Bhatti everything, but he will need her full attention. From what Teddy can tell, women are always distracted, trying to do too many things at the same time, always happy to go off on tangents; that's why they make good nurses and politicians but not good chefs or truck drivers. He also realises that he can't do it without his Mauser.

Teddy is one of those people who are only articulate when they talk about cricket. The rest of the time they rely on a combination of grunts, hand gestures and repeat snippets of what other people have just said to them. He also has very little experience of sharing his feelings.

He has been a customer of women and occasionally their tormentor, but never a lover. He believes that being a lover is something that falls somewhere between paying them and slapping them around. Twice he has come close to conceding love. Once he gave a fifty-rupee tip to a prostitute who looked fourteen but claimed to be twenty-two. Encouraged by his generosity, she also demanded a poster of Imran Khan, and that put him off. Teddy promised to get it but never went back because he had always believed that Imran Khan was a failed batsman masquerading as a bowler. On another occasion he only pretended to take his turn with a thirty-two-year-old Bangladeshi prisoner after a small police contingent had shuffled out of the room. He just sat with her and played with her hair while she sobbed and cursed in Bengali. The only word he could understand was Allah. He had walked out adjusting his fly, pretending to be exhausted and satisfied, even joking with the policemen: it was like fucking an oil spill.

But Teddy Butt can be very articulate, even poetic, with a Mauser in his hand, and after much thought this is what he decides to do. He tries practising in front of the full-length mirror in his room. 'You live in my heart.' With every word he jabs the Mauser in the air, like an underprepared lawyer trying to impress a judge. He worries that his gun might send the wrong signal, but he is convinced that he will be able to explain himself. People always try their best to understand when their life depends on listening properly. He changes the dressing on his thumb as if preparing for a job interview.

'You can't go around the Ortho ward with that.' Alice Bhatti has emerged carrying a bedpan in one hand and a discarded, blood-smeared bandage in the other, and starts admonishing him while walking away from him. 'Don't waste your bullets, this hospital will kill them all anyway.' Teddy feels the love of his life slipping from his grasp, his plan falling apart at the very first hurdle. He grips the Mauser, stretches his arm and blocks her way.

Alice Bhatti looks confused for a moment and then irritated. 'What do you want to rob me of? This piss tray?'

With the Mauser extended, Teddy finds his tongue. 'I can't live like this. This life is too much.'

'Nobody can live like this.' Alice Bhatti is attentive now and sympathetic. 'If these cheap guns don't kill you, those Boldabolic pills will. Get a job as a PT teacher. Or come to think of it, you could get a nurse's diploma and work here. There is always work for a male nurse. There are parts of this place where even women doctors don't go. Charya Ward for example hasn't had a . . .'

Teddy doesn't listen to the whole thing; the words 'PT teacher' trigger off a childhood memory that he had completely forgotten – a very tall, very fat PT teacher holds him by his ears, swings him around and then hurls him to the ground and walks away laughing. The other children run around him in a circle and decide to change his nickname from Nappy to Yo Yo. Teddy puts the gun to Alice Bhatti's temple and snarls in his little girl's sing-song voice, 'Give me one good reason why somebody wouldn't shoot in this hospital? Why shouldn't I shoot you right here and end all my troubles?'

Mine too, she wants to say, but Teddy's hand holding the Mauser is trembling, and one thing Alice Bhatti doesn't want in her life is a shootout in her workplace.

He orders Alice to put her tray and bandages down, which she does. She has realised that Teddy is serious. Suicidal serious maybe, but he is the kind of suicidal serious who in the process of taking his own life could cause some grievous bodily harm to those around him.

Ortho ward is unusually quiet at this time of day. Number 14, who is always shouting about an impending plague caused by computer screens, is calm and only murmurs about the itch in his plastered leg. A ward boy enters the corridor carrying a water cooler on a wheelbarrow; he sees Alice and Teddy and stops in his tracks. Embarrassed, as if he has stumbled on to someone's private property and found the owners in a compromising position, he backtracks, pulling the wheelbarrow with him. Alice doesn't expect him to inform anyone.

'What do you want, Mr Butt?' Alice Bhatti tries to hide her fear behind a formal form of address. She has learnt all the wrong things from Senior Sister Hina Alvi.

You live in my heart, Teddy Butt wants to say, but only jabs the air with his Mauser, five times. In the Borstal Alice heard many stories about men in love brandishing guns, and in all of them when men are unable to talk you are in real trouble. She looks at him expectantly, as if she has understood what his Mauser has just said, likes it and now wants to hear more.

Mixed-up couplets about her lips and hair, half-remembered speeches about a life together, names of their children, pledges of undying love, a story about the first time he saw her, what she wore, what she said, a half-sincere eulogy about her professionalism that he was sure she would appreciate, her shoulder blades, all these things rush through Teddy Butt's head, and then he realises that he has already delivered his opening line by pulling out a gun.

Now he can start anywhere.

Alice Bhatti thinks that she should not do Sunday shifts any more and instead help her dad with his woodwork. If she lives to see another Sunday, that is.

She looks beyond Teddy. At the top of the stairs, a man sits facing the sun like an ancient king waiting to receive his subjects. His legs amputated just above the knees, he sits on the floor, wearing full-length trousers that sometimes balloon up in the wind. He has a stack of large X-rays next to him. He picks them up one by one, holds them against the sun and looks at them for a long time, as if contemplating old family pictures.

Teddy Butt decides to start with her garbage bin. 'I go through your garbage bin. I know everything about you. I see all the prayers you scribble on prescriptions. You never write your own name. But I can tell from the handwriting.' He sobs violently and holds the Mauser with both hands to steady himself. The muzzle of his gun slides down a degree, like an erection flashbacking to a sad memory. Alice sees it as a sign from God. *Bless our Lord who art descended from the heavens.* She is a tad too quick in her gratitude. God accepts it with godlike indifference. And Teddy straightens his gun. He seems to have found his groove and starts to speak in paragraphs, as if delivering the manifesto of a new political party that wants to eradicate poverty and pollution during its first term in power.

'The love that I feel for you is not the love I feel for any other human being. The world might think it's the love of your flesh. I can understand this world and their thinking. I have wondered about this and thought long and hard and realised that this is a world full of sinners, so I do understand what they think but I don't think like that. When I think about you, do I think about these milk jugs?' He waves his Mauser across her chest. Alice looks at his gun and feels nauseous and wonders if the peace and quiet of this corridor is worth preserving. 'I think of your eyes. I think of your eyes only.'

The octopus of fear that had clutched Alice Bhatti's head begins to relax its tentacles.

In her heart of hearts, Alice, who has seen people die choking on their own food, and survive after falling from a sixth floor on to a paved road, knows that Teddy means every word of what he has said. And he isn't finished yet.

'I was standing outside the hospital, hoping to catch a glimpse of you. It was a full Rajab moon. Then I looked up at the balcony of Ortho Ward and saw you empty a garbage bin. I saw your face for a moment and then you disappeared. Then I looked up again and saw that the moon had disappeared too. I rubbed my eyes, I shut them, I opened them again. I stood and kept looking up for forty-five minutes. People gathered around me. I held them by their throats and kept asking them, where has the moon gone? And they said, what moon? We have seen no moon. Did you just escape from Charya Ward? And then I knew that I can't live without you.'

A thick March cloud has cloaked the sun outside. The perfect spring afternoon is suddenly its own wintry ghost. The man with the X-rays is trying to shoo away a kite, which, confused by the sudden change in light, thinks it is dusk and swoops down in a last desperate attempt to take something home. The legless man is fighting the kite with the X-rays of his missing legs.

The final bell rings in the neighbouring St Xavier's primary school and eighteen hundred children suddenly start talking to each other in urgent voices like house sparrows at dusk.

Alice Bhatti bends down, picks up the piss tray from the floor and holds it in front of her chest. She speaks in measured tones. 'I know your type,' she says. 'That little gun doesn't scare me. Your tears don't fool me. You think that a woman, any woman who wears a uniform is just waiting for you to show up and she'll take it off. I wish you had just walked in and had the guts to tell me you want me to take this off. We could have had a conversation about that. At the end of which I would have told you what I am telling you now: fuck off and never show me your face again.'

Teddy Butt flees before she is finished. He runs past the legless man taking a nap with his face covered with an X-ray, past the

69

ambulance drivers dissecting the evening newspapers, past the hopeful junkies waiting for the hospital to accidentally dispense its bounty.

As he emerges out of the hospital he raises his arm in the air, and without thinking, without targeting anything, fires his Mauser.

The city stops moving for three days.

The bullet pierces the right shoulder of a truck driver who has just entered the city after a forty-eight-hour-long journey. His shoulder is almost leaning out of his driver's window, his right hand drumming the door, his fingers holding a finely rolled joint, licked on the side with his tongue for extra smoothness, a ritual treat that he has prepared for the end of the journey. He is annoyed with his own shoulder; he looks at it with suspicion. His shoulder feels as if it has been stung by a bee that has travelled with him all the way from his village. His left hand grips the shoulder where it hurts and finds his shirt soaked in red gooey stuff. He jams the brake pedal to the floor. A rickshaw trying to dodge the swerving truck gets entangled in its double-mounted Goodyear tyres and is dragged along for a few yards. Five children, all between seven and nine, in their pristine blue and white St Xavier's uniforms, become a writhing mess of fractured skulls, blood, crayons and Buffy the Vampire Slayer lunchboxes. The truck comes to a halt after gently nudging a cart and overturning a pyramid of the season's last guavas. A size-four shoe is stuck between two Goodyears.

School notebooks are looked at, pockets are searched for clues to the victims' identity, the mob slowly gathers around the truck, petrol is extracted from the tank and sprinkled over its cargo of three tonnes of raw peanuts. Teddy with his broken heart and the truck driver with his bleeding shoulder both realise what is coming even before the mob has made up its mind; they first mingle in the crowd and then start walking in opposite directions.

A lonely fire engine will turn up an hour later but will be

pelted with stones and sent away. The truck and its cargo will smoulder for two days.

In a house twenty miles away a phone rings. A grandmother rushes on to the street beating her chest and wailing. Two motorcycles kick-start simultaneously. Half a dozen jerrycans full of kerosene are hauled into a rickety Suzuki pick-up. A nineteen-year-old rummages under his pillow, cocks his TT pistol and runs on to the street screaming, promising to rape every Pathan mother in the land. A second-hand-tyre-shop owner tries to padlock his store, but the boys are already there with their iron bars and bicycle chains. A police mobile switches its emergency horn on and rushes towards the police commissioner's house. A helicopter hovers over the beach as if defending the Arabian Sea against the burning rubber smell that is spreading through the city. An old colonel walking his dog in the Colonels' Colony asks his dog to hurry up and do its business. A bank teller is shot dead for smiling. Finding the streets deserted, groups of kites and crows descend from their perches and chase wild dogs, who lift their faces to the sky and bark joyously. Five size-four coffins wait for three days as ambulance drivers are shot at and sent back to where they came from. Carcasses of burnt buses, rickshaws, paan shops and at least one KFC joint seem to have a calming effect on the city. Newspapers start predicting 'Normalcy limping back to the city', as if normalcy had gone for a picnic and sprained an ankle.

During the three-day shutdown, eleven more are killed; two of them turn up shot and tied together in one gunnysack dumped on a rubbish heap. Three billion rupees' worth of Suzukis, Toyotas and Hinopaks are burnt. During these days Alice Bhatti is actually not that busy. When people are killed while fixing their satellite dish on their roof, or their motorbike is torched while they are going to buy a litre of milk, they tend to forget

71

about their various ailments; they learn to live without dialysis for their kidneys, home cures are found for minor injuries, prayers replace prescription drugs. Alice has time to sit down between her chores, time to take proper lunch and prayer breaks. Between cleaning gunshot wounds and mopping the A&E floor, Alice Bhatti has moments of calm, and finds herself thinking about that scared man with the Mauser, his mad story about the disappearing moon. She wonders if he is caught up in these riots, if he is still having those dreams. She wonders if she has been in one of his dreams.

On the fourth day a fisherman bicycles slowly through the rubble with a wicker basket brimming with his home-made fishing net. With his back to the city he dips his toe in the seawater, likes its cold-warm-cold feel, rolls up his trousers, and starts laying his net for the night.

NINE

SENIOR SISTER HINA ALVI doesn't ask Alice Bhatti to take a seat, and looks at her as if she is seeing her for the first time, as if it has never occurred to her that this junior nurse is capable of doing anything that has not been explicitly ordered by her.

Hina Alvi's hands move briskly, paan is rolled in fast forward, and instead of tucking it into the side of her mouth, she starts chewing it fiercely and speaks in a raspy, nervous voice. 'Just because there is no police case, just because Qaz's family haven't launched a formal complaint, doesn't mean they are going to forget about it,' she says. 'In fact you should be more scared that they haven't registered a case against you. It means they want to deal with it on their own. It means they want to deal with *you* on their own.'

Alice Bhatti hadn't reported the VIP room incident to Sister Hina Alvi or anyone else. In fact she went home afterwards as if she had carried out a minor surgical procedure or given someone a tetanus shot. She had hoped that no respectable man – and Junior, with his team of bodyguards and raw silk suits and a mother dying in the same VIP ward where he had been born, was nothing if not respectable – would go around complaining about a little cut on his private parts. And she was right. He hasn't complained. Now Sister Hina Alvi tells her that she should be scared because he hasn't complained.

'I think *I* should have complained. And I didn't because I thought they were your friends.'

Sister Hina Alvi looks at her with hurt eyes, as if Alice has accused her of running a pimping racket. 'I am not that old. Now sit down and tell me what happened.'

* * *

73

People on the night shift had heard screams. Patients sleeping in the corridor had assumed it was some VIP dying. They had seen Sister Alice Bhatti walk out of the VIP room taking off her gloves and coat and shaking her head as if she had just lost a patient she could have saved. Soon after, they had seen a man running to his Devil of the Desert Surf pressing a white hospital bedsheet to his crotch. And they had connected the dots and come up with the most obvious explanation: that Sister Alice Bhatti and the man running with the bedsheet were involved in a kinky sex game in the VIP room that had gone too far. These people won't stop having fun even when their mother is on her deathbed, they speculated. Maybe the mother on the deathbed is part of the fun. She had bitten him off in the heat of passion, and then taken it home, one rumour went. He had chased her all the way to the edge of French Colony, but had to stop and turn back because you can't track anything down in French Colony. Even if someone has slashed your dick and disappeared, you don't go there. Then there were those who always hear a shot during such incidents and they swore upon Allah that they heard a shot. And then there are those who always hear an autorickshaw's silencer misfiring when they hear a shot. Nobody even remotely believed Senior's bodyguards' version: that it was a minor accident in the VIP room's loo, that Junior had tucked his handgun in his raw silk shalwar and it had gone off. Only a scratch. A bad scratch but only a scratch, the bodyguards told everyone, and in turn had to field some silly questions. 'Did you see it? The scratch?' they were asked. 'With your own eyes? Is that part of your job? To take care of the scratch?' At which point the guards started mumbling curses and fiddling with their guns.

'What would you have done in my position?' Alice Bhatti asks, as if enquiring about her options in a basic medical procedure. Do you go for stitches or do you just sterilise and put on a bandage?

Sister Hina Alvi swallows a bit of betel juice, licks a drop that is about to dribble off her lower lip, smiles and leans forward. For a moment it seems she is about to share a fond memory from her past, but then she leans back in her chair as if she has just remembered that she is a senior sister with senior sisterly responsibilities and must resist the temptation.

'I have learnt my trade at the bedside, on the job, not in some second-rate nursing school. I would not let them go that far, I would not have let the situation get out of hand. This is not some Pashto film that you are living out. This is real life. That thing that you slashed was a real cock.' Sister Hina Alvi emphasises the word 'real' as if the country was full of fakes.

'And he was waving that real cock of his in my real face.' Alice Bhatti feels that Sister Hina Alvi understands perfectly what she is talking about but doesn't want to agree with her because that might compromise her official status. She doesn't want to be misquoted later. Sister Hina Alvi feels powerless but doesn't want to admit to being powerless. God knows how vast the Senior's family connections are. God knows how long Sister Hina Alvi has known them. What if she herself has been through the same situation? She obviously wouldn't want to bring that up. She wants to start blaming the victim before the victim can blame anyone else. She wants to be remembered as a solid administrator.

'You are not the first one and you wouldn't be the last one to occasionally get something in your face,' Sister Hina Alvi says, throwing her hands up in despair. 'But your duty is to convince them to put it back in their pants and zip up. That's what you are trained to do. You are not taught to go around hacking them.' Sister Hina Alvi slashes the air with her right hand like a mad TV gardener.

'And how do you suppose I should have done that? He had a gun to my head.' Alice Bhatti is angry now, as she remembers the large plate with a little sandwich on it, the smell of green

75

tea and thousand-rupee notes. She mimes a gun with her hand and holds it to her own head.

'Cut out this gun-shun business. Everyone is holding a gun to everyone else's head. If guns could get anyone to do anything, then this country would be sorted by now. Just count the number of guns you see on your journey here from your home and tell me if it has done anyone any good. Where is home, by the way?'

'French Colony.'

'Nice place. I hope they keep their own neighbourhood clean, your people, I mean. Because they are definitely letting this city drown in its own filth.' Alice Bhatti knows that people think that everyone in French Colony is a janitor and works for the Corporation. But she refuses to be drawn into this discussion. It never goes anywhere. 'I don't know anyone in the Colony,' she says. 'I just moved there and it's as clean as any other place I have lived in, which means not very.'

Sister Hina Alvi realises that she has touched on a topic that Alice Bhatti does not want to discuss. 'What about family? Any brothers, sisters?'

Suddenly Alice Bhatti feels that she is being interviewed for a marriage proposal. She feels she might be asked if she can cook and sew, whether she would be OK living with an extended family.

'Look, what alarms me is that they haven't called, they haven't complained, they haven't even written. I know their mother passed away and nothing will happen for forty days. But I can't say what will happen after that. I went to offer my condolences and they were very polite. They thanked me. They are an old family, they have long memories. They can also be very creative when it comes to taking revenge.'

'Do you think I should go to the police? It was self-defence, you know that.' Alice knows she will not go to the police – she has struggled half her adult life to keep away from the police – but she wants to see what Sister Hina Alvi has to say about this.

Sister Hina Alvi shakes her head in despair, as if Alice Bhatti is that stupid child who is always asking why, if the earth is round, people on the other side don't fall off into space. 'In our VIP room you had to deal with one man. In the police station there will be a room full of them in your face. You'll need a chainsaw.'

Sister Hina Alvi reaches into a file and pulls out a typed sheet of paper. 'This is the best I can do. I am suspending you for two weeks. I haven't written it on the suspension letter, but you'll get paid. I'll try and get the word out that you have been punished and hope that will calm them down. Consider it compulsory leave. Relax. Things will be better when you return.' She says the last sentence looking down, as if she is sure things will never get better.

Alice Bhatti takes the paper and starts to fold it carefully. 'So basically I am being punished for resisting an armed assault.'

Hina Alvi lifts her enormous bag from the floor, plonks it on the table and starts rummaging through it.

Alice is already wondering what she is going to do for two whole weeks. She can't think of a thing. Will she have to find a hobby? Or listen to Joseph Bhatti's rants about the state of Christianity? The prospect makes her even angrier. 'I thought you were my colleague. I thought you knew these people; after all, you put me on that shift. I thought you would take some responsibility for this. At least pretend to be on my side.'

She stops abruptly as Sister Hina Alvi produces a palm-sized gun out of her bag and holds it towards her. 'Keep it. I hope you don't have to use it. I have had it for four years and I have never had to. I don't even know if it works.'

TEN

NOOR SEES ALICE AND Teddy walking out of the Sacred, hand in hand, and starts to suspect that love is not just blind, it's deaf and dumb and probably has an advanced case of Alzheimer's; it's unhinged. Look at them holding hands, whispering to each other, smiling, walking out of the hospital like they are leaving this world of pain behind for ever. Alice is pretending to have lost her eyesight, holding on to Teddy's finger and walking with her eyes shut. She has probably lost her brains too. Noor has walked for too long holding Zainab's hand to find anything remotely cute about anyone pretending to be blind. To have eyesight is to be blessed. Pretending to be blind when you have a perfect pair of eyes seems to him grotesque blasphemy. And to derive some kind of sexual pleasure from it is downright perverse. Noor wishes there was a government department where he could report this offence. Surely if there are laws against non-believers pretending to be Muslims, there should be a law against people with perfect eyes pretending to be blind.

Love, he concludes, is a runaway charya.

It started with a casual enquiry. Alice Bhatti came over when Noor was massaging Zainab's feet, nudged him aside and started kneading her feet and ankles with expert fingers. 'Where is that police tout friend of yours?' And when Noor looked at her quizzically, she pulled out what looked like a toy gun and pointed it towards Noor's head. 'Answer before I shoot,' she laughed and lowered the gun. 'I need his help with this. I want to be able to shoot moving targets.'

'You definitely need help,' Noor sneered. 'But I am not sure if my friend is the man. My friend doesn't have a permanent address. But I'll let him know when he shows up next.'

How can there be love between these two? Noor wonders. How can there be *anything* between these two? Noor knows that Alice likes sucking toffees in her breaks. He also knows that Teddy carries Accu-Chek in his front pocket to monitor his sugar level and can inject insulin while riding a motorbike. She is trying to bring order to a world full of sick people, administering IVs at two a.m., holding old women's hands, pretending to be their daughter, reading the Kalima with them as they breathe their last. He rides high on entropy; he pees right under the sign where it says *Look, a dog is pissing here.* Sometimes when he sees an approaching beggar he puts his hand in his pocket, and as the beggar hovers around in anticipation he takes out a comb and starts to groom his hair. He waxes his body hair every week; she shaves her underarm hair only at Easter and Christmas, when she goes to church and wears a sleeveless dress. She looks left and right at least half a dozen times before crossing the road, sometimes walking half a mile to find a pedestrian bridge or a safe zebra crossing. He rides his motorbike at full speed on the wrong side of the road and expects traffic to part for him, and it usually does. He watches National Geographic Channel in his free time.

Alice has never had any free time.

It's only when he sees them walking out of the Sacred compound holding hands and getting into an autorickshaw that Noor realises that he might have played a role in this fucked-up love story.

Noor had conveyed to Teddy the basic facts, in the most casual way.

'Junior Nurse Alice Bhatti has been looking for you,' he had said as he took the bandage off Teddy's thumb. The multiple fractures had started to fester and it smelt of impending gangrene.

'Was she angry?' asked Teddy, biting his tongue; he seemed to be reliving a painful memory.

79

'She is always angry,' said Noor. 'She was carrying a gun and she was asking about you.'

Noor knows the old saying about opposites attracting each other, but these two belong to different species. It's like a cheetah falling for a squirrel or bats trying to chat up butterflies. Noor keeps his analogies to himself, doodles an occasional bat in the margins of his register and follows this unlikely love as it takes shape amidst the dying chaos of the Sacred Heart, which Ortho Sir has started calling Slutsville after hearing rumours about Alice and Teddy.

Noor sees them just before sunset behind the A&E building, Alice and Teddy's right arms outstretched, Teddy's chin resting almost on her shoulder, his hand steadying her hand as it aims the gun. Noor sees that their shadows overlay each other and stretch a long way, right up to the Sacred's back wall. Noor thinks this is the saddest afternoon of his life.

In the last few days there have been other moments, little gestures that should have alerted him. Teddy curling his lips when he sees a patient talking to Alice in a loud voice, Teddy holding a door open for her for a second longer than he should, Teddy walking behind her and trying to fall in step with her, Teddy appearing at lunch breaks with fried fish wrapped in newspaper, Teddy pretending to read the newspaper, Teddy riding in the passenger seat of the police jeep rather than sitting in his designated place in the back. Noor has no idea whether Teddy is following a road map or has just woken up one day with ideas of self-improvement and coupledom. He knows not where this story is headed. Or maybe he has known all along but doesn't want to believe it.

'This thumb is festering,' Alice Bhatti had said, without any reference to their earlier attempt at gunpoint romance. 'How did you manage to break it in so many pieces?'

'Yes, Teddy,' Noor chimed in. 'You shouldn't go around

putting your hand in dangerous places. What were you trying to do? Make mincemeat for Inspector Malangi?'

Alice Bhatti cleaned the wound with a cotton bud soaked in spirit. 'You need a course of six antibiotic injections. Miss one and we'll have to start all over again.'

It was at that moment that Noor realised that Alice had crossed the line that care providers are supposed to watch out for. It was the kind of moment that professionals are trained to take in their stride, and this was unprofessional behaviour of the most basic kind. You are supposed to manage pain, not share it. Cutting, disinfecting, injecting, stitching is all in a day's work. But here, when Teddy lies with his face down on the stretcher, on this very shaky wheelie stretcher on which Alice and Noor have shared their Borstal memories, something shifts in Alice's heart. Teddy's hands flail helplessly in the air to stave off the needle. He clenches his hairless butt, his face contorts into a cartoonish grimace, his hands close into tight fists, this bundle of hard muscle tries to save himself from the tiny prick of pain; this is when Alice Bhatti feels that feeling that people call a tender moment, the feeling that you feel when a baby is about to fall off a bed and your instinctive reaction is to scoop it up in your arms. Sister Alice obviously doesn't scoop Teddy into her arms, but she puts her hand on his shoulder, an instinctive, comforting touch, not a touch that promises copulation, or the kind of touch that hints at a lifetime together and healthy babies winning school prizes, but a casual touch that says, look that was all, that was all the pain I was going to cause you, look, it doesn't hurt any more, does it?

But this small, spontaneous gesture is enough to convince Noor that Teddy is in love, and that his love has been accepted and reciprocated. Not only is he in love, but Alice Bhatti approves this love, accepts it with her hand on his shoulder, and believes that their hearts have been connected somehow in this moment through the needle injecting that fluid into his body which will protect him against all infections. Now their hearts must remain connected till the time one of the two stops beating.

Teddy is also determined to banish all competition, to protect this tender shoot of love against every kind of bad weather.

Teddy doesn't really think that Noor is competition, but he looks at him and sizes him up: why is this boy always glued to Alice's side? Teddy will have to talk to him soon.

Together what will they become? Alice Bhatti Butt? Alice Butt? Alice Teddy Butt?

There are people in his life who call him Teddy and there are people in his life who call him Butt Sahib. When someone addresses him as Teddy Butt Sahib, he knows that he'll be asked to do something humiliating. Nobody has ever called Alice Bhatti anything but Alice, Sister Alice or – in private wards – Sister Bhatti. Mostly people call her 'daughter' or 'sister' and then do exactly what they would do with their own sisters and daughters: they treat her like a slave they bought at a clearance sale.

Noor might be only seventeen but he knows about love, what it entails: to see the beloved drink water, to see them open their eyes, to try and guess if they are asleep or awake, to try and guess what dream they are dreaming when they are asleep, to kiss somebody when they are sleeping, to feel their early-morning nausea, to feel scared when they are scared, to feel your ears get hot when they are embarrassed.

Noor is a man; he thinks he knows that Teddy can't get out of that nine-second cycle. But what does Alice see in him? Does she like him because he rescued her from Charya Ward? But it was Noor who first warned her and then sent him in. Do you want to marry someone because they pulled a gun at you and professed their undying love? This whole business of love, he concludes, is a protection racket, like paying your weekly bhatta to your local hoodlum so that you are not mugged on your own street.

Noor knows all of this, but even when he sees them walk out of the Sacred gate hand in hand, he can't imagine them feeling any of those things for each other. He can't imagine reading their names together except maybe in a tragic news headline.

ELEVEN

'I HAVE A SURPRISE for you,' Teddy Butt tells Alice fifteen minutes before she is about to finish her last shift before Ash Wednesday. Joseph Bhatti had placed a box of sweets in the kitchen this morning and she had found a rosary hanging from her doorknob. She likes it when Joseph Bhatti tries to play her mother; but she can't stand it when he expects her to play her own mother. She doesn't mind starving herself for the day, but what's the point of singing *There is no fees in the school of the crucified one* along with a couple of hundred other people most of whom have never seen the inside of a school?

Teddy is dressed in starched white shalwar qameez and embroidered shoes and looks like he is going to attend some-one's engagement party. Alice Bhatti is not easily surprised. Teddy has been writing her lovesick notes that she suspects are copied from *100 Best Love Songs of the Past Twenty Years* but she thinks he should get credit for trying. Any man who reaches for a book when he thinks about you is a man that you should think about. She has been giving him an occasional smile and Lexatonils and accepting small trinkets with a wry smile; they have reached a level of resigned intimacy.

'Surprise me,' she says, sounding bored and not believing for a moment that Teddy is capable of an original thought. Teddy Butt's ideas of love are derived from any song that might be topping the charts at the time. His ideas about the logistics of love are learnt from the wildlife documentaries he watches on National Geographic, lions copulating by the lakeside and grass-hoppers serenading other grasshoppers while licking morning dew off their wings. Sometimes he dreams of carrying Alice in his jaws like when a lioness transports her cub to a safe place.

Not another pink teddy bear, not another singing greetings card, not another bargain from the perfume bazaar, and definitely nothing from Gentlemen's Squad's lost and found stores, she secretly hopes. She suspects that he gets his gift ideas from the same shopping channel where he orders his protein supplements. But she also feels that she is his teacher and must not discourage him. He is learning. At least he is turning up to meet her without pretending to be sick. And without his Mauser.

She has been expecting to be asked for something. She is not sure what. Maybe she'll be invited out for lunch in one of those Irani cafés where couples sit behind curtained booths. She has been apprehensive that she might be asked to go to the zoo to see the new pair of South African lion cubs that Teddy has been obsessing about. She doesn't really know what her answer would be but she has been hoping that she'll have an answer when she is asked. Now she is being asked.

'You have to shut your eyes first,' he says in a lilting voice, looking into her eyes. Either he has been mixing his Lexatonil with something else, or he is just sleepy with love. A black butterfly appears out of nowhere and does a little dance between their locked eyes before it flies away. Alice likes this swirl of black velvet so close to her face. She imagines herself submerged in a sea of black butterflies. She is intrigued. She shuts her eyes properly. And as soon as she does, she begins to yearn for a proper surprise. If she was dreading a cheap little trinket before, now suddenly she wants an oil-tanker-sized surprise. She wants a surprise so big and so heavy it could flatten her in the middle of the road. She wants a tied-to-a-rocket-and-launched-into-space kind of surprise. She wonders why she isn't thinking of flowers and candy and why she suddenly yearns for large, heavy, speedy objects. It's futile to predict what love will make of you, but sometimes it brings you things you never knew you wanted. One moment all you want is a warm shower, and the next you are offering your lover your chest to urinate on. 'Yes, surprise me,' she whispers.

85

He takes her left hand and wraps it around the middle finger of his right hand and asks her to hold on to it.

She has checked his pulse before. She has dressed his mangled thumb, which initially looked like a dog had chewed it and spat it out. He has pretended to read her palm: *Oh, the distance between your thumb and forefinger, that's a sign of your compulsively generous nature. I have never seen such a generous hand. And this thumb, such willpower, leadership qualities, stubborn maybe. This is definitely a Gandhi hand. Always principles over pleasure. Now show me the other one.* But never have they held hands without a tacitly agreed cover story. She feels as if she is holding a live little animal. She clutches it tightly.

'You'll have to walk with me. Walk carefully,' Teddy says.

As she emerges from the A&E department, Alice catches a whiff of rotten fruit, and a familiar old woman's voice jeers at her from a distance: 'Look at you playing blind man while your patients are dying out here. I am dying out here. Give me something for the night. The nights are becoming longer.'

Alice Bhatti smiles with her eyes shut. It is the old legless junkie who goes around on a skateboard and is always threatening to start swallowing broken electric light bulbs. 'Wash your arse once a week,' she shouts back. 'That's all you need. Nobody dies of lice.'

'Kafirs have all the fun in this country. This country was made for Muslims, and poor Muslims can't even get any Valium around here,' the old woman shouts back at her.

Alice Bhatti walks on. She doesn't walk very carefully. She doesn't want a calibrated, mild kind of surprise. She wants to rush headlong towards her destiny and surprise it before it can surprise her.

In the hospital compound where patients with all kinds of impairments walk around with all kinds of supports – teenage boys taking piggyback rides on their old fathers' backs, teenage girls carrying their mothers on improvised stretchers, the polio battalion steering their skateboards – Alice walking with her eyes shut, holding on to Teddy's finger, is a very ordinary sight.

Teddy puts a stiff, shy hand on her back and helps her into a waiting autorickshaw. Alice doesn't want to hear whatever it is that Teddy is whispering to the rickshaw driver. She wants their destination to be a surprise. She feels the tincture-disease-hunger smell receding as the rickshaw bumps and swerves its way through heavy traffic. It doesn't occur to her to let go of Teddy's finger; she squeezes it every time the rickshaw jumps over a speed breaker. She lets her body press into his every time the rickshaw takes a tight corner. She feels Teddy's whole body stiffen, and tremble lightly at every turn. Alice feels she can go anywhere pressed against this hard, warm, trembling body draped in starched cotton.

The traffic thins, the rickshaw drives faster, the air becomes salty and moist. A fine shower occasionally sprays her face. The rickshaw stops. Teddy helps her out. She shivers slightly when he puts his hand on the small of her back to give her support.

She wishes for a lifetime of alighting from rickshaws with his hand on her back.

She knows that she is on a boat, a motorboat. She has never been on a boat before. Now she remembers where this surprise might have originated. During a random conversation with Teddy on a slow afternoon, she vaguely remembers telling him that she has never been on the sea. 'Surely everybody has been to the sea. It's right there,' he had said. 'No, you fool, I have been to the beach but I have never been on a boat,' she had replied. 'All those waves rocking you up and down. Must be fun.'

He has remembered something she mentioned to fill an awkward silence between them. She feels angry for a moment. What right does he have to act out her private little whims? Then a wave hits the boat and she finds herself holding on to his shoulder. Seawater sprays her face and she doesn't have to worry about her stinging eyes. Seawater washes away her tears.

'Should we get married?' Teddy asks in a whisper, but she hears it clearly above the roar of the sea.

'Here?' she shouts.

'No. No.' He sounds reassuring, trying to clear up a minor misunderstanding. 'There.' He points to the distant blurred shape of a giant boat, which seems to have emerged from the depths of the sea. 'But you promised to keep your eyes shut.'

Whatever happens afterwards, actually happens in this moment. Alice Bhatti wanted a solid, feet-on-the-ground-type surprise. But after the ride on the motorboat, they climb a ladder, and when she opens her eyes, instead of the certitude of a carpeted road or the soft sand of a beach, she finds her feet unsteady on the stern of a bobbing submarine on the very moody waves of the Arabian Sea.

Who knows what she was really hoping for? Maybe a walk by the seaside, maybe a corn on the cob while watching a monkey do a gun salute, as the waves lapped around her ankles; what she ended up with was an impromptu marriage proposal followed by an impromptu wedding in the middle of the Arabian Sea.

She couldn't have guessed it. The surprise was, well, a surprise.

The story of what happened between them on that submarine has many versions, mostly narrated by Alice. Teddy has only one version and he always sticks to it: I have friends in the police who know some people who know people in the Coastguards who work with people who work in submarines. They're like a family. When she opened her eyes, Alice squealed with delight, but then she didn't. They served biryani. She chose her own name. Aliya. No, it wasn't pre-planned. Who can plan something like that? How come there was an imam to perform the nuptials on a submarine? That's plain ignorance about naval matters. There is always an imam on every submarine. She gave her consent. It was she who said that she'd go back to her house in French Colony and move in with me in a few days. I could have waited for as long as it took her. It wasn't as if I was in a hurry to jump into bed with her. A man thinks of a woman every nine seconds but he doesn't marry them all.

If you are being asked to marry someone on a submarine that may or may not be operational, you probably can't squeal for long. You have decisions to make, or maybe you have already made decisions by travelling this far.

They go down a narrow staircase. The dining cabin has a slim table with seats that you can only put half your arse on.

Alice would never mention squealing. But her versions would keep changing depending on who her audience was. She would never admit to converting and would always insist that religion was never mentioned. She would admit that she did say 'yes' thrice. She was not sure whether she said yes to the question about taking Teddy as her husband in exchange for a suspended dowry of thirty-two rupees, or if she said yes when in a moment of confusion someone started addressing her as Aliya. Her versions would vary. Sometimes she would recite half a Kalima, which would lead people to joke, in bad taste of course, that maybe she became half a Muslim. The only thing she would always remain consistent about was that there were dozens of sailors in white shalwar qameezes, all calling her bhabi, and that there were three seagulls in the sky squawking like old friends trying to put some sense into her head and stop the wedding.

People asked her: 'What does a submarine look like from the inside? Where do they keep their torpedoes? Is it true that the junior sailors have to sleep standing up?' And she would always get irritated with them because she thought they were interested only in trivia. 'It looked like a dead eel from the outside and inside smelled of sailors' farts,' she would say.

What Teddy and Alice would never know was that the smell of Alice Bhatti's jasmine bracelet lingered in the submarine for days. Sometimes there were heated discussions, once even a punch-up, about the exact colour of her lipstick. She was quite fair-skinned for a Christian, a midshipman insisted. There was the obvious gossip about how a police tout like Teddy Butt got lucky.

There was a consensus on one point, though: that Alice didn't look or behave like a typical Christian lady, although she was the only Christian lady they would ever meet in their entire lives.

TWELVE

ALICE BHATTI WALKS PAST the shop owned by Jesus Bhatti, who sells cigarettes, milk and, when business is bad, pints of his own blood at the Sacred. Next to the shop is an empty shack from where the only entrepreneur in French Colony used to operate, stealing manhole covers and then selling them back to the Corporation. The open drain is clogged, its surface shimmering with all the plastic bags dumped in it. When Alice Bhatti was still a student, she used to mull over this question: if half the population of French Colony is responsible for clearing the garbage from the whole city, how come they can't keep their own streets clean? Now she knows better and walks carefully trying to avoid the open sewers. She observes a gang of cats jumping the drain, playing a lazy game of catch.

Every married life in French Colony starts with a trip to the tailor's shop, and this is where Alice Bhatti is going: to Dulhousie Tailoring, the only business in French Colony that has been around for forty years and also has a branch in Lahore and, according to the signboard outside the shop, now one in Toronto as well. She waits for a moment outside and through the frosted glass door surveys the inside, full of shadows hunched over sewing machines. The shop's glass doors keep out the stench, or 'the French perfume' as outsiders call it. The aroma of steaming irons pressing Lawrencepur wool makes the customers feel rich, or at least tricks them into believing that they are not in French Colony any more. Senior Dulhousie has spent his life stitching cassocks for clergy, suits for churchgoing Catholic businessmen and wedding dresses for their daughters. Alice has never stepped inside the shop before, always aware that her father is as much of a Choohra in her own colony as he is outside it. By studying seven books in four years and marrying a semi-employed Musla, she is hoping to rise above the stench that is her daily bread. While in Borstal, she never missed her own home. She missed a home that she didn't have as yet. She would hear the stories of other inmates who had tried to kill their husband or husband's mistress or mistress's husband and these stories always had at the centre a home: a hand pump, a stove, a charpoy or a little courtyard with a jasmine plant. Was that what she was yearning for, a home she could call her own?

She is relieved that everything has happened so suddenly; she hasn't had the time to examine her own motives, otherwise her love story would have turned into an anthropological treatise about the survival strategies employed by Catholics in predominantly Islamic societies.

Dulhousie is a smart businessman; he can recognise ambition when he sees it, and although someone from French Colony getting a nurse's job is not unusual, a trainee nurse coming out of the household of Choohra Joseph Bhatti, whom even other Choohras consider untouchable, is a sign that the next generation is ready to move on. Dulhousie has seen enough Bhattis in his life and, dear Lord, they shun upward mobility as if Yassoo had explicitly forbidden it. He has seen their stubbornness forged over generations, their fortitude like an infectious disease that catches them young and is their only companion right up to their deathbed. The ambitious ones might send their women to slave in the big houses, but otherwise they think that the government owes them a living, a meagre, below-the-gutter living, but still a living. And now, if they are managing to go to schools and colleges, they have already risen above the Bhatti mindset that enslaves them. If they are ready to dress better, if they want a tailored suit, they want better manners, they want better houses, they give more to the Church. For him, sewing fine dresses is not just a matter of earning an honest living but also keeping his Lord's lambs in an optimistic mood;

a community that dresses better will ultimately become a happier community. So when he sees people like Alice Bhatti walk into his shop, he doesn't hold his nose, he doesn't send her off to any of his half-dozen students bent over their Singers, he adjusts his glasses and greets her with a smile so bright it could light up the farther corners of French Colony.

As is his habit, Mr Dulhousie offers a short prayer before he starts to take her measurements. This is the first time Alice has been measured, and every part that Mr Dulhousie takes in with his faded measuring tape becomes more real, human, marriageable.

Alice's body is one of those miracles of malnourishment, which has resulted in a thin, brittle bone structure with overgrown breasts. Dulhousie knows that she comes from the kind of household where starvation is passed off as fasting, where during every last week of the month dinner is bread soaked in water, where milk is taken without sugar and tea without milk, where meat is had when someone gets married or dies, where dhal and rice is a Sunday special and every fourth Sunday of the month is compulsory Lent. In these households, even empty stomachs gurgle *Yassoo be praised*.

With this dietary regime she has acquired a body that many girls of her age would kill for, or sometimes kill themselves while attempting to achieve. Her ribs can be counted through her shirt, her collarbones stick out like sharpened boomerangs, her ankles look like a display from an anatomy lab; but her breasts have somehow survived lack of proper nourishment, in fact seem to have thrived on the lack of a balanced diet, like Persian cantaloupes that only grow in the desert and die if it rains more than once every season. At the age of fourteen, she performed in an Easter play and at school afterwards had to stand in front of the cross to get her picture taken. An old nun quipped that she looked like a cross with tits. From then on, she has refused to go near a large cross.

Mr Dulhousie wraps the tape around her ribcage, making

sure that only the tips of his fingers touch her body, and whispers, 'By Lord's grace many rich Christian ladies starve themselves to acquire this kind of figure. I remember your mother, I made her wedding suit too. Same size. I could just look up my old register and come up with the exact same dress.' He says this with a smile and then takes off his glasses and wipes a non-existent tear from his eye. 'How tragic that He took her from us in her youth. But our Lord shuts one door and opens another. At least you were able to finish your education with all that settlement money. I hear you were even living in the hostel. That is what our people need to do more. Get out more often, mingle, learn to live with people outside the Colony.'

Alice Bhatti doesn't quite know how to deal with a neighbourhood tailor speculating on her family history. 'Yes, He took her,' she mumbles.

Dulhousie gets busy with measuring her and whispers another compliment. Alice can only make out something about how it's a privilege to have a natural figure like this.

Alice is painfully aware of this so-called privilege but has always found it a curse. Because people always stare. She is constantly pulling down the hem of her shirt to deflect their attention. What is she hoping to achieve? Does she really expect people to stop staring at her breasts and instead focus on the hem of her shirt? Or to be able to deflect their naked gaze to her fingers, fidgeting, pulling her shirt down nervously?

For work she chooses a loose shirt and then over that loose shirt covers her chest with a dupatta, makes sure that even the back of her neck is covered, ties her hair back, then makes sure that her shalwar covers her ankles. And only then does she set off for the Sacred.

Alice could probably have learned to ignore the stares, steeled herself against hungry eyes, managed to avoid the rubbernecks. She could have learned to live with the life lesson that men think that the best use of their eyes is to weigh a woman's anatomy, but, as she embarks on her professional life, she has realised that people are not content just looking. Suddenly they want to touch her as if not sure what they have seen is real. She is aware of the fact that different rules apply outside French Colony: some people do not want to drink from the same glass that she has drunk from, others will not take a banana from the same bunch that she has taken a banana from. Their problem. She can live with being an untouchable, but she desperately hopes for the only privilege that comes with being one. That people won't touch her without her explicit permission. But the same people who wouldn't drink from a tap that she has touched have no problem casually poking their elbows into her breast or contorting their own bodies to rub against her heathen bottom.

They try to exploit her professional standing as well. When she started as a nurse she was quite easy with her hands, taking pulses, pressing flesh for invisible tumours, tracking down that evasive source of pain. On a field trip to Sargodha district she was stopped by elderly men again and again who wanted her to check their pulse. She obliged readily, her trained fingers lightly picking up their sturdy, peasant's heartbeats; then she gave them the good news that they were in fine fettle. She even volunteered to look down their throats, tapped at their chests. One day she was standing beside a scenic well complete with a pair of shiny black bullocks taking weary but purposeful steps around it and little kids chasing chickens and goats when she took a stately grandfather's wrist in her hand and closed her eyes for extra concentration. She opened her eyes to give him the good news about his robust heart when she noticed that Grandpa's other hand had parted his dhoti and was tugging at a long, thin, flaccid penis. When she kicked the old man in his shins and started to walk away, she heard him mutter: 'I'll cut you up and throw the pieces in that well.'

Now she has lived long enough to know that cutting up women is a sport older than cricket but just as popular and equally full of obscure rituals and intricate rules that everyone seems to know except her.

Alice Bhatti is not interested in understanding the rules, but she also doesn't want to be the kind of girl who attracts the wrong kind of attention and ends up in the wrong place. She doesn't want to be the kind of girl who is groped on buses, poked in service kitchens, who cannot walk a block without giving people the idea that she should be travelling blindfolded in a car boot. She doesn't want to be someone who walks around demanding to be hacked to bits and buried in a back garden.

During her house job she worked in Accidents and Emergencies for six months and there was not a single day – not a single day – when she didn't see a woman shot or hacked, strangled or suffocated, poisoned or burnt, hanged or buried alive. Suspicious husband, brother protecting his honour, father protecting his honour, son protecting his honour, jilted lover avenging his honour, feuding farmers settling their water disputes, moneylenders collecting their interest: most of life's arguments, it seemed, got settled by doing various things to a woman's body. A woman was something you could get as loose change in a deal made on a street corner. Rarely, but very rarely, there was a woman who settled a score with the competition. Alice had met some in the Borstal who had bumped off their husbands, taken pride in what they had done, but still managed to look like widows in mourning. To her young mind, which had stayed away from newspapers and television which covered this sport with the same relish with which they covered every other sport, it seemed the city was full of serial killers. There was a murderer in every kitchen; sometimes there was a murderer even when there was no kitchen in the house, sometimes even when there was no house, no boundary wall, no roof. Even nomads living in improvised tents could catch the honour bug and settle a game of cards that had gone on for too long in the night by trading in a woman. And what she learned was that nobody was surprised; there were no police detectives sitting around matching clues, no parliamentary subcommittees discussing ways of saving this endangered species. It was as inevitable as the fact that it will not rain in March, as preordained as the rule that no matter how many speed restriction signs you put up, somebody, somewhere will manage to get run over by a motorised vehicle.

It's understandable that Alice Bhatti thinks about these things. She looks at these battered bodies on the floor of the A&E and tries to figure out the rules of this sport. Like any logical, thinking person she has begun to believe that there must be a reason why these women get killed and not the other fifty-six million in the land. Their names might be on the list but they manage to get away. Some of them complain of a fate worse than death but Alice Bhatti has seen many of the fresh arrivals in A&E, and she knows that getting hacked at the hands of a father, lover, brother is definitely a fate worse than being run over, accidentally, by a truck driven by your own offspring.

Alice Bhatti has made her observations and thinks she has identified the type of woman who attracts the wrong kind of attention, who stumbles from one man who wants to slap her to another man who wants to chop off her nose to that final man, the last inevitable man, who wants to slash her throat.

And she doesn't want to be that kind of woman.

She knows that a lot of the time these women are beautiful. Not ordinary beautiful but a strange kind of beauty that calls attention to itself. They could be wearing a hijab or covered in swathes of loose, man-repelling fabric and they would still draw attention to themselves. It is the kind of beauty that screams, 'Look, I am here, look, I am sitting, now I am standing, these are my legs, I am walking on my legs, this is my neck, can you feel the ice-cold Pepsi going down my throat, here is my nose, do you think it will look better with a nose ring?' When they open their mouths they sound common enough, but their eyes look at the person they speak to with regal contempt: aren't you sad you are not me? Aren't you sad you can't have me? Is your life worth living? I am leaving now, I have places to go, things to do, private things, intimate things, with other people, not with you. You can stay here and live your miserable life. You can keep looking as I walk on these legs and go away from you.

Of course you don't have to be a head-turning beauty or possess a pair of eyes that taunt to end up on the A&E's floor. Alice Bhatti has seen women so old, so haggard, so beaten by life that cutting them seems like a waste of time. But they do it anyway.

Alice Bhatti is not taking any chances. She doesn't want to be that kind of woman.

She tries to maintain a nondescript exterior; she learns the sideways glance instead of looking at people directly. She speaks in practised, precise sentences so that she is not misunderstood. She chooses her words carefully, and if someone addresses her in Punjabi, she answers in Urdu, because an exchange in her mother tongue might be considered a promise of intimacy. She uses English for medical terms only, because she feels if she uses a word of English in her conversation she might be considered a bit forward. When she walks she walks with slightly hurried steps, as if she has an important but innocent appointment to keep. She avoids eye contact, she looks slightly over people's heads as if looking out for somebody who might come into view at any moment. She doesn't want anyone to think that she is alone and nobody is coming for her. She sidesteps even when she sees a boy half her age walking towards her, she walks around little puddles when she can easily leap over them; she thinks any act that involves stretching her legs might send the wrong signal. After all, this is not the kind of thing where you can leave your actions to subjective interpretations. She never eats in public. Putting something in your mouth is surely an invitation for someone to shove something horrible down your throat. If you show your hunger, you are obviously asking for something.

Mr Dulhousie is looking at her with a benign smile as she takes out crumpled hundred-rupee notes and puts them on the desk in front of him. She has also perfected no-touch transactions. If your fingers touch someone's fingers, what might they make of it?

Before leaving the shop, she gives Dulhousie the only instruction that matters to her. 'When you stitch the shirt, can you please make my privileges look a bit flat?'

THIRTEEN

TEDDY BUTT'S G SQUAD family, having failed to arrange a proper wedding party for him, try to give him a proper wedding night, the kind they would have liked to have for themselves. Most of them come from upcountry, where their own wedding involved only a telegram from home saying apply for leave, send money, you are getting married on such and such day. So it's understandable that they want to celebrate the first ever love marriage in G Squad in style. They raided the stolen property store in their own offices, haggled with some flower sellers, threatened to throw the owner of a bedware store into jail, and in a last generous bid to give Teddy a perfect start in his married life, picked the locks of a crockery warehouse.

When Teddy comes to fetch Alice from the Sacred, she has changed into her two-piece wedding dress stitched by Mr Dulhousie.

'Where is Madame Bhatti going?' Noor asks her.

'Somewhere nice, I hope,' she says.

When Teddy, with Alice on his arm, enters his flat in Al-Aman apartments, he finds himself surrounded by strings of marigolds hanging from the ceiling. Alice notices that some of these strings are made of paper flowers. There are a few macramé ones too. On the wall in the living room, red ribbons are Scotch Taped to read *Happy WeddingS*.

Although Teddy isn't an official member of the squad – no rank, no promotions, no pension plan – they take good care of him. In return, he acts as a crime-scene cleaner, comforter, errand boy, towel holder, cheerleader, doorstopper, gun-cleaner, replacement court witness, proxy prisoner, fourth card player, but more importantly a companion to people who have been caught but not yet killed, a companion for the passengers on their last journey.

'Soothing the doomed slut' is the nearest he has come to having a job description.

Teddy expected something from them for his wedding, maybe an invitation to use one of the safe houses for his honeymoon, or some trinkets, and he definitely expected some advice about life after marriage. He gets all of that and a house full of flowers. They have decided to give him a sizeable dowry. A dinner service for his grubby single-stove kitchen, half a dozen teacups with saucers, even a matching tea cosy, Chinese blankets with wild animal prints, silk bedsheets and a carton full of towels, marked *For Export Only*.

After the ceremony on the submarine and before Alice arrived at his flat, they took him to a safe house for what they called a warm-up night. 'We were looking for a virgin for this special occasion, but then Inspector Malangi reminded us that our bhabi is Yassoo's follower, so we went looking for a Christian virgin. And you know what the pimp said? He said the last one was taken more than two thousand years ago.'

Malangi, being an elderly gentleman and the founder of the squad, only smiled, while the others slapped their thighs and laughed out loud. Then they got busy with a game of cards that would decide their turn; it was understood that Teddy Butt being the bridegroom would obviously get to go first. They were models of good behaviour that night and the party broke up at four in the morning with a still unfinished quarter-bottle of Murree Millennium.

The only note of discord came when the Christian girl confessed after two drinks that she was actually a Hindu from Nepal. Malangi became sulky and threatened to set police dogs on her, then scolded his colleagues. 'First I get away from one wife and three daughters, that is four women, just to be with my friends. And I end up with yet another woman who, like all other women, lies and cheats. Why didn't I just stay home?'

The girl was businesslike with them, encouraging them to take their game of cards seriously, giving special attention to the bridegroom. And when she told them that she knew how to say fuck in eight languages, they all cracked up and insisted on repeating it after her in a chorus. The night ended with them shouting *fok jou, na ma low, khahar kosse, chodhru, ma ki kir k*.

And yes there was marital advice for him, if only as an afterthought. But it sounded sincere and urgent.

'No disrespect to our bhabi, your wife is just like our sister but these mushkis are very hot, so save yourself. You have worked hard on this body, she'll suck all the juices from your bones.'

'Go easy, take breaks, come with us on little trips.'

'Come and take a boy from our lock-up occasionally. It keeps the balance in the universe.'

'Love can only survive if it comes with a ration card.'

On the big night, the G Squad have made an effort. They have hastily thrown a black silk bedsheet on the mattress, its price tag still attached. On the sheet they have strewn some rose petals and in the middle sits a teddy bear the size of a class-five boy, in its lap a red box of sweets from Fresco. Teddy picks it up and thinks he should offer some to Alice, but then its extremely light weight puzzles him. The time spent with the G Squad has taught him to be suspicious about things that don't measure up; there is something unusual about the box. He opens it and shuts it immediately, embarrassed. He opens it again and picks out a slip of paper nestling on a pile of used condoms from the warm-up night.

'We'll pick you up at four in the morning.' Inspector Malangi's handwriting is like that of a child trying to fake a sick note. Getting to work is Teddy's own responsibility. Whenever he is offered a ride, he knows that they really need him. It means they have got someone special to deal with, or someone really nervous. He hates dealing with the nervous ones. He also thinks that it is a nice reminder that the business of life must go on despite marriage, despite a wife, despite a house full of crockery and vague expectations. Despite his new life, he will be able to pay regular visits to his old life.

He also realises that tonight he is the nervous one. He has dreamed about it for so long that now, finally faced with the object of his fantasies, he feels short of breath. It reminds him of how he feels before big competitions, a certain hesitance, not knowing whether this is what he really wants in life. He feels like one of those lion cubs who manage to corner their first prey but then don't know how to kill it, can't yet find the jugular vein. As he waits for Alice to come out of the bathroom, he wants to be with the G Squad racing down a highway with some deadly criminal squirming in the back of their van. Or just hanging out in the office, making a list of dangerous criminals who might one day end up in the back of their van.

Now he feels as if he himself is in the back of the van.

He realises that Sister Alice is standing just behind him, very close. He still thinks of her as Sister. Alice. He feels her hand on his shoulder. He turns around in panic as if she has read his thoughts. He finds himself in her arms. She nuzzles his nose with hers, wedding-night drunk.

'I didn't expect all this. You planned it. For how long have you been planning? How did you know this would work out? What if I had said no?'

Teddy's body is limp against hers. He puts his arms around her and he cracks his knuckles. He knows in that moment that he probably hoped that she would say no. That he had never thought about the life that would follow if she said yes. He was mentally ready for a lifetime of yearning and mournful songs but he had never actually planned for a woman, any woman, and Alice is suddenly nothing but a woman who has come to live in his apartment. Now he knows how it feels to be one of those criminals in the back of the van; they are shorn of their deadliness, squirming and pleading, promising a lifetime of innocent compliance. He knows what happens to them.

'My friends from work. They did it all. I don't know where to buy flowers and teacups. They are all married, so I guess they know.'

'So you have a job as well?' Alice runs her fingers along his spine. Teddy squirms, then stops himself and pretends he is ticklish. 'Such a responsible man. What more? Now do you want to tell me the names you have chosen for our babies?' She holds his face in her hands and makes to kiss him on his lips. Confused, Teddy turns his face away and her lips end up on his ear. Both his hands grip her buttocks, but then he realises that there is no need to hurry, she is not going anywhere; they have the whole night, hell, their whole life in front of them. He moves his hands up and holds her by her waist. He has an unannounced, almost sickly erection.

'Do you want some tea?' he asks.

'I'll make it,' she says, holding his arms and putting them by his sides, patting them, as if reassuring a hypochondriac.

In the kitchen she finds a tea set still wrapped in old newspapers, tears open a family pack of Lipton tea bags, scrubs a kettle that has fungus on its lid, puts it under a tap that has more fungus growing in its mouth, and waits for a few seconds, for a thin dribble of water to fill the kettle. After spluttering and hissing, the flame from the stove almost licks her nose, and it is only after she has put the kettle on the stove and found a lid to cover it that she stands back and thinks that this is her new life. And she hasn't told Joseph Bhatti about it yet.

She tries to imagine a conversation with him that'll never take place. 'If he is not a Choohra, it doesn't matter. You have married outside French Colony, it doesn't matter. What does it matter if he is a Yassoo man or a Musla? What does it matter who he is? Welcome home, memsahib. But always remember, wherever you go, you won't be very far from French Colony.'

Alice Bhatti puts two empty cups on saucers, smiles as they sit side by side and comes out of the kitchen.

Teddy stands just outside the door with his heart beating. She comes to him with open arms. Teddy Butt is accustomed to a certain amount of coy bargaining from women in these situations. *I'll take my shalwar off but you have to promise you won't touch my bra.* Or sometimes breathy cooing in the ear used as delaying tactics. *You big man, first tell me about your life.* Or, *Look, you can do anything you want, just don't spoil my hair. Can you at least wash your hands? You have to wear two of those, they look too flimsy. Hurry up, the last bus is in one hour.* Or, *What's the hurry, I am not running away with your money.* Or sometimes just glacial passivity and silent tears, as if they were homesick for a place that has been obliterated in some obscure war.

But the way Alice embraces him is the way men are supposed to embrace each other, open-chested, arms around each other, loins locked.

There is no warning, no build-up, he hasn't even kissed her properly yet. He just touches her, shudders, and a wet patch spreads in his starched shalwar like spilt ink. A few drops dribble down to his ankle. Teddy is the type of man who hates nothing more than his own seed. He has a separate set of towels for this very purpose on his bedside table. But surrounded by strings of plastic flowers, real rose petals on the bed and Alice breathing heavy in his arms, he has to pretend that nothing has happened. He tightens his grip around her, as if trying to block this scandalous information from reaching her.

'I know this happens sometimes,' Alice says, and snuggles his neck with her chin.

'What happens? What has happened?' Her knowledge frightens him. How does she know? he wonders, and then suddenly it dawns on him. What else does she know? After all, there is not much he knows about her. How has she come upon this knowledge? And now she stands there cuddling him in mock sympathy. She knows that it happens to other people. How does she know that? She has never been married before. How can he be sure? Has she been with other men? Suddenly he feels that she is complicit in every premature ejaculation in the city.

'So this has happened before? To you? I mean to someone with you?'

'Not really.' Alice tries to evoke the coyness she thinks she is entitled to as a bride. And then adds by way of explanation, 'But I did go to school.'

'So this is what they teach you there?'

'I went to a nursing school, remember.'

'But still, what kind of class do you go to, to learn this? Do they draw pictures? It's not really an illness. Or is it an illness?'

'Of course it's not an illness. They don't teach it there. I just know. I also know what happens after that.' She reaches into Teddy's trousers and gropes around, and finds that his thighs and groin are waxed.

'I need to go to the toilet.' Teddy grabs a towel from the bedside table and rushes away. 'And where's that tea you promised me?'

At three in the morning he sits on the edge of the bed, washed, changed, wrapping and unwrapping a handkerchief around his hand.

'Come to bed, go to sleep,' says Alice.

'I need to go to work.'

'At this time? What kind of shift starts at three in the morning?'

'It starts at four, actually. It's police work. It can start any time.' He feels he has already said too much.

'This is not the kind of work you can bring home with you.' He remembers Inspector Malangi's advice. 'This is not the kind of work you discuss over a family meal.'

'I'll be picked up.' He feels that should be explanation enough. It should also tell her that it's not some lowly job where you have to take a bus to work. It's official. There is an official vehicle on its way. To take him to work.

But it's only 3:15 a.m. He wishes it were already four. Or at least that Alice was properly asleep. His heart sinks at the thought that from now on not only is he responsible for his own sleep, he is responsible for hers as well.

He watches her face closely. She is back in some dream, smiling. He thinks that this married life is not fair. He is responsible for her sleep but has no control over her dreams.

FOURTEEN

By the time the G Squad Hilux screeches to a halt in front of the Al-Aman apartment block, Alice Bhatti is fast asleep, with her head in Teddy's lap. She is not one of those girls who grew up dreaming of various scenarios about their married life, but this is one of the things she had imagined herself doing: sleeping with her head on her husband's lap.

Teddy has been staring at her face, and panicking every time her eyes twitch and a smile spreads. She seems to be in a dream where there are things to smile about. Teddy has an urge to keep sitting, keep looking, until she wakes up and tells him about her dream. But he can hear the Hilux revving its engine downstairs. If you have a job to do at four in the morning, there is a reason that it needs to be done then. It's not the kind of job that would fit into a nine-to-five routine. It is obviously not the kind of job that can be done after sunrise or before sunset. It needs to be done at four a.m.

Teddy puts his right hand under her warm neck and slips a pillow under it. Alice shivers in her sleep, smacks her lips, then smiles as he pulls a light blanket over her. 'Lord be with you,' she mumbles in her sleep, her fingers gently scratching his spine. Teddy is startled and looks at her as if he has woken up with a stranger whose name he can't remember.

There is no time to wake her and ask her what she means with this lord business. Is this what she has been dreaming about? A lord? Her Lord? He has never really given religion much thought, but this is his house and if there is going to be a lord around here, it has to be him. I'll talk to her when I come back home in the morning, he thinks. He doesn't like to leave home with unanswered questions. His shoulders feel

108

heavy. He tries to think of an excuse to escape from the mission, but then looks around at his new life – strings of macramé hanging from the roof, the new bedsheets, the Chinese blanket – and knows that he can't escape from this. One night of married life and it seems he is already trapped, weighed down by his new demands. He shuts the door gently and races down the stairs. The driver has switched off the headlights on the Hilux but its engine is still running, its red and blue flashing lights playing quasar with the new minaret of the neighbourhood mosque. The old crumbling minaret has been refurbished with thousands of little irregular-shaped mirrors, probably leftover shards from a mirror-shop wreck. He doesn't see Inspector Malangi before he appears from the shadows, puts his arm around Teddy's shoulders and starts walking him towards the Hilux. 'Don't worry, we'll be back before she wakes up.' He points vaguely towards the upper floor of Al-Aman. Inspector Malangi never jokes during one of their pre-dawn missions. He becomes polite and methodical and caring, like a devoted father getting his children ready for school: uniforms, homework, pocket money, a loving pat on the back.

'We are taking him to meet his mother for half an hour because of his good behaviour. To Buffer Zone. Then we are taking him to Central Jail, and then it's up to the lawyers and the judges.' Inspector Malangi pauses to light a cigarette; his walrus moustache needs a trim, his eyes look tired. 'But he just won't stop crying. I haven't even touched him for the last two hours. Do something.' He gives Teddy a friendly slap on the back, hands him a TT pistol and a flashlight. Then he produces a tiny perfume bottle, Teddy extends his palm and he pours a few drops on it. Teddy rubs his hand under his nose. Inspector Malangi believes that bad smells are disorienting, not good for your focus.

'I don't know how you do it, Teddy.'

Teddy Butt ignores the compliment. He needs to preserve all

his communication skills for the job at hand. The Hilux takes off as soon as he climbs into the back. A huddled, shawl-wrapped figure in the corner stirs, and after great effort and clinking of chains, a face looks up. Teddy switches on his flashlight. He can usually tell the value of the target by looking at the weight of metal on them. This one seems pretty heavy. A chunky pair of handcuffs, a nylon string around his ankles; this arrangement is reinforced by a set of iron rods that join his handcuffs to iron rings around his knees. It's unfathomable how this creature can stay in any human position for long: if he sits, his knees are around his shoulders, if he tries to lie down, the iron rods threaten to pierce his loins; he can't even roll himself into a ball and lie on the floor of the Hilux. These arrangements are usually made for the kind of people who tend to jump out of speeding jail vans, or for the sort of prisoners whose friends and comrades ambush police vehicles or barge into courts with RPGs blazing or blow up bridges to take back their man.

Teddy removes the shawl from the prisoner's face and holds his flashlight close to it. The face is boyish and covered in tears and snot. One eye is a reddish, swollen mound. The lower lip is broken, and behind it a couple of teeth have probably been knocked out. He whimpers like an animal that has been half slaughtered with a blunt knife and is now waiting for its soul to leave its body. He is in that sad state where a swift death seems like a reasonably better option.

Teddy takes a corner of the boy's shawl and starts to clean up his face. The whimpering gets louder.

'We'll take these off when we get to your mother's place,' Teddy says in a casual voice, not reassuring, just explaining standard operating procedures.

The Hilux honks at a donkey cart with spinach piled high and the driver asleep stretched out on top. The donkey, used to early-morning speedy traffic, swerves and makes way for the Hilux. A streetlight flickers on a small signboard, the kind that have cropped up all over the city. It depicts a wooden coffin: *Say your prayers before prayers are said for you.*

When asked to do this duty, Teddy feels like one of those ancient fabulists he has heard about on National Geographic. When men still lived in caves, they sat around fires and told each other stories so that they could stay awake and not get devoured by wild beasts. Teddy feels he is doing the same thing, in a slightly different way: keeping them awake, comforting them, cajoling them through the night, making them feel alive till such a time when they are not alive and don't need to hear any more stories to stay awake.

The boy raises his head with a great deal of difficulty, looks into Teddy's eyes and sobs. 'I know you are taking me away. I know you won't bring me back.' Teddy gets up from his seat and sits beside the boy, putting his right arm around him. That is usually half the job, developing a physical bond with them, holding their hand, being their family. You just need to tell them a story, any story, preferably something unexpected. 'I gave them all the names.' The boy's sobs get louder. 'Everything I know. They said if I gave them all the names, they'd send me to jail. But you are not taking me to jail.' He starts bawling like a child who has just realised that his favourite toy is broken beyond repair and he won't be given a replacement.

Teddy gets them all the time. *I didn't do it. They made me do it. I was told I was doing it for my country. I was at home asleep. My uncle is a lawyer.* He knows how to deal with them.

'I got married last week,' Teddy says. 'Tonight was my first night with my wife. And here I am at four in the morning being dragged out to Buffer Zone.' He looks at the boy's face to see if he is interested in his story. If the mention of Buffer Zone has brought back any memories. 'I know what you are scared of,' he whispers in his ear. A whispered word of kindness in his trade can be as effective as pliers in a police investigator's hands. 'We both know that they do those things. But why would they drive so far out? Any open sewer in the city centre would do.

Do you know why they have brought me with you? Because they don't want your family to see their faces. See, I am not even in the police. Would they drag a policeman away from his new wife? I am just somebody they want to use so that your family doesn't come after them. I am not saying you'll live happily ever after. Who knows what will happen tomorrow, or when they take you out next time. They don't always bring me with them. But you know, tonight we are all right.' Teddy shrugs his shoulders, challenging the boy to share his meagre optimism. He switches off his flashlight and whispers, 'If I were you, I wouldn't trust them. I would note down their names and remember their faces, their ranks. See the number on their belt buckles? That's their ID number. I would drag them to court after this is over. If I were you, I would go and talk to the media, name names. I know a crime reporter, but you must not mention me. This is my livelihood, and now I have got a family to support. Did I tell you that I just got married?'

A truck with its lights on full beam speeds past them on the wrong side. Teddy catches a glimpse of skinned buffaloes hanging in the back on rows and rows of hooks, their heads intact, horns curled and eyes wide open. He moves forward to block the boy's view. He doesn't want him to see dead buffaloes hanging upside down at this hour of the night. Teddy doesn't want the boy to get any hasty premonitions about what lies ahead.

'So I got married last week. Guess where the wedding took place? I can bet you'll never be able to guess. Come on, three guesses. But who would have thought that I'd be spending the first night of my married life with you? My new wife definitely had no idea that I'd go to sleep with her but by the time she woke up I'd be with a pretty boy like you.' Teddy slaps the boy's thigh and laughs. He notices that the boy is not whimpering any more. He is trying to say something. That is always a good sign. Teddy wants to encourage him. 'You must be someone important? You must have really impressed someone.

They wouldn't put so much metal on a pickpocket. Are you married?'

'My name is not Abu Zar.' The boy's voice is melodic, cultured, as if he has been taking singing lessons. 'That was my friend's name. I mean that was the name he took. My name is Afzal and my mother doesn't live in Buffer Zone. None of my family lives in this city.'

For a few moments there is complete silence. They have entered an area of total darkness. They leave streetlights behind as they approach Buffer Zone. Teddy can hear not-Abu Zar breathing. Something pops in his nostrils like little crackers going off or a broken bone finding its lost home.

Confusion in such circumstances might seem tragic or tragicomic depending on what you find funny and what makes you sad, but it is a very useful tool in Teddy's line of work. If they insist right to the end that they are somebody else, then they live in the hope that the confusion might be cleared up at the last moment. Even when you feel the barrel on the back of your neck, you can say to yourself that they are killing someone else, not you. You go down protesting and hoping to correct a mistake that someone made in an official file, which is better than going down weeping or even worse just going completely silent with fear.

The Hilux makes its inevitable stop fifty feet from a phone booth. On these nights Inspector Malangi behaves as if it's him who is going to die, so he always wants to call his family first, wants to talk to his children.

Teddy accompanies him to the phone booth. They climb over a pile of gravel and walk in silence like two sleepy night workers. He knows there is no point in bringing this up, but if he doesn't bring it up now, he'll have to think about it later. And this is not the kind of work he would like to take home. 'This guy we have got is not Abu Zar, he is just the driver; not even a driver, he just borrowed his motorbike. The real Abu Zar is in Sweden.'

Malangi holds the door of the phone booth open and turns towards Teddy. 'What do you think we should do? Raid Sweden? Our jurisdiction ends at that bridge over there. We can't even pick up a common thief from Clifton. Do you want to know how many people lay dead in Garden East after he and his friend drove by? One night with your wife and you are teaching me law enforcement.' He sighs. 'We all tend to go a bit soft. Look, Bakhtawar has her maths test today. Can I talk to her first?' Inspector Malangi shuts the door and starts dialling.

Far on the horizon, a cement factory exhales a cloud of milky smoke, and a faint red dawn struggles behind it.

'I'll pick you up from school, my dear. Don't forget to read the questions twice before you start answering them. Remember, read them twice, because you might miss something the first time.'

FIFTEEN

ALICE VISITS HER FATHER in the morning to get her things. French Colony seems filthier than she had left it a couple of days before. The walls are covered with posters announcing a two-day-long Quantum Healing Festival to be led by a visiting preacher, Edward Qaiser from Oklahoma, who claims to sell the thing that Catholic evangelists all over the world seem to sell, the promise that the lame shall walk.

And when they can walk, Alice Bhatti wonders, where will they go? How about real miracles, like the drains shall remain unclogged? Or the hungry shall be fed? Or our beloved French Colony shall stop smelling like a sewer?

In his youth it had been suggested to Joseph Bhatti that he should start charging for his ulcer cures. 'God gives me a gift and you want me to sell it?' he retorted. And then he would add, probably in jest, 'And the gift I have is not even mine. It's a gift from the Musla god. He probably mistook me for a potential Musla. You can't sell what's not yours. You don't choose your neighbour and your neighbours don't choose their own god. And you shouldn't provoke your neighbour's god.'

As she approaches her street, Alice Bhatti has a slight sense of trepidation. She feels no emotional pull, no sudden rush of childhood memories; she looks away when she sees a vaguely familiar face approaching. She is ashamed of the fact that she is embarrassed to call this place home. Before she went to the Borstal via nursing school, Alice had never really felt like a grown-up; she was always defined by her father, his profession, French Colony, Reverend Philip and his insistence on framing all life's problems in wedding parables. In fact it was during her time in the Borstal that she first felt free. No mother to tell her to keep her hair tidy, no father to tell her to keep the tidy hair covered. Just a lot of women with bad teeth and memories that wouldn't go away.

She finds the door to her house open, but there is no sign of Joseph Bhatti. Then she hears the sound of wood being chopped in the backyard. She starts taking out her clothes and putting them in a gym bag that she has brought from Al-Aman apartments. She takes her toothbrush, two lipsticks, a moisturiser and some imitation jewellery and puts them in a little vanity case. It's only after she has placed her bag in the middle of the bed that she realises how little she's taking from this home: twenty-seven years of life and she is taking with her a beggar's dowry.

Joseph Bhatti appears in the doorway, wiping his brow. He is wearing a white vest and his dhoti is folded up and tucked above his knees. The grey hair on his chest is covered in fine sawdust. He is surprised to see Alice Bhatti but he doesn't seem displeased.

'I see you are all packed up and ready to go. You could have waited for me to go first.'

Alice Bhatti has never figured out how a certain kind of man can manage to play victim and saviour in the same breath. He wouldn't have noticed if she hadn't come back for a couple of years, but now he is giving her that 'see, I am being abandoned again' look.

He thinks he was abandoned by Alice Bhatti's mother. And who abandoned her mother in the first place?

At the age of twelve, Alice Bhatti is not sure if her mother has just passed away, or has died in a tragic accident, or left this world to become Yassoo's eternal bride. They keep telling her that He took her and she wants to ask why, but everyone is too busy cuddling her, patting her head, as if she hasn't become an orphan but won a prize at school.

Three days after Alice Bhatti's mother's funeral, Joseph Bhatti goes back to work and comes back with a baby peacock, except that Alice can't tell that it's a peacock because it's covered in black mud and is either fast asleep or dead. It smells of rotting fish.

'Look, Mother of Alice, what I found,' Joseph Bhatti shouts as he enters the house. He is startled for a moment when he realises that Mother of Alice is not home, she is in paradise with her new husband, Yassoo Masih. Alice stares back at him from beside the tap that is used to wash clothes and crockery as well as for Sunday showers. She is scrubbing a pan slowly, her mind still struggling to accept the fact that her mother is not coming back from work. She saw the coffin, walked behind it, joined in when they sang *pity on the soul of thy handmaid*, but her twelve-year-old brain still can't comprehend concepts like everlasting salvation and the perils of the mortal life. So if Mother of Alice is never coming back, who will cook, who will do the dishes, who will wash her hair? is all she thinks. And then she picks up the dishes and sits under the tap. She doesn't want her mother to find filthy dishes when she returns from her tryst with Yassoo.

Joseph Bhatti can't remember how he addressed his wife before Alice was born. He called her nothing; just *oye*, or *listen*, or *what's for dinner?* or *did you hide my bottle?* or *here is my salary* or sometimes when he returned from work with a salvaged object, *look what I found*. Now, standing in the doorway, cradling a bird dripping black filth, Joseph Bhatti is startled by his own voice and the lack of response to it. Nobody says: Father of Alice, you have brought home more kachra, you can't stay away from garbage even when you are off duty.

They always referred to each other as Mother of Alice and Father of Alice, as if they had been waiting to become parents so they could abandon their old names. They always referred to his work as duty, as if his duty was not clearing up clogged sewers but directing the traffic or standing watch on a glacier to defend his country's borders.

Joseph Bhatti stops in his tracks for a moment when he realises that he'll never be called Father of Alice by anyone again, but then he continues as if Mother of Alice's accidental little death should not get in the way of a sweet habit nurtured over twelve years.

Alice Bhatti is not used to being addressed by her father. He makes toys for her, little birds from discarded wood usually, but he is not the kind of father who hugs his child or cuddles her to sleep, especially if the child in question is a twelve-year-old girl. But when Joseph Bhatti sees Alice sitting under the tap, furiously scrubbing a pot, trying to be her own mother, he comes to her and puts his hand on her shoulder and says the words that she has been hearing since they brought her mother home covered in a white sheet: 'What can we do, my child? He took her.'

Before the funeral, it seemed they hadn't merely covered her body but prepared her for export to some far-off country with strict packaging regulations. With two clean knots at both ends of the shimmering white shroud, she looked like a giant vegetable being sent to cold storage. Reverend Philip, who conducted the funeral service, seemed more excited than sombre and kept saying, *He took her.* In fact he was so excited that to Alice it seemed that Reverend Philip had given Him a hand when He was taking her. Or at least that He had consulted Father Philip before taking her.

'Our Lord took her away when she was in the prime of her youth; now she looks down upon us from the heavens and smiles upon us and her smile lights up our lives. She wasn't ours to keep, she was Yassoo's bride, and there she lives with Him in paradise, and this arrangement will last for eternity. But she left us a gift of life; she gave us the gift of Alice. Our hearts are filled with His blessings that He took her from us but in taking her from us He returned her to us for all eternity. Our hearts are full of memories of her and our memories are filled with her generous heart. But our hearts go out to our brother Joseph Bhatti who is still grieving.'

How did He take her from them?

Alice Bhatti's mother died at work. At somebody's house where she worked full time. She had quit her three part-time cleaning jobs at three different houses to get this one job because they wanted someone full time. This house was so big it could have housed all the three houses where she had previously worked. In fact the whole Bhatti household could fit under their travertine marble staircase, which needed to be washed and polished every day. It was on this staircase that she slipped and died. He took her. It's entirely conceivable that if you are washing travertine marble with soapy water you can slip and crack your skull, you can die. When He wants to take you, He can make the marble staircase slippery. He can make you put more soap in water than required for travertine marble. He can make you trip over that bucket of soapy water you put on the stairs and forgot.

But it is not very likely that when you slip on that staircase you'll also accidentally scratch yourself on your left breast with such violence that those who wash your body will see four parallel sharp gashes drawn with human nails. It's also unlikely that during that fall on the staircase you'll somehow manage to spill someone's sperm on your thighs.

He took her.

There were rumours that Reverend Philip had accepted a gift of ten thousand rupees on Joseph Bhatti's behalf to stop the autopsy and let the owners of the house with the staircase off the hook. But the truth is that even those who believed this rumour – or maybe even started this rumour – didn't believe for a moment that the owners of the house with a marble staircase of that size would let any hook sink into them.

So yes. Maybe it was He who took her.

A gardener from the house with the marble staircase from where He took her turned up at the funeral service, and the way he behaved it was clear to everyone that he was a Musla and had never been to a Catholic service of any kind. Whenever

Reverend Philip mentioned Mother of Alice's name (which by the way was Margaret Bhatti, and many people heard her name uttered for the first and the last time at her funeral service), the gardener started to wail in an injured animal's voice. And when everyone stood up to join the choir singing praises to the Lord who took her, he kept sitting with his hands covering his face and muttering something in Bengali. The congregation believed he was offering some Musla prayer, as they clearly heard him say the word Allah repeatedly.

After the service, over a pot of biryani that Reverend Philip had generously donated, the crying stranger at the funeral service was discussed in whispers. The person sitting on the gardener's left, who was the only one who had spoken to the stranger and hence found out that he was a gardener from the house from where He took her, insisted that he had heard him saying 'murder, murder, murder' during the prayer. The person sitting on the right of the gardener accused the person sitting on the left of spreading vicious rumours and violating the sanctity of a post-funeral meal. He even offered to swear on the Holy Bible to prove that the stranger was actually saying 'martyr, martyr, martyr'.

The stranger himself had left immediately after the funeral prayers, without attending the biryani feast. He was never heard from again.

'Mother of Alice.' Joseph Bhatti lowers the bird into Alice's arms and says, 'It's not a hen. It's a peacock.'

Alice Bhatti has never seen a peacock in her life, except in her year-one class book where P stood for Peacock or Pakistan. But this bird in her arms looks nothing like the one in the picture. It looks and smells like a piece of wet garbage. She holds it under the water tap, and as the mud starts to wash away, she sees crescent sheens of green and blue under it, the patterns of yellow and gold emerge slowly and as the soap washes away the mud, spots of red and brown complete the picture from her book. She uses her bar of Capri soap, which is reserved for their Sunday baths, and starts to scrub it. The peacock squirms in her hands, puffs up its wings and shudders violently, sending soapy water drops all around. Some goes into Alice's eye, and she rubs it with the back of her hand, managing to get more soap into it. She is crying but Joseph Bhatti can't tell. He goes into the corner with the stove and asks, 'So what are you going to make for supper?'

This is how Alice becomes Mother of Alice, and she does not like it one bit. 'Nothing,' she says. 'Or do you want me to cook this?' She lets go of the bird, which stretches its wings, takes a short flight, then hops around the courtyard trying to find a place to hide.

'What are you making?' Alice Bhatti asks her father, as if enquiring about dinner arrangements. Joseph Bhatti wraps his dhoti around his knees, sits down on the bed, picks up the bag as if checking its weight to guess how long she is going for, and seems satisfied with its light weight. 'I have been working on a cross, with my own hands, but I can't show it to anyone before I have finished it. I will send it to Italy. You'll see. Everyone will see.'

'A cross? That's what this world needs. Another cross.'

'Yes. The world needs this one. You know that our Lord Yassoo's faith didn't spread beyond Egypt until they learned to mass-produce wooden crosses,' he says, emphasising every word, as if trying to explain the Old Testament to high-school students. 'What we need to do now is make our own, with our own hands. Stop this merchandising.'

'They are everywhere now,' says Alice Bhatti. 'You can buy them really cheaply, in all materials, all shapes. I have seen some that double as telephones and alarm clocks. There are Chinese ones that can recite the Holy Bible in thirty-one languages.'

'You should have brought him with you,' says Joseph Bhatti. 'I know that whoever he is, he is not a Choohra. I hear he is a Butt. Probably fair-skinned, traces his ancestry to Central Asia via Kashmir. But just because they became Muslas doesn't mean that they are any better than us.'

'He is at work,' says Alice, picking up her bag. 'He does night shifts, but I'll bring him over soon.'

Alice used to tell her dorm mates at the nursing school that if Yassoo came back to life today and roamed the world and saw it full of so many crosses, wouldn't he conclude that it was a world of perpetual pain?

And for once, He would be right.

Joseph Bhatti will one day sit down to write what will be called his last testament. It will be published in some newspapers as an open letter; in *Catholic Monthly* it will be described as 'the last desperate plea of a wronged man'. The *Good News Weekly* will call it 'the sad rant of a grieving father'. It will go on to describe him as 'someone who divided the community, someone who was against the very concept of community, someone who practised religion as if it was black magic, who brought his already beleaguered Church into disrepute by openly hobnobbing with black magicians and spiritual quacks and then petitioning the Vatican against his own church. He washed his dirty linen in the holiest of holy places.'

Joseph Bhatti has never believed in daily, mundane suffering. He has always hated their little petitions, their letters to the editor; he always leaves the room when he hears the word 'persecution'. He doesn't know yet that late in his life he will be forced to write a petition. But then what kind of father wouldn't demand justice for his daughter?

He still has his tumbler and set of candles. But these days he is mostly called for stomach cancers, and that too only when patients have been sent back home from hospital to spend their last days with the family. He can still light a candle. He can still recite Sura Asar one hundred and one times without getting breathless. But life has beaten him into submission. Now he says things like 'It's Allah who cures, I only light the candle and speak his words.' And after he has done his procedure and knows in his heart that it will not work, he doesn't stay, doesn't accept any hospitality: 'No thank you, I already ate. I don't drink tea.'

He feels that finally they have pulled Yassoo down to their level, as if Yassoo wasn't the saviour of all mankind but a janitor who went around cleaning their streets, then sat in a corner drinking his Choohra chai from his Choohra cup until the day he quietly died and ascended to a Choohra heaven.

SIXTEEN

'DO YOU KNOW WHAT happens to men after they get married? Teddy Butt asks not-Abu Zar as he massages his stomach. 'And do you know what happens to women after they get married? Here's a clue: it's not the same thing and it has nothing to do with sex.'

The Hilux roars past a huge billboard that announces Spanish villas with french windows and imported kitchens. A shiny couple with a child peer through what must be a french window. Not-Abu Zar looks up and listens with concentration, as if Teddy were giving him career advice.

'Men feel hungry, all the time. I feel an army of rats marching in my stomach and I have been married less than a week. I'll ask them if we can stop for breakfast on our way back.'

Not-Abu Zar shakes his head enthusiastically, as if he has always worried about the connection between coupledom and hunger. The swelling on his right eye has subsided, the blood has congealed around his lips; he looks like a boy who has botched up his face paint.

'Men constantly feel hungry and women constantly feel sad. That's what marriage does to them.'

The Hilux leaves the Super Highway and swerves on to a dirt track, and then starts taking what seem like random turns, slowing down then speeding up. In normal circumstances it might be seen as an attempt to lose a tail, but the veterans of G Squad know that at this point Inspector Malangi likes to introduce a bit of confusion in his own team. He doesn't want them to remember where and how they reached their destination. He doesn't want any of them to lose their mind in the future and come sniffing back to relive the memory. There are

124

rumours of Malangi's predecessor losing his three-year-old daughter and becoming so affected by it that he ended up digging up lots of places in Buffer Zone in an attempt to give his victims a decent funeral. It was a huge embarrassment for the department. Malangi doesn't want any of his men to end up like that. A bit of disorientation also gives a certain edge to the proceedings. The members of G Squad become more alert, they want to do their job and get out. They have come to realise that they are not here to enjoy the scenery.

'Hunger I understand, because you know a man has to work hard every night, sometimes he has to work hard more than once at night, but why do women get sad after getting married? I mean, shouldn't they be happy? They have found their mate, the father of their future children, the man they will force to work so hard that after his demise they'll become much sought-after widows.' Not-Abu Zar murmurs something, but Teddy thinks it isn't a good idea to let him talk at this stage. 'Have you heard the one about why the cow looks sad? Did Abu Zar, I mean the real one, your friend in Sweden, ever used to tell you dirty jokes? Or did he think that laughter was bad for the health of the nation? So this man asks a cow, why do you always look sad? The cow replies, if someone squeezed your tits twice a day but screwed you only once a year, you'd feel sad too.'

Not-Abu Zar nods his head and speaks in a voice that is low but clear. 'You have to believe me. I was the driver. Abu said you can drive my motorbike and I did. I have never touched a gun.'

Teddy suddenly feels angry at this boy's stubbornness. By the time this hour of the night arrives, they all lose their ability to think, but this boy is determined to fool the world right to the end. And he is not even pretending to play along. Teddy has had people here who have told him heart-wrenching stories about being abused as children. Some he managed to soften up to an extent that they plotted picnics and revenge after the night was over. And when all else failed, he would tell them cricket jokes, mostly about Imran Khan and his real bat, and they would laugh till their torture wounds would start bleeding and Teddy had to calm them down. This boy seems to have no sense of humour.

Teddy leans forward and says in the boy's ear, 'So why did Abu do it? Did someone pay him? Maybe he wants to get his seventy-two virgins? Did he tell you that? But remember, all the seventy-two will become sad very soon. And does Abu's driver not get anything? You must get something? What was your deal with him? That you could watch while he fucked those seventy-two?'

Not-Abu Zar looks at him with hurt eyes, as if he had considered Teddy a friend and hadn't expected such a filthy suggestion from him. Not-Abu Zar manoeuvres himself into a praying position, folds his handcuffed hands into his lap and starts reciting Sura Yaseen. Teddy turns off his flashlight in despair. They are moving through a thicket of bush now, branches crunching against the sides of the Hilux.

Teddy's knowledge about which Quranic verse should be recited at what occasion is vague, and second-hand, but even he knows this one. This is the one they recite by the deathbed to ease the passing of the soul, because when a soul leaves the body it's like a fine silk shawl being dragged through a bush of thorns. It is recited to steady the hand of the angel of death. Sometimes it resounds in the corridors of the Sacred. Sometimes the death-row prisoners are allowed to carry nothing but a copy of the Yaseen or receive a visit from someone who can recite it.

Teddy's knowledge of these things comes from his friend whose name is also Yaseen. He went off to Kashmir and returned to a hero's welcome when he brought back a severed turbaned head and claimed that it had belonged to an Indian major. Teddy never saw it, but those who did said that the Indian major, even in his death, looked very scared. Yaseen went off again to Kashmir, or maybe some other place that needed to be liberated, and never returned. Nobody ever heard from him. Nobody brought back his body or his head. It was as if there was nothing left of him. Yaseen was a good friend and he had a balanced personality: not only did he know appropriate suras for every occasion, but he also knew quite a bit about stock markets, oil prices and the latest technologies developed by NASA. He had that core that this not-Abu Zar boy also seemed to have.

Like any self-respecting professional in this situation, Teddy Butt feels like a failure. This man chained to the bone, sitting on the floor of a speeding Hilux, is reciting verses that are a preamble to his own death. Teddy feels this boy has something he will never have: a core that keeps him centred, that frees him from the fear of death. Not-Abu Zar might be running rings around G Squad, but he knows where he has come from and where he is going. He might even be mistaken. Maybe he came from nowhere and is going nowhere and what he recites means nothing, but he has something that keeps him connected to the universe. Would Teddy be able to recite something if he was in a situation like this? If Teddy had so much metal on him, would he be able to manoeuvre himself into a position like this and sit still?

And what if the circumstances were different? What if he was dying in a hospital or at home from a slow incurable illness? Someone close to the dying person usually sits next to their bedside and recites Sura Yaseen. Does Teddy have anybody who will do it for him? He has Alice. Ah, Alice. Can she be taught? After all, she does know how to recite the Kalima. Will she learn it for him? He looks outside and realises that they are in the Zone now. The Hilux drives between clusters of aloe vera and wild shrub; it slows down, then picks up speed again, and by the time it comes to a halt, Teddy has lost all appetite for his job.

As he frequently does, he starts contemplating a career in

private security and reminding himself that you get to travel in the front seat, you carry your own repeater and you don't have to make small talk with anyone. In fact, keeping quiet is a kind of job requirement.

Inspector Malangi is the first one out of the Hilux, and he thumps the side of the cabin. 'What do we want?' A gentle breeze stirs an aloe vera bush and the perfumed air comes to them in tiny whiffs. Part of Teddy's duty is to figure out what is the last thing his companion would like to do. Choices are usually limited in the middle of nowhere; it comes down to a drink of water, time out to take a piss, but mostly people ask for a cigarette. Teddy has no idea what not-Abu Zar wants. He doesn't want Malangi to know that their journey might have started off well but now it seems as if he has been butting his head against a wall. He has no clue whether not-Abu Zar smokes or not, and whether he wants some bladder relief before he is relieved of his life. Not-Abu Zar is oblivious now, hunched over, his chin almost touching his knees, and he is reciting at top speed as if aware of the fact that Yaseen is a long sura and he must finish it before he gets off the Hilux. 'My friend here wants to take a leak,' Teddy says, and before Inspector Malangi can ask his team to take positions, he adds, 'But first he wants to finish reciting his Yaseen.'

Malangi seems to have no problem with the suggestion. Not-Abu Zar is rocking now, moving slowly back and forth with the rhythm of every verse. Teddy can't see his lips in the dark, but it seems Inspector Malangi is repeating the words after not-Abu Zar. Inspector Malangi wouldn't trust anyone else to recite on his deathbed, so he has probably learnt the verses by heart. He also seems to know when the sura comes to an end, because as soon as not-Abu Zar stops moving, Malangi says, 'Jazak Allah' loudly. He gives Teddy a bunch of keys. 'Take him.'

If it doesn't involve any undue risk, they usually like to take the handcuffs and any other metal off their prisoner. They all become very squeamish when they have to remove anything from a corpse, as if by putting a bullet in somebody they have contaminated them. Also for some reason the handcuff marks stay longer if removed afterwards.

The recitation seems to have calmed not-Abu Zar: he is relaxed and passive as Teddy unlocks four sets of locks from his hands and feet. There is a bit of a struggle with the nylon rope, but soon not-Abu Zar is standing beside the Hilux rubbing his wrists, stretching his back and ferociously scratching his armpit. Teddy inspects their operational area by moving his flashlight up and down. They are in the middle of a clearing in the wild fig bushes, full of green thorns and ripe little buds ready to bloom at the first sign of sunlight.

'I can't do it standing up,' not-Abu Zar says to Teddy, ignoring Inspector Malangi, who has got his Beretta in his hand now.

'You can kill forty-six people in six minutes, all the while riding a motorbike, and you can't take a piss standing up? Hurry up, behind the bushes.' Inspector Malangi is impatient. The recitation has thrown him off course. According to his time line, they should have been driving back by now.

'Let's go.' Teddy holds not-Abu Zar by his right arm and starts to move. He hears Malangi mutter behind him: 'The bloody sun is about to come out.' Teddy lets go of his arm and pulls out his TT pistol and shows not-Abu Zar the way with his flashlight. They walk about ten steps and find themselves in bush so thick the Hilux headlights seem distant. Teddy turns his light to the other side and says, 'OK, take your time, I am not looking.' He faces the bush and suddenly has a feeling that the wild figs are alive. Nothing moves, but there is a slight rustle, and he has a distinct feeling that the bush is breathing. Then he sees a pair of eyes sprouting from the bush on his left, one all black, one all white. He moves the light up and down and finds that there are other pairs of eyes that look like the buds have suddenly bloomed in the bush. Before he can straighten his TT, a black dog bares its teeth and jumps at him.

Four others follow, their barks full-throated and ferocious, and they come at Teddy as if they have rehearsed their attack. One of them, a tall, lean, malnourished specimen, all black with white legs, stays back, raises his head to the sky and howls as if reading Teddy the terms of his surrender.

SEVENTEEN

ALICE BHATTI PUTS A box of sweets on Senior Sister Hina Alvi's table and begins to walk out as Hina Alvi emerges from the bathroom adjusting the hem of her shirt with one hand and coiffing her hair with the other. She looks at the box of sweets, then looks at Alice Bhatti, who blushes like a new bride. Sister Hina Alvi breaks into spontaneous laughter. Then she comes over and, still laughing, gently hugs Alice Bhatti.

Hina Alvi beckons her to sit. She cups her chin in her left hand and looks at Alice with amusement and pity, as if saying, look at you, all grown up, who would have thought? 'So ten days of suspension from work and you return with a husband? I tell you, girls these days get bored so easily.'

Alice forces a courteous smile. 'If something has to be done, one might as well do it when one has a lot of free time.'

'Before I congratulate you, can I ask you something?' Sister Hina Alvi drags her chair closer and sits down. 'I don't expect you to take advice from me, and I hate to interfere in my colleagues' personal lives for the simple reason that I have absolutely no curiosity about their domestic matters. I am just mildly concerned about you: why would a girl like you marry? Why would a girl like you marry a boy like him? What kind of man waxes his body hair? You might as well have married me.'

Alice Bhatti has expected a catty remark or two, and that's why on her return to the Sacred she has come straight to Sister Hina Alvi's office. She wanted to tell Hina Alvi herself before anybody else told her, but she didn't expect such directness. She is beginning to wonder why Sister Hina Alvi is getting all personal with her.

'He is a bodybuilder. They are supposed to do it. It's a

requirement for their job. Like we wear white coats. Black coats would make more sense, save us all that washing. But nobody really thinks about these things.'

Sister Hina Alvi looks at Alice as if she can't believe that a professional nurse would harbour such unprofessional thoughts. She drags out a dustbin from under the table, bends down and spits her leftover paan into it. She takes a tissue from the Dry Nights box and wipes her mouth.

'It's none of my business really, but just tell me one thing: can he actually make a living lifting dumbbells? And you know that building his body is not all he does? Isn't he always hanging out with that horrible Inspector Malangi? Always riding in police vehicles. Why would anyone want to be friends with those people?'

Alice Bhatti feels Sister Hina Alvi should have given her this talk before her trip to the submarine. She wonders if Hina Alvi is envious as women sometimes are when you go off and get married without seeking their approval first, like betraying a supposed best friend. Every match made in this world has some detractors. It would never have occurred to Alice Bhatti that hers would be Sister Hina Alvi. 'He works with them. On a contract basis. It's freelance work. He says he doesn't want to get a regular job with them because then he can't work out regularly.'

'So he is the law's little helper? What you are saying is that he is a police tout, does their dirty work for them. Rent-a-witness. Replacement prisoner. Beat up this little guy while I bugger his sister, that kind of part-time job. Look, I don't know why I am going on about this. It's none of my business. This is a free world. But you have to find your own freedom. And if you think you can find freedom by hitching yourself to someone like him, then good luck. Congratulations. I should be happy for you. But I am worried. I hope you are not doing it just to get a different name. A married Muslim nurse is not much better than a single Christian nurse. You just become a slave multiplied by two.'

Alice Bhatti appreciates Sister Hina Alvi's concern. She is

trying to be the mother Alice Bhatti doesn't have, although she knows that Hina Alvi would hate to be described as anyone's mother, let alone a grown-up married woman's mother. But at least she cares, and more importantly she is not scared of showing that she cares.

'Thanks, Sister Alvi. I should probably have consulted you before jumping into it. But I myself was surprised. It all happened very suddenly. I have always thought I can live without a man. I always thought a proper job was all the security I needed. But that incident in the VIP room . . . that made me rethink.' Alice is startled at what she has just said. She hasn't thought of this before. But now that she has uttered these words, she thinks that there might be some truth in it.

'Oh, OK.' It seems Sister Hina Alvi is having a moment of private regret that doesn't last more than a moment. 'And you didn't even bother to go out of the Sacred gate to look for a husband,' she says. 'You got hitched to the first piece of trash you came across.

'You probably realise that girls from my background are not really bombarded with proposals. In fact, he was the only one who showed any interest. I mean, there are those who show interest, but you know what kind of interest that is. At heart he is a decent person.'

Hina Alvi looks into Alice's eyes as if trying to decide whether this conversation has already gone too far; she has given this silly girl an opening and now she won't stop till she has told her whole life story.

'First love,' Hina Alvi says, 'is like your first heart attack. Chances are that you'll survive it, but you don't outlive it. That first gasp for air is the beginning of the end. You have managed to breathe some air in, and you think you are all right. You might think it's a matter of lifestyle, quit this, cut out red meat, walk, run, get a personal trainer, try shitting standing up, but . . . it'll get you in the end.' Sister Hina Alvi sighs, and puts both her hands on the table.

'Look, I am not the right person to give anybody marital advice. I have been married thrice. And I am single now. I married the same man twice. Just to be sure. But the result was the same. In fact the second time it was worse. I didn't even feel depressed like I used to the first time. I just felt bored. I did it for the same reason that everybody else does it: that you need someone to snuggle with, wake up next to, bring you yogurt when you have a bad stomach, that kind of thing. But I never really got any of that. It was I who ended up comforting them and waking up next to them and being their doctor. Maybe you'll be luckier. But you don't seem like the kind of girl who attracts luck.' She realises that she shouldn't have said that last sentence, but she is not the type to take back her words.

'I think both partners need to understand that it's always a compromise. If people give each other space . . .'

'Men don't understand. Just remember that. They don't.' Hina Alvi, it seems, has had enough of the wisdom of the newly-wed. 'I mean, they might have a fine understanding of how a carburettor works or how a human brain is wired, but ask them to understand your sadness on a sunny afternoon and their brain starts doing push-ups. They want to physically lift your sadness and smash it to bits. God, sometimes they want to tie RDX to your sadness and put a timer on it. They think understanding means climbing up a mountain and disappearing into a cave. And that man, your compromise, it does seem that he was locked up in a cave for a very long time. Who knows, maybe you can teach him to live in this world.' Hina Alvi starts to open the box of sweets. 'Congratulations. We all crave sugar sometimes, but you work in a hospital, you have seen those gangrened limbs. That was all sweet sugar once.'

EIGHTEEN

THE DOGS TIGHTEN THE circle around Teddy and then take turns barking at him, as if arguing about what to do with this man who stands in their middle, frozen, the only thing moving a tremulous circle of light emanating from his right hand. 'What are you doing there?' he hears Inspector Malangi shout in the distance behind him. 'Castrating stray dogs? We have a job to finish. Bring back the boy.' Teddy hasn't even noticed how and when not-Abu Zar disappeared. For the moment he stands still and listens to the dogs.

Teddy knows exactly what to do when confronted by a mad dog or dogs in a pack who behave in a mad fashion because of peer pressure. He learned his lesson when he was in class seven, on a sweltering June day when he had limped back home, a big gash on his right calf, blood streaming into his shoe, canine teeth marks on his hand. As he entered his home, his father, the PT teacher, started to bark at him, his big jowly cheeks expanding and contracting like fish gills. 'You are running away from dogs, you sissy puss? You didn't know there were dogs on this street? You never noticed that sometimes they challenge people? What was all that training for? A Scout is never taken by surprise; he knows exactly what to do when anything unexpected happens.'

For Teddy's father, everyone who was born after Partition was a sissy puss, because nobody quite met his criteria of not being a sissy puss: how much buffalo's milk had they drunk? Had they ever been injured in a real bull race? Had they ever bicycled three hundred miles to watch a Shanta Apte film? Had they ever stolen a government horse? Hell, had they ever stolen anything? And no, electricity didn't count; you were still a sissy puss.

PT teacher hooked his thumbs into the braces that held his khaki-coloured shorts around the girth of his belly, stared at Teddy and bared his teeth. 'You are always supposed to be what?'

'Prepared,' Teddy murmured, and felt as if he had run away from a pack of mad dogs only to be confronted by the leader of that very pack.

PT teacher blamed Teddy for the attack. 'It's your fidgety self, the fear inside your Teddy heart that attracted the dogs to you. They can smell a faggot from miles away. Come with me. I'll show you if the same dog dares to attack me. Hell, let's see if that dog even raises its eyebrow. And you will think it's because you are small and I am large. Now, if you have ever studied science, you'll know that dogs can't tell the difference between big and small. A dog doesn't care about your size; a dog can smell your heart, read your thoughts. And your heart is nothing but a big blob of fear. Ask yourself. What are you afraid of? A dog can bite. So? You have got teeth too. A dog can jump, you can jump. But a dog can't plan ahead, can't formulate strategies. In short, a dog can't *prepare*. But you can. You can also think, but your brain works like a woman's brain: always worrying what will happen next, when will the roof fall? The roof will not fall. Or the roof will fall when the roof falls. Your sweaty hands and your shivering legs can't stop the roof from falling.'

PT teacher starts to unbuckle his belt, hands trying to find the loop, lost in no man's land between the abrupt descent of his belly and his rising thighs. Teddy goes into a corner and assumes the position, looking down at his shin where blood has begun to congeal in the shape of a dog taking a nap. Teddy hears howls of laughter. 'See, I am trying to breathe here and my son thinks that I want to thrash him. Is that all I do in this house? Don't I work all day to put food on the table? Who works hard all day to keep this roof over your head? But you and that mother of yours always pretend I am some kind of slave master holding you hostage.' Teddy turns around embarrassed, pain momentarily forgotten. PT teacher is sitting on the mat, his belly resting almost on his knees. 'Come and take them out,' he says, and then mumbles his mantra: 'The spirit is there in every boy; it has to be discovered and brought to light.' Teddy kneels beside him and wriggles his hand into the left pocket of PT teacher's shorts. His shorts are frayed but made of expensive cotton material. Butter jeans, he likes to call them; apparently the only factory that made them was burnt down during Partition.

PT teacher scratches his armpit, then opens another button on his shirt, licks his finger and starts caressing his nipple, which is swollen and seems to be on fire. With practised manoeuvres Teddy manages to hook the earrings into his forefingers and pulls them out of the pocket. Two gold circles studded with fake pearls. He puts them into the sweaty hand of PT teacher, who places them in front of him like a Hindu priest making an offering. Teddy's mother appears as if in response to his offering, carrying a plate of food. She puts it in front of him and scoops up the earrings and starts to put them in her ears.

The ritual is repeated in reverse every morning. Before leaving home, PT teacher shouts for Teddy's mother. Teddy's mother comes scurrying in, puts the plate of breakfast in front of him and starts to remove her gold earrings, the only jewellery she owns, in fact the only thing she owns in the entire world, then puts them on PT teacher's outstretched palm. PT teacher starts eating his breakfast after putting the earrings in his pocket.

The breakfast consists of a raw onion and stale bread from the previous night. PT teacher believes that onion is the elixir of life; it cleans the blood and keeps his vision clear. He can still read the newspaper without glasses and shoot a ball into the hoop from twenty yards. He never reads the newspaper, though. 'An apple a day only keeps the doctor away,' he often lectures Teddy. 'But an onion keeps the devil away. It keeps your blood clear and keeps the bad thoughts out.' The only bad thought that Teddy has ever had is about PT teacher collapsing and dying in front of the school assembly as five hundred boys in their white PT kits shout: 'We are prepared.' Teddy has tried eating onions to purge himself of his bad thoughts, in the hope that PT teacher will pick him for the school band.

PT teacher has told his colleagues that during the Partition riots somebody cut off his mother's ears to get her earrings, and he doesn't want that to happen to his wife. His fellow teachers think that he is a mistrustful, stingy old bastard who believes that if he keeps his gold in his pocket when leaving home then his wife will not elope with anyone. There is a rumour that he did have another wife, who ran away with someone, taking all her jewellery. Others say that his wife eloped because he was spending all his time with the young members of his Scout troop. There is yet another rumour that at the time of Partition, as a teenager he went around cutting off refugee women's ears to get hold of their earrings and now obviously doesn't want that to happen to his wife. He can't quite get it into his head that Partition happened more than half a century ago, at a time when the clip-on earring hadn't been invented.

As the son of a PT teacher, Teddy sometimes expects special status at his school, a front-row place in the PT class, vice-captaincy of the football team, or at least to be allowed to ring the school bell once a week. But PT teacher also doubles as the Scout master and believes in the Baden-Powell principles, so Teddy must first deserve, then desire; he must prove that he practises the principles of fairness and equality and that every day he does at least one thing that should count as a service to the community. There are boys in PT teacher's troops who get special gymnastic training, go on camping trips, spend after-school hours in his office learning to tie reef knots. Teddy is singled out to go and sit under a tree all by himself and practise drums with sticks and a pair of bricks. *Under the shadow of this flag, we are one, we are one.* He practises the same beat day after day in the hope that if he can prove his commitment, he'll get a proper drum to practise on and then be chosen to play in the school's marching band and maybe get the silver stick to lead it.

It's on one of those after-school afternoons when Teddy is under the tree with his sticks beating a pair of bricks that the boy who is already the head Scout and the football captain and inter-school gymnastics champion emerges from PT teacher's office with PT teacher's arm around his shoulder and the band leader's silver stick in his hand.

Teddy stopped eating onions after that day and let his bad thoughts run wild. After school he stayed back, went into the corner and smashed one brick over the other, all the while mumbling, *Under the shadow of this flag we are one we are one.* He didn't stop till both the bricks were smashed into little pieces.

Here, surrounded by six dogs with not-Abu Zar nowhere in sight, Teddy feels as if he is back under that tree, a mad drummer punishing a pair of bricks as someone else walks away with the prize.

Later, over breakfast at a roadside café, Inspector Malangi doesn't touch his tea, but makes sure that Teddy eats properly. Teddy tries to push his plate away after one helping of omelette, but Malangi orders more toast, another omelette. Another cup of tea? Maybe a bit more sugar? Come on, eat all your eggs, you are newly married, you need the fuel.

It's only when it's time to leave and Teddy lays his flashlight and TT on the table that Inspector Malangi puts an arm around Teddy's shoulders and takes him aside. 'You have to find this boy if our family is to stay together. I'll be asked questions.

139

Thirty-six years of service . . .' He fingers the epaulette on his shoulder. 'They will laugh at me that I fell for "Oh, I need to pee." Even pickpockets know better tricks. And we are talking a high-value target here. I should have known. I didn't believe that boy for a moment. I didn't believe him when I had two hundred and forty volts running through his testicles. My only mistake – and let me emphasise that I don't believe it's a mistake *yet* – was that I trusted you.' Inspector Malangi walks him out, close to the edge of the road, not caring about the trucks that whizz past.

'I still feel maybe we should have looked a little bit longer in the bush. We could have set up a checkpoint on the Super Highway,' Teddy mumbles. His stomach full of eggs and toast, he suddenly feels very sleepy and yearns to be in his bed, under the blanket, with Alice. Inspector Malangi sighs and loosens his grip on his shoulder. The thought crosses Teddy's mind that Inspector Malangi is planning to push him under one of the speeding vehicles.

'Of course there was no guarantee what else might be waiting for us in that bush. We couldn't even tackle a bunch of mutts.'

Teddy shakes his head as if he agrees. But in his heart he still believes that he is only partially responsible for not-Abu Zar's escape. What were the others doing? Where was the cordon? Why didn't anyone turn on the searchlights when they heard the dogs bark? How did they let not-Abu Zar get away without firing a single shot?

'When you told me that this boy wasn't Abu Zar, did you believe it?' Inspector Malangi steers him away from the road, as if he has just realised that they might be run over.

Teddy breathes in and stands still for a moment. He understands that his fate depends on this question. Not only on his answer, but how he frames it.

'I do believe that he was telling the truth, but not for a moment did I believe that . . . I mean, not for a moment did I waver . . . But you see, it's complicated. He was definitely not

Abu Zar. In fact I think that even the other Abu Zar, the one in Sweden, is not Abu Zar. You can only be Abu-something if you have a child. And both of them are single and the other guy lives in Sweden. I think they were lovers and then something went wrong. We may never find out, but the very fact that he has gone to Sweden . . .'

'So we are agreed. You believed him. And I believe you. If he is not Abu Zar, and if even Abu Zar is not Abu Zar, then he could be anybody. He could even be you. So it's in our interest that you go and find him.'

NINETEEN

'WHAT KIND OF MAN comes home from work with a full stomach?' Alice Bhatti turns the knob on the stove and looks at Teddy with complaining eyes. He is leaning on the kitchen door looking sheepish, as if he was waiting to be scolded for coming back late. He even has a long story ready, a little present to give. He hadn't thought about the consequences of the large meal he was forced to eat after losing not-Abu Zar. 'I am really full.' He moves his hand over his stomach, as if presenting a reliable eyewitness. He doesn't know how to explain to Alice that in his line of work, kindness and cruelty are badly mixed up. *Have you eaten? Eat some more. Now die.*

'Don't do that,' says Alice, coming towards him, then stopping a few inches away. 'After eating a meal, if you touch your stomach, it grows and grows.' Teddy laughs. His shoulders sag, as if he has just put down a large weight he was made to carry all day and was not expecting to be rid of so easily. He lifts up his T-shirt, grabs her hand and presses it against his hard belly. 'Twelve years of lifting weights . . .' He sucks in his stomach as Alice throws a couple of light punches at it. 'I must have lifted this whole city in weight. This is not going to go anywhere. Even when I am old and dying in your arms.'

Alice runs her fingers over his stomach, counting the flesh ridges. 'I want one like that.' She can't remember if she has ever made such a direct demand to a man. Or to a woman. Marriage, she suddenly realises, is a liberation army on the march.

'It was not always like this. It was very difficult in the beginning.' Teddy puts his hand on her shoulder. 'I have never liked the taste of eggs.'

'You have six every morning. Raw,' says Alice.

'That's work.' He taps his stomach. 'Those yolks slosh around in my stomach till noon. But the omelettes that the inspector made me eat this morning, those almost killed me. Kindness kills me.'

'I still want one like that.' Alice pokes his stomach with her forefinger. 'Even if I have to eat all those eggs.'

'We can start right now,' says Teddy, caressing her hand. It seems that for the first time in his life he has been asked for something he can readily give. 'A woman's tummy won't become this hard. It'll become flat, though. Actually it *shouldn't* become hard.'

'And why is that?'

'You don't want to suffocate the baby.'

Alice blushes, as if it has never occurred to her that their marital intimacy could lead to babies.

'There is a special routine for women. It involves breathing exercises. Let's try that,' says Teddy.

'You told me you never knew a woman before you met me, so how do you know these women and their special routines?'

Teddy lifts the hem of her shirt, runs his hand over her belly then grips the part where her ribcage gives way to the slightly protruding bulge of her stomach. 'I know people who know people who know women. They make a living selling flat tummies. Now inhale.'

Alice takes a quick, deep breath. 'No, not like that,' he admonishes her and playfully pinches her flesh.

Alice is excited, not in a carnal way, but at the thought that her new husband is teaching her how to breathe.

'You are a trained professional and you don't know how to breathe,' says her new husband, running his fingertips along the length of her throat, then slowly bringing his hand down between her breasts to her lower stomach, tracing the trajectory of air travelling through her body. She inhales slowly. He makes encouraging sounds. 'Hold it there and count to three,' he says, when she can't take in any more air. He puts his hand just below her ribcage. 'Exhale,' he says, and she exhales slowly, feeling slightly dizzy as her lungs deflate.

Alice opens her eyes and sees that there is a look of intense concentration on Teddy's face, as if he is trying to extract a bullet from someone's head, someone not dead yet.

'Now when you exhale, suck your tummy in, first inwards, then upwards.' His palm pushes her stomach in, then upwards, as if trying to force it to retreat behind her ribcage. 'No, no, as soon as you start sucking it in, start thinking of sucking it up, there should be an overlap halfway through. Women are supposed to be able to do many things at the same time and you can't do two things with your own tummy?' He pretends to be annoyed. Her ribs tickle and she bursts out laughing. 'Look.' Teddy lifts his T-shirt, tucks it under his chin and breathes in with his eyes shut. When he exhales, his stomach contracts and then disappears under his ribcage, leaving behind a steep concave that reminds Alice of the starving Buddha. Or was that Yassoo's body as he lay in that cave afterwards?

Later she is stretched out on his bench press looking at the ceiling, her arms raised, holding the weight bar. Teddy stands above her and takes two five-kilogram bumper plates from the plate tree and slips them on to either side of the bar. Her arms tremble a little. He bends down, puts his hands on her shoulders and presses them firmly down on the bench. He adjusts her posture, parts her legs slightly and brings her feet in, then presses her knees with his hands and asks her to start. She brings her arms down and lifts the weight with her full force. 'No jerks,' he says. 'No rush. You are not in a weightlifting competition. Let them become part of your body and then move with them, like you are putting a baby to sleep: rock them gently. Arms up, breathe in. Arms down, breathe out. Don't carry the weights, let the weights carry you.' Every time she raises the bar, she feels a tug in her lower stomach. Her trembling arms become steady. He watches her with the beaming eyes of a proud father and the intense concentration of a punishing guru. A flock of birds rushes through her chest every time their eyes meet.

After she has counted up to twenty-five, he takes the bar out of her hands and puts it aside. She feels the light has gone out of his eyes, as if he has suddenly remembered something he was trying to forget. He is rubbing his eyes, as if he has seen too much.

'You look exhausted, and I lifted all the weights,' she says, taking the hem of his T-shirt to wipe her brow.

Inspector Malangi had once given him a lecture about how to make women happy; it was the easiest thing in the world. 'You don't need to give her gold bangles, not silk, not flowers. You don't need to write poetry or massage her feet. Just put a hand on her shoulder when she is least expecting it. Look her in the eye when she is busy chopping vegetables. And she is happy like a child who has seen his first elephant. That's the easy part. But *keeping* her happy, any woman happy – and it doesn't matter if she is your mother or daughter or your Friday whore – that, my friend, is impossible. You can become a clown in a circus and learn to swallow real swords, but it won't bring a smile to her face. There is a deep hidden well of sadness in every woman, as inevitable as a pair of ovaries, and on certain afternoons its mouth yawns open and it can suck in every colour in this world.'

Teddy knows that this is not that afternoon. He'll be gentle and patient when that afternoon arrives.

'I have got something for you.' He extends a folded newspaper towards her. She stares at the newspaper in confusion. She turns it around and sees a picture of the famous twins conjoined at the head. A pair of monkey faces with very large eyes stare at her. *Only one will live. But which one?* asks the caption under the picture.

145

'Open it,' says Teddy. Alice unfolds the newspaper gingerly, as if the life of the conjoined twins depends on her careful handling of the newspaper. She finds a damp, thorny sapling, one tiny leaf yellow-green and young, another large one almost black and moth-eaten. There is a tiny green bud hidden under the leaf, like a promise made in all honesty but forgotten when the season changed. The newsprint around the sapling is damp and the words seem blurred. Alice realises, and is puzzled, that without any reason, tears have clouded her eyes.

TWENTY

When Alice Bhatti finally meets up with Noor, first they talk about a cancer diet, and some tentative ways of delaying the inevitable for Zainab. In between, she tries to make a man out of him.

She walks in with bendy legs, cheeks flushed, carrying a stack of boxes of sweets in one arm and swinging a plastic shopping bag in the other hand, as if she has just been bargain-hunting. 'I got married,' she announces, putting the gift-wrapped boxes on the table.

Congratulations. Now we can all become police informers and live happily ever after. Noor doesn't say that, of course, and keeps quiet, too surprised to speak. Alice Bhatti comes to him and hugs him. Noor doesn't move, his arms stiff at his sides. He has heard the news many times over, but he has heard so many versions of it that he has decided that it can only be a rumour.

Dr Pereira was the first one who barged in and asked, in a stark whisper, 'Have you heard the rumour?'

'Sir, if I were you I would ignore it,' Noor had said without looking up from his register. He had assumed that in his chronically understated way Dr Pereira was referring to the giant banner that had been strung up overnight at the entrance of the Sacred. It accused the doctor, in three rhyming lines, of being an Indian dog, a Jewish agent and a land grabber.

'The rumour about Alice Bhatti. That she has converted. At the hands of that acquaintance of yours, Mr Butt.'

Noor had suspected Teddy Butt of all kinds of police-sanctioned crimes, but he had never suspected that Teddy went around the city converting people to his faith. How exactly did he do that? By hitting the soles of their feet with a stick? By tying their hands behind their back? By dunking their heads in gutters? What was his faith anyway? Last he saw Teddy, getting some attention from Alice Bhatti seemed to be the only faith he had.

Ortho Sir made a rare appearance, his goatee bristling with some private indignation. 'So you are a matchmaker now?' He stroked his goatee and fixed Noor with a steady glare. Noor stood up in confusion, wondering what he was being accused of. 'No, sir, as far as I know, Alice has not converted.'

'I knew it.' Ortho Sir banged his fist on the table. 'These people have turned this place into slutsville.' Ortho Sir said this as if slutsville was a Toronto suburb he had been denied entry into. 'All they do is fuck around, and when they get into trouble, they use religion, nay they abuse religion. I'll make sure that these people are exposed.' Ortho Sir stomped out. Noor sat there wondering why, if Alice had actually gone ahead and married or converted or married and converted, she was trying to hide it. It wasn't as if there was an army of heart-broken suitors who would take offence. He put the rumours down to their mock shooting lessons in the Sacred compound. Sometimes these things can appear to be more intimate than they actually are.

Now she waltzes in as if she is living her life in a shampoo advert, bringing with her the smells of new marriage and an air of optimism last seen in the hospital when the first colour TV arrived three decades before. There she stands, hugging him, announcing that she has got married. Noor doesn't ask her who and why; he is more concerned about where. He has heard a rumour that she got married on a nuclear submarine.

Pakistan doesn't have nuclear submarines, he knows that, he has read it in the papers. 'Are you sure you got married on a nuclear submarine? They wouldn't allow you on it. They wouldn't allow a non-Muslim on it. I mean, they would allow them if they worked on it, of course, if they had a proper pass and uniform.'

Alice is too busy writing notes on the boxes to take in anything. 'Got married on a boat. Yes. Everyone should get married on a boat.'

'Are you sure you didn't end up on an Indian submarine? Indians do have nuclear submarines. And if you did get married on one of those, I don't think it would be considered valid here. It's OK to marry Junior Mr Faisalabad, it's your choice, mixed religious marriages have their problems, I mean the kids will grow up confused and everything, but I don't have anything against them per se.' Noor is trying to block out mental images of Alice in a red dress, sprawled on the stern of a white yacht, her head in Teddy Butt's lap, his hands playing with her hair. 'I am just wondering if it's a real marriage. Because marrying Junior Mr Faisalabad on a submarine that belongs to another country, in international waters, I don't know what the proper term is, which laws apply. If it had happened on land, then it would be quite simple.'

'Are you going to congratulate me or just lecture me about maritime law?' says Alice. 'First Sister Hina Alvi tells me that marriage is some kind of incurable disease, and now you.'

Noor stops rambling and tries to focus on the little plastic bag that she is holding so carefully, as if it contains the secret to her new happy marriage.

Alice Bhatti has brought with her a little brown book wrapped in a polythene bag and a handful of rice that seems to have been soaked in a cheap red dye. 'Waiting at the bus stop I found this.' She unwraps the polythene bag with the kind of care she shows only when unwrapping bandages from multiple fractures. *Home Cures for Cancer*. The title is hand-written. Inside, on the cheapest possible newsprint, is the most indecipherable mumbo-jumbo that the Urdu language could sustain without being confused for a divine language.

149

Noor counts three couplets in the first chapter, two in Urdu, one in Punjabi. The first one praises Allah, the second reminds the readers that they are all doomed and worms will eat their innards, and the third eulogises a variety of herbs that He has created. 'Are we going to sit here and recite poetry? Zainab has never shown any interest in poetry. She doesn't even know what poetry is.' Noor looks at Zainab, who has been in a slumber for thirty-six hours, waking up only to suck on an orange. He hasn't slept for thirty-six hours. He feels delirious, like a seventeen-year-old who has to keep vigil at his mother's bedside while watching out for his own untimely bouts of lust. He tries not to think about Alice taking off her red dress. And if the wedding really took place on a boat, was she wearing a sailor's white shirt? He tries not to think about Alice Bhatti's shirts. He achieves this by conjuring up Teddy's upper torso, taut and slippery and smelling of mustard oil.

'No,' says Alice, grabbing the copy from his hands. She flips some pages and turns to Chapter Two: Growing Your Cures in Your Back Garden.

She starts reading aloud, at first haltingly, then with the confidence that comes from being married for three whole days. There are too many words that Noor doesn't understand, exotic plants that he has never heard of – banafsha, ajwain, nazbo – and seasons that he doesn't even know exist: *towards the end of spring collect the blooms that have only withered for three-fifths of a day.* The text blurs the distinction between gardening and the growth of cancer, as if the lump around Zainab's liver isn't a poisonous tumour eating her innards but a lump of wet earth about to sprout end-of-winter gardenias.

Noor listens as Alice reads. She asks him to jot down strange ingredients for strange concoctions. He makes circles around the ingredients whose names he can't recognise.

They seem like two travellers lost in a desert who have just stumbled upon a treasure map and for a moment have forgotten all about their thirst and lack of direction.

If Noor had been a bit experienced in these matters, he might have seen through Alice Bhatti's heroics. He might have noticed that she was dreamy-eyed and saying things like *river of life* and *fresh beginnings* and *balancing your personal universe*. Noor himself doesn't know what he wants or what he wants first or what he is willing to swap for what he doesn't yet know he wants. He wants to save his mother's life, but failing that, he wants her to die without pain – or maybe he just wants Alice, newly married Alice or the old, not-converted, not-married Alice. He asks himself trick questions at night: what if Zainab is saved but he can never see Alice again? What if Alice leaves Teddy but Zainab has to suffer more? He knows this is not logical. But are three types of cancer logical? Is it logical for him to sit at his mother's bedside and wonder if Teddy Butt is doing all those things with Alice that he claims he has done with a variety of other women?

When Alice Bhatti assumes the role of Zainab's saviour, Noor is grateful, but she assumes the wrong role. He doesn't want her to be a saviour. He wants her on his lap. He is at that age where he could even be on her lap. The hormonal rage is such that he could make love to that chair warmed by her, the latex gloves she has discarded; he could live happily ever after with that stethoscope she has snaking around her neck.

In the confusion caused by his raging hormones and impending grief, he doesn't remind Alice that they have no back garden to grow their cures in.

An oncologist on a charitable visit from Houston stops by Zainab's bed, looks at her latest reports and says, 'Six weeks. I think you should probably take her home.' Everybody around the bed looks down. Nobody wants to tell the charitable oncologist that this *is* her home. Alice Bhatti escorts him to the next patient and Noor hears the good doctor from Houston cooing, 'What an interesting case, what a rare strain of non-Hodgkin's.'

Alice Bhatti returns later and tries to reassure Noor. 'Who does he thinks he is? A TV doctor? Did you see his teeth? So white.' They don't mention six weeks again.

With Dr Pereira spending more and more time with patients who are not on six weeks' notice, Alice Bhatti elevates herself to the role of oncologist and cancer diet specialist.

Noor marks dates on a mental calendar, but he can't really tell what the doctor from Houston meant when he said six weeks. She is there, suffering, in pain but still there. She goes to sleep, she wakes up, she takes her pills, she pees and she drools and feebly scratches the dry patches on her legs. How could it get any worse? Will she die a little bit every day, until the last day of the sixth week, when nothing will remain of her? He wants to ask someone.

Noor can't ask Alice Bhatti any of this. They talk about uncooked food instead, which Alice's manual tells her is the best way to fight cancer. 'It's feeding on you, so you feed yourself what cancer doesn't like,' Alice Bhatti reads out from her book.

'What if we give her uncooked vegetables only?' Noor says to Alice, who has her rubber gloves on and is picking syringes from a stainless-steel tray and putting them into recycled cellophane sheaths. The top button on her white shirt has come off and it's held together with a safety pin. Noor catches a glimpse of her skin-coloured bra, its lace frayed on the edges. 'Or pomegranate juice. I read somewhere that pomegranates are full of antioxidants. That will be good for her. Yes?'

Alice starts to unpeel her gloves. 'It will not cure her,' she says, unfolding the gloves carefully and turning to throw them in a bin.

Noor wonders if her panties are also skin-coloured. His cheeks become red and he starts to massage Zainab's feet. 'But it will stop it from spreading,' he says. 'Her cells will resist, fight back.'

'Good idea,' says Alice. 'You fetch pomegranates and I'll get this ready.' She takes out six Leukeran generics from a packet, puts them in a little white stone bowl. Then she opens a drawer, produces a cylindrical black pill pulveriser and starts pounding the pills. Noor looks at her hand around the stone pestle and blushes again.

As the days go by, they start thinking of themselves as a team that will find a cure for cancer and defeat the inevitable. But they are going through the motions, playing a part written for them. In his heart, Noor knows that despite the luxury bed and an abundance of very expensive painkillers sourced by Sister Alice, Zainab is slowly moving towards her six-week deadline.

If you have spent most of your life in hospital, you know that there is only so much all the scanners and antiseptics and radiation machines can do. The injections that Zainab and Noor could never have afforded are administered regularly. But Zainab seems to be slipping into longer and longer comas.

When she wakes up, Noor slips a little piece of sweet in her mouth. She chews it slowly, then a smile spreads around her lips as if she has just recognised a long-forgotten flavour. Noor sees her smile and gets excited. 'Alice,' he tells her. 'She got married. Our Alice from the Borstal. She is married now. She brought these sweets.'

'Why are you shouting? I am not deaf,' Zainab says. 'I know all about marriages. I got married once. Is it a love marriage?' She doesn't wait to hear his answer and slips back into sleep, as if all those happy memories have tired her out or she doesn't want to think about what happens in a marriage necessitated by love and made public with things made of milk, flour and sugar.

The boxes of sweets that Alice distributes are meant to bring the rumours to an end, but people want confirmation. They come to her, congratulate her and then ask: so what is your new name? 'Why should I have a new name? Don't you like my name? I like my name.' Alice tells everyone the same thing and they leave whispering a bit more: *See, she has not converted. For all we know she is not even married to that Butt man. Were you invited to the wedding? Was anyone invited? Even her lapdog Noor wasn't invited. What kind of wedding is this where the only evidence is a box of cheap sweets? They are probably living in sin.* People touch their ears and sigh as they imagine all the sinful things that Alice and Teddy are doing in private, and hiding behind a few boxes of sweets.

They don't even notice Alice's devotion to her new cause. Zainab may not survive her cancer, but her cancer will be fed the best food and medicine that Alice can scrounge from around the hospital. She walks the corridor, goes on her rounds, smooths a sheet, cleans dribble from someone's face, thrusts an unnecessary thermometer up someone's rectum. But she always comes back as if there is only one patient who matters.

Zainab's breath rattles like a lumbering train as she gets closer to her destination, and Noor's work suffers. His reports become erratic. He mixes up headaches with hepatitis, brain tumours with tuberculosis, fractured ribs with spontaneously bursting gall bladders. All references to real people start getting deleted, pages go by without any reference to Dr Pereira. In the 'Time of Report' column, every one is reported at 1200. With his register open, Noor keeps staring at Zainab's pale face, her shrinking limbs, hoping for some sign of improvement, listening out for the approaching footsteps of death. He doesn't hear anything except Zainab murmuring in her sleep.

Their home cures only seem to have left her more dazed. She reaches into her past and tells him how her mother once beat up her father in the village square and her father laughed out loud at every blow as the whole village stood by and applauded.

If a woman can't drag her man to the middle of the square

154

and thrash him once in a while, the marriage is doomed, she advises Alice.

Dr Pereira throws the register at Noor. He actually slams it on the table, and then plays drums on it with his knuckles. He works himself into a rage in these situations, but today even his anger seems distracted. 'Is this what I told you to do? Where is the truth? Where is the rhythm? I asked for a straightforward recording of the facts. Just a simple description of what goes on in this place. Who does what. I don't want a misery list. All I am getting is a list of names, ailments, people admitted, discharged, expired. If somebody was to read this in a few years' time, all they would learn is that there once was a hospital that had a lot of sick people suffering from every possible disease humankind has ever known. A child could have told you that. A hospital by definition is full of sick people. What about the others, the attendants, the workers?' He is basically asking Noor, how come I am not here? If there is all this toil and trouble, where is the saviour? Who runs this place?

He is not here to help Noor and Alice save Zainab. That cause, he knows, is doomed. He is doing this for posterity. 'Some people work around here. Others just want to live in TV sitcoms.' He looks at their collection of herbs and books with handwritten titles, and shouts, 'This is a hospital, not a Sunday hobby club for herbalists. If you want to practise your mumbo-jumbo medicine, go and do it somewhere else.' Then he looks at Noor and says, 'I mean, get back to your real job.'

Dr Pereira's impatience towards Alice Bhatti and Noor is that of a privileged person towards someone less fortunate, someone who has been granted an opportunity but is hell-bent on squandering it. Someone refusing to come out when the weather is nice. Someone insisting on wallowing in their own misfortunes when there is dancing on the street. Someone refusing to take part when history is being made. Dr Pereira is human enough to realise that Alice and Noor are not the authors of their own misfortunes, but he is not imaginative enough to recognise their desperate attempts to rewrite them.

Noor has spent enough time in the hospital to know what they really think: they think that Sister Alice grew up in a gutter and still carries that stench. They think that Noor was born in a jail and grew up in these corridors and carries that odour associated with people who are born into slavery. Noor doesn't know yet what real misery looks like. He will know only once he sees an open grave, a gash in the earth and Zainab draped in six yards of white cotton washed in Zamzam water from Mecca.

'Something needs to change in this place,' says Dr Pereira, scribbling in the margins of Noor's register. 'Change is always good. Sister Hina Alvi tells me our maternity ward is a mess. Baby slaughterhouse, she calls it. That delivery room is a gambling den, she says. Everyone comes out a loser. You both are probably needed there. At least there are lives there that are worth saving.'

TWENTY-ONE

THE FIRST RAINS OF his married life bring the first murderous
thoughts Teddy has ever had. And these are not even related to
his search for not-Abu Zar or his attempts to stay away from
Inspector Malangi. His rage is domestic; he is not sure if it's
because of his wife or the weather.

Three days of torrential rains and the streets around Al-Aman
turn into a swamp. Nobody can go out except little boys who
have turned discarded tyres into their private pleasure boats
and chase each other using cricket bats as oars. Teddy hasn't
left home for three days and increasingly feels like a trapped
animal, rattling his cage, eyeing his fellow inmate with suspicion. Humidity crushes them like a fallen roof. The ceiling fan
throws down hot gusts of wind like burning debris from a
building on fire. Alice is lying on her back wearing just a shirt
and no shalwar. What kind of woman goes around the house
without her shalwar? He is not used to having Alice here during
the day, and he is certain he'll never get used to having Alice
here without her shalwar during the day. He keeps thinking,
shouldn't she be at the Sacred? Aren't people drowning or being
roasted by faulty electric wires? Alice has been trying to tell
him about some dead rich begum with the unlikely name of
Qaz, and her unruly brats in the VIP room. Is there a rich
begum in the world who doesn't have unruly brats? What are
you supposed to do in a VIP room if not behave badly? What
is wrong with a Surf and bodyguards? He himself drives around
in a Hilux with bodyguards. Does that make him a devil?

For the first few days, marriage smelled like lemony disinfectant and love-soaked bedsheets. Their comings and goings
gave their lives a certain rhythm; little surprises in the pot on

the stove, mock scolding about did you do your weight training today, and their hurried lovemaking on the doormat as Alice kept whispering, I am getting late for work.

Now, as Teddy is housebound and Alice goes around taking down curtains and washing them, clearing out kitchen cabinets and screaming every time she sees anything that looks like a cockroach, Teddy feels he is being throttled by the wet rag that Alice has just used to wipe the bathroom floor. Must be the weather, he tells himself. Then he notices that Alice has rearranged his weights according to their size. But in the wrong order. No, it's not the weather. He wants to take that twenty-kilogram bumper plate and crush her head with it. He is alarmed at the visuals that accompany that thought in his mind and looks at Alice to see if she can tell what he has been thinking. She is sprawled on the sofa. Still no shalwar. Teddy lies down at her feet. They are like two beached crabs, disoriented, not sure which way they should crawl to get back to the ocean.

Teddy has never had any murderous thoughts before. In fact, he has almost no flair for physical violence. Those who have followed his career might think that he does it for a living, dashing from one atrocity to another, but no, he has only ever been what is called an accessory to murder, the clean-up guy, the one who keeps watch, the one who removes the wallet and ID cards and any other valuables from the body but has never aspired to the main job. He has always done it with a certain level of detachment. He has never had any personal motivation, so he has never felt angry, and hence there has never been any remorse, no nightmares about gagged men pleading in animal voices, no visions of slit throats and foreheads with bullet holes. Basically, he only provides valet parking for the angels of death. He has secretly planned that if he does get a full-time job offer from the G Squad, he'll take it but later get himself transferred to Traffic, where you never have to touch anyone and people start stuffing your pockets as soon as you take out your challan book. Though now that not-Abu Zar seems to have disappeared

158

from the face of the earth, Teddy is not likely to be offered a proper police job. There is more chance of him being forced to take not-Abu Zar's job, which would last about half a second. All he'll have to do is to wait for a bullet in the head.

He thinks maybe he'll branch out into personal training or private security. He knows that people run post-pregnancy-flat-stomach-in-three-weeks workouts and make more money than the sharpest member of the G Squad. He also knows that someone of his build can be sitting in the front seat of an air-conditioned Mercedes, holding doors open and waiting outside wedding parties where you get to eat the same food that the guests eat. But doing squats with young mothers or providing armed protection to rich kids has always seemed a bit effeminate to him. When he sees fitness instructors with their gym bags and second-hand Nike tights, or personal security guards with their cocked berets and Uzis slung off their shoulders, he sees nothing but glorified Filipino maids. He might as well start wearing a kimono and become a waiter in a Chinese restaurant. Or are those Japanese?

But these decisions are not his to make. He is not going anywhere till he finds not-Abu Zar, and how can he find not-Abu Zar if he can't leave the house? How can he even plan a proper search if his woman walks around all day without a shalwar?

He was going to go about it in a systematic way; he had got a sketch drawn and then had one thousand copies printed. Now one thousand images of not-Abu Zar sit in the cupboard, away from Alice's prying eyes. Official documents, she was told. Now he can't even go out and put these posters on the walls. Looking down into the deluge from the window, it occurs to him that maybe he should make paper boats out of them and send them out into the world.

Teddy tries to curb the onslaught of images of heads being crushed under bodybuilding plates. Malangi has told him that most murderers are stay-at-home types. He should get out as soon as the water recedes. Malangi has also told him that when trapped at home, look at your woman from a different angle, pretend she is someone else's wife ('Don't pretend that she is Mrs Malangi, because, trust me, you don't want to'). Forget what she is saying; try and get to know her body.

Teddy concentrates on Alice Bhatti's shapely ankle and reminds himself that it is his wife's ankle. This leg is his wife's leg. He kisses her ankle and then cups her kneecap as if marking her body bit by bit, convincing himself that it belongs to him. 'You smell nice, Mrs Butt,' he says, nuzzling the back of her knee with his nose.

'I smell like something the cat dragged in,' she responds, withdrawing her leg, then she puts her heel on the nape of his neck and gently massages it.

Teddy Butt can see all the way up between her legs where a few wiry hairs jut out of her white panties. He feels a mixture of disgust and desire, like a devout person who is hungry but can't decide whether the fare on offer is halal or not. The ceiling fan suddenly moves faster in its doomed assault on humidity.

'You can use my wax if you want,' Teddy Butt says kindly, as if offering her a lick from his ice-cream cone.

Alice grabs his hand, pulls it to her panties and presses it against herself. 'This is a woman's body, not a baby girl's. Did you want a baby girl as your wife?'

Teddy's face reddens and he gets a sudden urge to punch her between her legs. He doesn't fancy baby girls, he has never thought of baby girls; he thinks baby girls are babies. He controls his anger, withdraws his hand, then moves it on Alice's smooth calf, gently, like a bar of soap gliding on her sweaty leg.

'In our Book it says that women shouldn't keep those hairs longer than a grain of rice.' He can't remember where he has read or heard this, at a Friday sermon maybe, or in the Friday supplement of a newspaper perhaps; he is not sure, but he is certain that he is not making it up. It sounds authentic and reasonable. It's specific but not stingy, something that most women can comply with, a true hallmark of all universal religions. 'It's about hygiene, especially in a climate like ours.'

'Basmati?' Alice says. Suddenly it seems they are a couple trying to decide what to cook for dinner.

'You are making fun?' Teddy props himself on his elbow and stares into her eyes, trying to decide if she really is making fun of him. 'Are you making fun of my religion? You know that I am not very religious, but I don't think it's a good idea to make fun of anyone's beliefs.'

'No, I am just asking a practical question. No offence, but you don't really go shopping, so you have no idea. You go to Sunday bazaar and you ask for rice and they'll ask you which one. That's all I am asking. There are about twelve varieties. They range from this, to this . . .' She demonstrates with her forefinger and thumb, the whole range, from tiny broken grain to genetically enhanced, almost vulgar-looking Kala Shah Kakoo basmati. 'One needs to be specific. Especially if it's God's word. It can be dangerous if it's vague. Choose the wrong variety of rice and you burn in hell for eternity.'

Teddy is not sure if she is mocking him. Women make you weak and impotent because they make perfectly normal men feel they are fools, Inspector Malangi has told him. You go to work and people think you have an analytical mind, you are an expert of some sort on something. You walk down your street and people ask for your advice because they think you are a man of the world, and then you go home and you start discussing weather with your wife or the damp in the walls and she will prove in an instant that you are the world's biggest idiot. That's exactly how he feels now. You can't even have a conversation about body hair without being accused of paedophilia and bigotry.

He makes a mental note to ask a G Squad member who is an expert on matters of religion.

'Will you help me move this bed? We might get some air if we put it against the window.'

Teddy gets up quietly. Together they move the bed, and now they can see a broken-mirror-tiled minaret while lying in bed but there is still no wind.

'Will you try and get a regular job?' Alice runs her fingers up his back, hoping to change the topic.

'What is wrong with my job?'

'Let's see. Hours are strange. You don't really get paid regularly.'

'I do get paid.'

Teddy thinks that on some special calendar for wives, today must be humiliate-your-husband day.

'You also do night shifts.'

'But that's part of my work.'

'And what I do is not part of my work?'

Alice starts to massage his shoulders, which stiffen up under her prodding fingers.

'Your work is dangerous. I can never get sand out of your clothes.'

'We live in dangerous times. We live in a dangerous place. It's better to know the danger, to work with it, to tame it.'

Teddy wonders if he has begun to talk like Inspector Malangi. Soon he'll be worrying about his wife's shopping habits and his kids' homework.

Then he remembers his own homework: a pile of not-Abu Zar's posters waiting for him in the cupboard.

TWENTY-TWO

ALICE BHATTI SENDS FOR Sister Hina Alvi when she realises that the baby is stuck flat, a situation that she has never dealt with before. The girl has been in labour for fourteen hours. When Alice Bhatti took over the previous night, the eighteen-year-old mother was already fully dilated. Since then it has been a series of false alarms. Alice Bhatti is holding her hand, ignoring her screams, which alternate between yelling and chanting slogans of Ya Ali as if she was a new convert at a Shia procession. Alice Bhatti wishes Dr Pereira was here rather than supervising the breaking of bread and sipping of lemon bloody squash at the Holy Trinity church. There is no one to help except Noor, who follows her instructions with his eyes to the floor and refuses to look up. This screaming girl almost his own age thrashing around on the bed reminds him of certain nights in the Borstal. There was a teenage girl from Balochistan who started to scream when her period pains started and refused to shut up even when they locked her in a solitary cell. On those nights Noor would cover his ears and tremble through the night. Noor who doesn't flinch when he sees shattered limbs on the A&E floor, Noor who can do twelve stitches in three minutes, all the while reassuring his patient that anaesthesia is on the way, Noor who is generally immune to any kind of gore can't stand the battle that this woman on the bed is waging against her own body. Even now, between handing Sister Alice scalpels and spirits, he turns towards the wall and cups his ears with his hands, like a child turning away from a particularly horrific scene in a movie.

When Sister Hina Alvi enters the delivery room, this is how she finds Noor, sticking to the wall in a corner. Sister Hina

Alvi is fanning herself with her dupatta, her lips are chapped crimson and the first thing she does is expel Noor from the room. 'Somebody must have given you birth, or did you just fall out of the sky? Now run along, go see if your mother is dead yet. We need that bed,' Hina Alvi says, pulling on her gloves. She stands over Alice Bhatti, who is preparing a scalpel and scissors for a cut.

'When did you take her vitals?'

'Forty-five minutes ago. She is all there, strong as a horse. But this thing is like a brick, refusing to move.' Alice Bhatti puts the girl's file in front of Sister Hina Alvi.

'Why are you girls so fond of cutting up people? Let her do the hard work. Nobody tells them of the consequences when they open their legs for someone. When will she learn if she doesn't learn now?' Hina Alvi bends down to take a closer look, then starts massaging the girl's belly, first softly then vigorously in downward motions. She puts her ear to her stomach and closes her eyes for a few moments. Then she lifts her head, and Alice can tell from her eyes what thirty-five years of bedside experience has told her: Sister Hina Alvi believes that the baby is dead.

This irritates Alice Bhatti. This experience, this knowledge that brings you the news of death before you can see it with your own eyes. A death before birth. She feels as if she has failed in some basic way. Has she worked for fourteen hours to bring a dead baby into this world? Has this poor girl, with no father or any other relative in sight, nurtured this soul so that it is returned to the Lord before she can hear the baby's first scream?

Can He take something from you before He has given it to you?

Sister Hina asks for a scalpel and gets busy between the girl's legs. Alice Bhatti holds the girl's head in the crook of her arm, takes her hand and gently urges her to push. The girl pushes, but it seems she is trying to take an impossible shit. After fifty minutes of the girl pushing and Sister Hina Alvi prodding with the scalpel, a tiny hand emerges. It is bluish in colour and hangs out like a big wart. Hina Alvi stands up exasperated, takes a deep breath, then bends down again, pushes the hand back and tries to align the head in the right direction by inserting two fingers and manoeuvring them in an attempt to hook an elbow or the neck. She works with the resigned concentration of someone who has pulled out too many dead babies from their mother's wombs.

An hour later they bring into this world an oval wrinkly head, a smudge of a face with streaks of thin black hair. The girl has passed out from the effort. A shudder passes through her body periodically, as if the dead baby, still connected to her, is sending her signals, asking her to come with him.

Sister Hina Alvi turns the baby upside down, slaps its back. It hangs there like a skinned kitten, its body covered in splotches of blood, which is the only evidence that this thing might have been alive at some point. She wraps it in a sheet and puts it by its mother's side. 'She'll want to see the fruit of her love when she wakes up. Poor thing, I know, but it might teach her a lesson,' says Hina Alvi.

Nobody mentions the fact that the baby is a boy, a dead boy but a boy.

Sister Hina Alvi peels off her gloves and throws them in a bin. Alice Bhatti mops the blood on the floor, collects yards of bandages and heaps of absorbent cotton, and while doing it, glances at Hina Alvi and realises that she is crying. Silently. She is scrubbing her hands at the sink, but Alice is sure that she is crying. There are no tears, no sound comes out of her mouth, but Alice can see that her face is broken, as if someone has clumsily rearranged her features. Her upper body shakes and her silent sobs echo in the delivery room. Hina Alvi covers her head and part of her face with her dupatta, as if getting ready to offer her prayers, and then abruptly leaves the room without giving Alice any instructions.

165

She stands next to the sink, lukewarm water washing over her hands, her eyes dry. She feels cold.

She dries her hands with the hem of her coat and goes and stands beside the bed, staring alternately at the sleeping mother and the dead baby. Without thinking, she kneels down and takes the baby's hand into her hands. She opens the bluish fist and finds that the palm is smooth, with not a line, not a wrinkle. She holds the baby's palm in both her hands and starts to pray. She prays like she has never prayed before, like nobody has prayed before. It doesn't matter if there is a God listening or not, it doesn't matter if He is busy somewhere else trying to avert a war or working out the chemical make-up of a deadly new virus. She just conjures up her Lord Yassoo and gives it to Him. She holds Him by His throat till He can't breathe, she hangs from His robe till He can't take a step forward, she grabs His goblet of wine and flings it across the room, she heckles Him when he descends from the Mount of Olives and starts to give His sermon, she snatches the fish from His disciples and throws it back into Galilee. She sings Him lullabies when His mother goes outside the stable to look for firewood, but that doesn't last very long. When He washes His disciples' feet, she accuses him of being a deadbeat Lord leaving poor wretched girls to bring dead babies into this world; she actually starts cursing him in Punjabi when He starts to raise Lazarus. What she is doing is probably the opposite of a prayer. In the heat of her demented devotion, she even forgets to ask Him for anything. Exhausted, she puts her head on the baby's stomach and listens to Lord Yassoo's eternal silence, feels his glacial incompetence. She hears no flapping of wings, no thunder, no lightning, no chorus of hymns rising in the background. She hears a door creak behind her and she opens her teary eyes slowly. Before she can turn around, she sees a little blood bubble pop out of the dead baby's left nostril, then the toes on his right foot start twitching, as if he is trying to walk in his death sleep.

166

Alice Bhatti gets up in panic, turns around and sees Sister Hina Alvi looming over her, her face white with some unknown fear. Alice Bhatti's first thought is that she has done something monstrous, broken some fundamental rule in the Sacred, she has done something that she wasn't supposed to do, that Sister Hina Alvi was never meant to see.

'You have to leave now.' Sister Hina Alvi doesn't even look towards the baby. 'There are people outside looking for you, Senior's people. They were asking about your husband, but I am sure they are actually looking for you. I have sent them to the medico-legal's office but I know they'll be back. You'd better hurry up and leave through the back entrance.'

Alice Bhatti remembers the men in a uniform that is not the uniform of any institution she knows. She remembers their caged animals' eyes. She remembers their banter about the jail showers. It's only when she is hurrying out of the door that she hears the baby's first cry, followed by a series of faint squeals, as if he is posing a series of questions. What happened? Wasn't I supposed to be dead? Where are you going in such hurry? Who are you leaving me with? Can't I come with you?

TWENTY-THREE

ALICE BHATTI RECLINES AGAINST the trunk of the Old Doctor, left hand covering her half-closed eyes, right arm flung aside, a lazy Buddha biding his time. Others might come here to be healed or find spiritual sustenance or firewood. Alice comes here to take a nap under its cool shade. Her head fits snugly in the wedge formed by gigantic roots that snake out of the earth; not very comfortable, but solid to lean against. Alice needs that solid thing to lean against in her life, but she needs it even more after the incident in the delivery room. She is surprised that even when she was slipping away from Senior's men, clutching her pistol, she had been more worried about the baby than herself. That stubborn little baby has unsettled her. Not just the baby, but the people who now look at her as if she isn't a diligent professional who occasionally goes beyond the call of her duty, but a messiah who has forsaken her right to a regular lunch break.

A brown dog, with one ear missing, paws covered in black mud, tries to lick Alice's toes. Alice opens her eyes and doesn't move her feet, but fixes it with a stare that says: not today. The dog moves a little bit further away and lies on its back with its muddy paws and smoky pink teats pointing to the sky.

Through the dusty leaves of the Old Doctor, the afternoon sun comes to Alice in dribs, like the rusting shower in Teddy's Al-Aman apartment. Squinting her eyes, she follows the progress of a cow-shaped cloud and tries to count the moments before it will gobble up the sun. She is surrounded by patients waiting to be hospitalised, their families camped around them as if on a picnic that has gone on for too long. There are those who have been discharged and told to go home and pray, but who insist on sticking around, thinking that life owes them another chance, hoping for their black warrants to be revoked, or at least for the Old Doctor to perform an old-fashioned miracle. A man with an elephant's foot smokes a cigarette solemnly, as if taking his medication. A wiry old TB patient, his face covered in a white mask fashioned out of his young wife's white dupatta, curses him repeatedly. A sturdy old woman, whose only ailment seems to be poverty, comes and stands over Alice and demands money. Alice slips her hand into the pocket of her white coat and passes her a two-rupee note without looking up. 'What will I buy with two rupees? You can't even buy toffees with that. Give me Xanax, or at least Lexo.' Alice Bhatti raises her hand towards the old woman and asks her to return her money. The old woman puts the hand holding the money behind her back and gently shoves her toe into Alice's ribcage. 'Allah has blessed you with so much. Can't you give me some Valium?' Alice Bhatti shoos her away and tries to concentrate on taking a nap, tries not to think about the red bubble in the baby's nose, its curled toes moving and the horror on Sister Hina Alvi's face. She doesn't feel any fear for the moment. She shuts her eyes tight in an attempt to block out the sunlight, which is beating down now, piercing through the branches of the Old Doctor, penetrating her pupils. Then there is a whiff of cool breeze that seems to come from afar, the sun disappears, the temperature around her suddenly plummets and Alice Bhatti dozes off to a lush green valley where cows made of white wool float, politely discussing the side effects of various types of sleeping pills.

'Why are you perturbed, my child?' a soft caress of a voice says in her left ear. 'It was I who raised the dead baby.' Alice Bhatti smiles to herself. First at the thought that she is hearing Himself speak. Secondly at the thought that if it is really Him talking to her, then shouldn't He know her answer? She is not amused by the fact that He has chosen her lunch break to visit her. She doesn't believe for a moment in this raising-the-dead

169

nonsense. A trapped bubble in a blood vessel, a lung slow to start, a heart still in shock: there are probably a thousand prosaic, scientific explanations. It was no more His work than the Old Doctor's. She knows what faith is; it's the same old fear of death dressed in party clothes. And what kind of miracle is this anyway? He has raised the baby and taken the baby's mother. What kind of universe does He run? An exchange mart? Where was Himself when she was on the run from Senior's men, hiding in Charya Ward? Probably on His own lunch break. Or probably busy with this charya world that he has created?

Himself has visited her once before, when she was a first-year student at the Sacred Heart nursing school, and that visit had resulted in her being charged with 'disorderly behaviour and causing grievous bodily harm'. She was madly in love with Him and constantly recited His words: *The heart is eternally corrupt and ruined for eternity.* It was not only her favourite prayer but her standard reply to most forms of greeting, and she started and ended her exam papers with this declaration.

Her love for Him made headlines for a few days; it was the lead story in the *Catholic Courier – Sisters of Mercy Get No Mercy –* and even the *Pakistan Times* gave it a few inches on the back page, under the headline: *Stand-Off at Sacred Heart.*

Alice Bhatti was only eighteen and signed her name Alice J. Bhatti with the J crossed to look like a cross. Yes, she loved Yassoo. She knew she loved Yassoo because every time someone mentioned the name, every time she read the name, every time she heard a word that rhymed with Yassoo, she got hot flashes in her temples and her heart pounded with such ferocity that she had to shut her eyes and praise the Lord at the top of her voice. Sometimes when she was in a situation where she couldn't raise her voice, when she couldn't pronounce His name in public, she wanted to punch someone in the face. She didn't just believe in the Holy Spirit, she possessed it and didn't believe in sharing.

That was why when three other girls in her dorm chipped in to buy a Yassoo poster, she refused to contribute. 'What is the difference between you and those girls who have Wham! posters on their walls? Did Yassoo ever say that He wants to be a fifty-rupee laminated piece of decoration on a wall? Paste him on your heart if you can.'

She had not always been like this. In fact, after He took her mother, for four years she had a running battle with Him during the Sunday services. She dressed in her best clothes and turned up for the service but without taking a shower; in fact sometimes she took out dirty clothes from the laundry basket and wore them to church. During the service she pretended to act like everyone else, but when others sang *Crown Him with many crowns*, she mouthed gibberish; when Reverend Philip gave his sermon, she told herself all the dirty jokes she had ever heard, and since she hadn't heard very many dirty jokes, she just ended up making a long list of all the words she thought were dirty. When the congregation went on to sing *Alas did my saviour bleed*, she uttered *poo, piss, Musla, Protestant, Goan*; the last one was really difficult to carry when surrounded by a couple of hundred Sunday zealots glorifying their saviour's bleeding, but so determined was Alice to express her defiance, to soil His house, to punish Him for taking her mother that she carried on recklessly.

But then one day He took her father as well, or everyone assumed that He had taken Joseph Bhatti, and taken him in the way that was His favourite way of taking the faithful from the sanitary profession. When everyone had given up on Joseph Bhatti, trapped in a sewer for ten hours, after they had already pulled out two of his colleagues whose lungs had collapsed with hydrogen sulphide, Alice prayed for forgiveness, prayed not to be left alone. She knocked on Reverend Philip's door and confessed her Sunday-service sacrilege, He brought Joseph Bhatti back to life, and she returned to the flock. And like all those who return to the flock after going astray, she made it her mission to defend His name, to make up for all her little blasphemies.

There were some Musla girls on the Sacred campus who didn't like posters of any kind, Wham! or Yassoo. In fact their hatred for posters was so absolute that in their very first term in the college they had petitioned against anatomical charts in classrooms. According to their petition, the posters were pornographic and against the decent behaviour prescribed not only by Islam but by every other faith as well. Their petition was denied on the grounds that the anatomical charts were the very foundation of the profession. Dr Pereira, the honorary principal of the Sacred Heart nursing school, put this in his note: 'You cannot go to a school and then start campaigning against the alphabet.' He liked that last line so much that he had it typed in bold. The poster girls found other ways to carry out their mission. The reproductive organs from these charts began to disappear: ovaries were ripped out, black ink was thrown on mammary glands and penile depictions were mutilated.

When this same group descended on Alice's dorm, a place they had started calling 'the kafir den', armed with hockey sticks and a copy of the Quran and chanting slogans like 'Another Push to the Crumbling Walls' and 'Who Belongs to Pakistan, Musalman, Musalman', it was Alice Bhatti they faced. The other three Yassoo girls offered passive resistance, their eyes shut, knees trembling and Yassoo-save-our-souls-but-first-protect-our-mortal-bodies on their lips.

Alice Bhatti kicked the attackers in their shins, and bit a small chunk of flesh from a hand that tried to grab her throat.

Then she produced a bicycle chain and padlock – and nobody knew why she had a bicycle lock when she didn't own a bicycle, didn't even know how to ride one – and swung it in their faces. The attackers stepped back and called her a Yassoo slut and a Yahoodi spy. She countered by explaining to them that Yahoodis killed her Lord Yassoo so they should make up their minds about what exactly it was they were accusing her of. And then took a swing with the chain lock at one of the anti-poster campaigners trying to sneak up on her from behind.

Alice Bhatti learned an important lesson that day: her room-mates might be good, God-fearing, stuck-up, churchgoing Catholics, but they were completely useless in a campus brawl. What use was your faith if it didn't give you the strength and skills to break a few bones?

When they appeared in front of the college authorities for their disciplinary hearing, Alice felt that they were speaking for their fathers, or their father's churchgoing friends, not for themselves. They tucked their ten-rupee plastic Jesus lockets in their bras, which puzzled Alice even more. Why wear it if you have to hide it? Did Yassoo ever say he wanted to be crucified on a hairpin and then hidden in your undergarments?

They were let off with a final warning. 'Nurses might be doing God's work, but they are not supposed to bring God into their work,' noted Dr Pereira in his warning letter, but Alice Bhatti carried on preaching Yassoo's love on the streets of French Colony.

Her local diocese dismissed her as one of those born-again messiahs that French Colony produced every few years, who, more than anything else, needed a balanced diet and family life, or at least regular sex. Her prayers, although she prefered to call them offerings, were not for public consumption. Because she knew that the prayers didn't tickle Yassoo or make his suffering any less. They were meant to elevate your own soul.

For the next two and a half years, Alice became the lone soldier of Yassoo. She bought a bag full of plastic crosses and stuck one on the school noticeboard every day. She was spat at, expelled, readmitted, investigated, warned, warned again and told that she had already been given a final warning, but she battled on.

She was not even sure whether she was fighting her Lord

Yassoo's fight or just doing what she needed to do to survive in this bitch-eat-bitch world that was the Sacred Heart nursing school.

The bite you see on Alice Bhatti's shoulder is not a love bite. It's a bite. The moon-shaped scar that you see on her left cheek and which still glows when she gets angry is not the result of an accident in the kitchen. It's a stray bullet that kissed her. It seemed the poster girls had poster brothers in other colleges who had guns. The bullet was meant for her throat or maybe her head, she was not sure. But she was sure that nobody would shoot at someone's cheek. Even now when she drinks hot tea, she tastes hot metal in her mouth. She has a cut on her right eyebrow from the time when a lab door accidentally slammed in her face.

A cigarette burn mark on the side of her left breast is the only medal that she hasn't collected in a battle. It's the only evidence of a furtive love affair as short-lived as winter in this city. A chain-smoking doctor who professed to be the only communist on the faculty befriended her. He liked to cuddle before and after with a cigarette in his hand, and only put it aside for the exact duration of intercourse, which usually lasted as long as it takes a cigarette to burn itself in an ashtray. 'Can you not smoke in bed?' she had said as they lay together after a brief session of vigorous lovemaking. The smell was making her nauseous, a mixture of humidity and sweat and the unfiltered K2s he liked to smoke to show solidarity with the workers of the world. 'Why, why? Is this too cheap for you?' He tried to put the cigarette between her lips, she slapped his wrist, and the burning cigarette singed the left side of her breast.

Her twenty-seven-year-old body is a compact little war zone where competing warriors have trampled and left their marks. She has fought back often enough, with less calibrated viciousness maybe, definitely never with a firearm, but she has never accepted a wound without trying to give one back. And like all battle-hardened warriors she has managed to preserve her

174

gift for the fight but forgotten why she became a fighter in the first place.

Her serene charcoal-grey eyes shield that gift; it's the kind of serenity that only four years of fighting for Yassoo can bring, the kind of serenity that owes as much to her inner faith as it does to her twice-weekly fast. It can be forty-six degrees Centigrade with no electricity, or mild winter; nothing can distract her. She is an all-weather, all-terrain fighter.

It was during her fourth year in nursing school, when she thought she had reached a truce with the poster girls, as they all had their exams and three years' worth of syllabus to catch up on, that she experienced the limitations of her devotion. Himself deserted her when she needed Him most.

As a sharp-eyed final-year student nurse she was in the operating theatre and watching closely as an octogenarian surgeon, famous for cutting open patients' chests and then not stitching them back shut till he had counted his fees in cash, had a coughing fit and from behind his mask looked at Sister Alice as if it was her fault. A senior sister who was supposed to assist in the operation had called in sick at the last moment and they couldn't find a replacement because the famous surgeon was known for treating nurses in the operating theatre like garbage bins in uniform. With a pair of tweezers he was holding a vein that he had just cut, and on which he was preparing to tie a knot, when through his insistent cough he beckoned Alice to take over. Alice Bhatti held the tweezers and stared at the vein, which looked like the work of the Lord, and for the first time in her professional life she felt exalted, felt His presence. She felt tall and humble at the same time. She was holding a life between the tips of the metal tweezers. She also felt that it could only be a power higher than her, a power that kept the life-and-death ledger that had handed her the scales, and now it was up to her to carry out His will. The words of Lord Yassoo, who resurrected the dead, flashed through her head only for a second; otherwise she was completely consumed by

175

the task at hand. The surgeon's cough was out of control and he left the operating theatre, giving Sister Alice the thumbs-up sign as he went. In that fraction of a second she forgot to do what medical professionals the world over learn within their first three months in surgical procedures training: that every third heartbeat you should let a drop of blood spill, you let the vein breathe. Sister Alice, spurred by her Lord's approval, squeezed with the power of her faith till the vein couldn't stand the flow of blood any more and burst in at least seventeen places simultaneously, swivelling like a lawn sprinkler going crazy.

Wheezing like an old car, the surgeon returned, mask in his gloved hand, and started taking off his gloves and shaking his head in mock despair. 'What do they teach you here? Slaughterhouse skills?' Alice Bhatti was still holding the vein with the tweezers as if it was a baby snake, still not sure if the baby snake was dead or only feigning. 'You can let it go now,' the surgeon said. 'It's not going to run away.'

The relatives of the deceased had paid their surgery fees upfront to the famous surgeon. They paid a little bit more money to the police and a manslaughter case was registered against the Sacred. The famous surgeon paid half his surgery fees to a famous lawyer and got a pre-arrest bail. The police invited Alice Bhatti to the police station for an informal chat, to ascertain the facts of the case, as they told her. She was happy to be a witness against the surgeon, but after arriving in the police station, she found out that she was not a witness but the main accused. The Sacred nursing school had decided to get rid of its most troublesome student. Without any warning, she found herself in the police lock-up. Dr Pereira was told about it only after the case had been registered. A travesty of justice, he said to anyone who'd bother to listen. After much running around and convincing Reverend Philip to help by showing newspaper clippings from the *Catholic Courier*, which had described Alice as a 'soldieress of Yassoo', Dr Pereira got her shifted to a women-only police station. They beat her up there as well, but let her sleep for a few hours every night.

When Dr Pereira managed to get her out on bail, she headed straight for the famous surgeon's clinic, told the receptionist that she owed him some money and barged in. Before the famous surgeon could shout or press a buzzer, she took a marble flowerpot from the windowsill and aimed for his head. He fainted at the first blow and thus was saved, suffering a broken nose and losing four front teeth from his imported Swiss dentures.

Dr Pereira had tried to fight the medical malpractice charges, but he couldn't rally the community to contest the charge of 'causing grievous bodily harm with intent to murder' when the victim was a famous surgeon. The lawyer Joseph Bhatti had brought to the court had never heard the term 'medical malpractice'. That was why Alice Bhatti had to take her final exam from the Borstal and do her house job by improvising dyspepsia cures for the inmates.

'The world is a lonely place, you'll be lonely till you atone for your sins.' Sister Alice knows where Himself is coming from. She has spent a lifetime of Sundays hearing this gibberish about original sin and eternal salvation. You could not grow up in French Colony and not have God shoved down your throat, His presence as pervasive as the stench from the open sewers. Now she believes in Him like people believe in the weather; you have no control over it, you just have to deal with it. You can air-condition your house, plant a tree and maybe you'll be better off. But there are always hurricanes, sand storms and earthquakes that can shatter the most elaborate protective fences.

'For my flesh is meat indeed, and my blood is drink indeed.' A shudder runs through her body. A hospital like the Sacred is probably not the best place to glorify blood and flesh, she thinks. The voice recedes and rays of sun again start to pierce Alice's eyes. She calculates that her lunch break is probably

177

over. She feels ravenous. She buys a bun kebab from the canteen and gulps it in big bites, ignoring the greedy eyes of two children who sit outside the canteen wearing shirts and no trousers. She promises herself she will visit the church on the coming Sunday. Just to say hullo to Him and request to be left alone. She decides that she'll ask Sister Hina Alvi if she can keep that stubborn baby. Maybe she can name him Little Yassoo. Maybe that'll please Him enough and He'll leave her alone. Surely she can raise a little baby? Her husband may not come home very often, but she is married now.

TWENTY-FOUR

ALICE BHATTI DOESN'T NEED to piss in a bottle and take it to the lab to find out that she is pregnant. She opens the fridge in the morning to take out milk for her tea and the smell of a single mango hits her in the pit of her stomach. She burps violently. She runs to the bathroom, clutching her stomach, then her hand moves to her throat in search of the convulsing muscle and she retches in the sink for about half a century. She looks at herself in the mirror, tears clouding her eyes. She is relieved that Teddy is not around. She is relieved despite the fact that Teddy hasn't been around for three days. She washes her face and takes a small sip of water. The water tastes of rust.

She has been through this once before. She was nineteen, in her final year in the nursing school and in love with the communist doctor. She was spending too much time with him and as a result smelled constantly of love and cigarette smoke. But their actual lovemaking was so furtive and infrequent that despite all those classes on reproductive health, it never occurred to her that their sweaty moments together could lead to anything. Maybe at the back of her mind she was thinking that if you can't have unprotected sex with someone who teaches you gynaecology, who can you have it with? She thought on it for a few days. A marriage and a pram and birthday hats did cross her mind, but when she got around to telling him, she did it without any emotion, like a patient describing the symptoms of common flu. 'I missed my period,' she said, as if she had missed a bus that she really wanted to get on, but that it was OK, another one would come along soon. The communist doctor got excited. First he started to cry, then he chain-smoked for an hour and went through a list of baby names that included every possible combination from the names of the central executive committee of the Indian Communist Party at the time of Partition. Then he went out to get more cigarettes and didn't return for nine days.

'My mother has a heart condition, I am not sure she can take it. For generations there has never been a single marriage outside our Shia clan, let alone a marriage into another religion.' He appeared to have aged in nine days. 'My tears have run dry.' He kept rubbing his eyes. He seemed to have discovered that the only chains he couldn't lose were those forged centuries ago in some Arab tribal feud. So startled was Alice by his histrionics that she found herself consoling him.

He brought her two misoprostols and made sure that she took them in front of him. Nothing happened. She got really bad diarrhoea. After she recovered, he managed to secure a Mifeprex injection from the hospital pharmacy. She suffered six hours of gruelling pain and felt as if glass was being ground in her lower abdomen. He stood above her and watched as she rolled the corner of the bedsheet around her hand, bit it with her teeth, tried to shove her fist into her throat, then gave up and started screaming. She screamed at him to stop staring at her. And when he shut his eyes, she shouted at him for being a coward. 'Why are you standing there like that? Watching a monkey show? Do you think I want to see that face of yours?'

She swore off doctors with leftist tendencies and penetrative sex for the rest of her time at the nursing school.

She has never talked babies with Teddy and now she knows why. It would have involved a discussion about names, how the child would be brought up, in what religion. Would it be circumcised or baptised or first circumcised then baptised? Would it be easier if it were a girl? She would have settled easily on some neutral name, no Joseph or Judith obviously, but something that would have worked for both of them, something neutral like Salamat or Saleem maybe. But who gives their firstborn a neutral name? Does she even like the sound of Saleem or Salamat? They remind her of those people in French Colony who give their children these names in the hope that they'll pass as Muslas. As if there weren't already enough Muslas who were called Saleem or Salamat and who were as poor as the poorest Choohra.

And it would seem like a concession. Shouldn't a baby be a blessing and not some kind of half-baked deal? What kind of life begins with a compromise?

Like her own.

Her stomach settles down after a while and she craves an omelette. She has seen enough pregnant women that these contradictory cravings don't surprise her. The idea of a baby lolling around on her stomach fills her with a longing that she has never felt before. But the thought of naming that baby, bringing it up in Teddy's world, fills her with a nameless dread. And then a strange feeling. She tries to suppress it and tells herself that it's her hormones babbling, but the thought refuses to go away: she feels that she wants the baby but not the baby's father. And the only way to keep her baby is to get away from the baby's father.

Maybe she can take Little Yassoo and her own baby and live in the nursing hostel. The rooms there are tiny, though, and rat-infested. Her house in French Colony? Maybe she can get Joseph Bhatti to babysit them while she goes to work. She can see two little babies in Joseph Bhatti's arms. She forgets for a moment how hard she had tried to escape that place. She feels that if she was in French Colony, she could have given them whatever names she liked.

Baby's father barges in on the fourth day, when Alice has packed half a bag, made half a plan and counted all her money. The way Teddy goes straight to his cupboard makes it clear to her that he has only come for a change of clothes, not to reclaim his wife or hear the news about his imminent fatherhood. He rummages through the cupboard with such desperation, it seems his life depends on finding the right shirt.

'I have a lead to the target that we lost,' he says, still going through his wardrobe.

'What did you lose?' Alice says, eyeing her half-packed bag.

'We lost a high-value target. We had him and then we lost him. Actually, I lost him,' Teddy says, having found a lifesaving dull green silk shirt that always reminds Alice of the colour of steaming horseshit. He takes off his T-shirt and then sits down to unlace his sneakers. Alice pushes her half-packed bag under the bed with a sneaky shove of her toe. She is surprised at what she has just done. Then she realises it's not the bag she is trying to hide, but her anger. She doesn't want to ask him where he has been. How will she raise a child with a man whom she cannot ask a question as simple as that?

'You lost a high-value what? That sounds like a lottery or some kind of gambling. What are your friends up to now? Running gambling dens?'

'A prisoner escaped. A very dangerous man. Actually a boy, but a very dangerous boy. I have to find him or I am buggered. But I have a lead now.' He starts to unbutton his green silk shirt. 'I have to meet the superintendent of the police. They might announce some kind of prize for arresting him. Apparently this boy is wanted in three countries. Did anyone tell me that? He said he was just the driver, but now it turns out that he's a very dangerous driver. And I do believe that he was just a driver. If I don't find him, I guess I'll get buggered by three countries.'

It seems Teddy is desperately trying to tell her something. Alice has always known that Teddy never quite tells her what he has been asked to do at work. She wants to understand his situation. He never shares this kind of work information with her, especially when he has choices to make like now: catch a boy or get buggered by three countries. What is this stuff about three countries? Will three countries get together to deal with this lousy husband of hers? About time.

Alice also realises that he seems strangely excited, as if all his work so far has been a preparation for catching this boy.

Teddy disappears into the bathroom carrying his green silk shirt hoisted over a hanger and held high like a flag.

Alice picks up his T-shirt to put it away, and a piece of folded paper falls on the floor. She has never really looked into his pockets or opened his wallet to find clues to where he goes when he's away. It had never occurred to her that he was capable of hiding anything from her. She unfolds the piece of paper without thinking, then looks up at the closed bathroom door and waits to hear the sound of the shower. It's a pencil drawing of a boy's face, broad forehead, tiny sunken eyes, sparse beard on his pointy chin. It could be any boy in his age group, even Teddy if he was unshaven.

The face that stares back at her from the paper makes her anxious for the future of her own baby.

She begins to worry about Teddy. She begins to worry about herself. She realises that she hasn't thought about the logistics of raising a baby. Who will take care of the baby when she is at work? Certainly not her father, she has decided. She can send her to a nursery, but where will the money come from? She will drop her at school, and she can imagine herself walking a little girl in a blue school uniform, hugging her goodbye at the gates of St Xavier. But who will pick her up from school? She wouldn't want to take her baby girl to the Sacred. Noor could probably play with her or keep her busy, but the Sacred is full of all kinds of infections and diseases and ambulance sirens. The Sacred is no place for a baby to hang out. She resolves that maybe she should tell Teddy and see how he responds. Men change when they have babies. Her own father, Joseph Bhatti, hasn't been an ideal dad, a bit crazy at times, but he held down a job till the age of sixty-five, and even after retiring he kept doing whatever freelance work he could get. She looks at the sketch again, shudders, then folds it and puts it in the shirt's pocket. You are going to become a father: she whispers these words to herself. They seem fake to her, words remembered from a TV soap perhaps. Is this how people tell their partners when they find out they have been knocked up?

She is still struggling to find the right words when the WC in the bathroom flushes twice and Teddy comes out rubbing his face with a towel. 'I need some money. And if somebody comes asking for me, tell them that I haven't been back, that you haven't seen me since I left with the G Squad.'

Alice Bhatti starts rummaging through her handbag and counting her money again.

'How are you going to find the boy? There are millions of boys in this city. Let the police find him. It's their job.'

Teddy, who is carefully adjusting the crease on his trousers, turns his head and stares at her steadily. 'You don't look yourself. What's the matter? I ask you for some money and you start giving me advice about how to run my life?'

The decision is made for Alice as she looks at his cocked eyebrow, the utter incomprehension in his eyes. Then he makes it easier for her. 'I think you should go to your father's for a few days. I don't think you can handle the pressure. I'll come and get you when this is over.'

'How much money do you need?' Alice asks without looking up.

TWENTY-FIVE

ALICE BHATTI HAS LEARNT within one week that making miracles is hard work, as hard as being an underpaid junior nurse in an understaffed welfare hospital. She has brought all her clothes in a bag and is camping out at the hospital. She is living the life of an in-house messiah at the Sacred. Dr Pereira tries his best to deflect the rumours about miraculous cures in the hospital by putting up banners announcing a cleanliness week. When someone calls up to find out about the sudden plunge in the infant mortality rate in the maternity ward, he recounts the steps he has taken to improve the standards of hygiene and points to the banner announcing the cleanliness campaign.

Dr Pereira has never figured out how people find out about these things. Somebody whispers something in your ear, and before you can turn to them and ask how they know in the first place, the rumour has travelled around the city and somebody else is whispering a version of the original in your other ear. Here it was a sweeper who had been instructed by Sister Hina Alvi to make arrangements for the born dead on Bed 8. There is generally no rush with the dead babies, so the sweeper takes his cigarette break, goes to the storeroom, and on his way stops and talks to Noor about the comparative merits of various brands of powdered milk. By the time he returns with a white sheet and a small bar of soap, he sees that the baby's feet are pedalling in the air and he is making a ruckus, as if trying to convince everyone that they have made a mistake. And then the sweeper sees that Sister Alice Bhatti is kneeling on the floor surrounded by bloodied cotton and piles of gauze. Her hands are folded in front of her chest and she is praying. The sweeper thinks he has no option but to go down on his knees and join her in prayer. He is not sure what exactly has happened; Hina Alvi declared a baby dead when the baby is all here, very much alive, crying his lungs out. The sweeper will tell everyone that he felt the presence of the Holy Spirit. In reality he reached that conclusion by using logic. When he is down on his knees, he realises that the dead baby come alive is a miracle, but there is this other person who has made the miracle possible. The sweeper has seen many odd things in this place: he has seen quintuplets being born, he has seen two doctors having a punch-up in the operating theatre over who forgot to take out a pair of scissors before stitching up the patient, but he has never felt any holy presence, only human negligence. Sister Alice kneeling in a puddle of blood, muttering a long prayer in Latin that the sweeper remembers faintly hearing in his childhood, is the *presence*. She exudes warmth, she is oblivious to her surroundings, the crying baby, the blood on the floor. The delivery room's fluorescent light seems to bathe her in a holy glow.

The sweeper just has to go out and mention it to an ambulance driver whose wife has had three miscarriages, and the news start spreading like a riot, because once it starts, it finds its own momentum and travels through lapsed believers who have been waiting for a sign, and then it reaches the really needy ones who can't afford to lose hope. Soon it isn't just the dead babies who are getting a second chance at the Sacred. According to the rumours, there are miraculous cures for advanced diabetes, and pancreatic cancer heals itself if you manage to get past the OPD. Some obese people are seen hobbling around the courtyard hoping to burn all their fat overnight.

In the all-pervasive mood of hyper-optimism, people either don't find out or choose to ignore two basic facts: the mother of the baby quietly passed away while Alice was praying to save the baby, and the miracle-maker is a lapsed soldier of Yassoo but still a Catholic, a woman, and a junior nurse. Although the Catholic Church had adopted a number of borderline pagan habits, falling into the local customs of burning incense at the mention of anything holy and covering every slab of marble that carried a saint's name with garlands of marigold, it had never allowed a female member of its congregation any role that didn't involve carrying a bowl of holy water, washing the dead or preparing the native cuisine for visiting clergy: Goan prawn curries for foreign bishops and aloo gosht for common priests from Punjab. The Catholic Church hears these rumours but ignores them, as for decades it ignored rumours about her father Joseph Bhatti's ulcer cures.

Alice Bhatti is so busy that sometimes she forgets the little baby that she allegedly saved. Nobody turns up to claim the mother's body and it gets the usual quiet burial after a seven-day wait. Alice Bhatti is living out of her bag. Sometimes it seems to her that the seven thousand patients in the hospital, hundreds crawling in the corridor, thousands more out in the compound using bricks as pillows, are feeling a bit better because they are in the hospital compound, only a few metres away from operating theatres, labs and drug dispensaries. But really they are here to seek the Bhatti cure. They have heard the tales about dead kids coming alive, the old no-hoper cancer patients going home on their own feet. They are here to seek her intervention. There are long queues whenever she is on shift.

Alice Bhatti knows that after the freak incident with the baby, the other so-called miracles are mostly the result of a non-literal implementation of the working nurse's manual, sometimes applied with a bit of inspired improvisation, half a Prozac added there, an antibiotic deleted from another prescription, but mostly a generous helping of disinfectant, constantly boiling pots for syringes and needles across the hospital, fresh cotton and gauze, bleach in the sinks and bathrooms. Not that her fellow paramedics cared at the beginning. They were happy to get some positive press and gave her all the industrial-strength chemicals she wanted.

'What miracle?' In the beginning they would laugh when

187

people started turning up. 'Anyone getting out alive from this hospital? Yes, that is definitely a miracle.'

Sister Hina Alvi walks in with a new junior nurse in tow cradling the baby, whom everyone still refers to as the dead baby. The baby is covered in a new pink blanket, its head shaved, its cheeks already beginning to fill out. 'How is our God's little healer coping?' Hina Alvi is the only one who isn't impressed. 'I hope you haven't begun to believe all this nonsense.'

Alice comes forward, takes the baby from the nurse's hands and starts rocking it. 'People will believe what they want to believe. I am only doing my job.'

Alice Bhatti means to sound modest, but her statement comes out as grand.

'Well I guess if they say it's a miracle, we can't mess with them. I don't know what this world is coming to,' says Hina Alvi. 'As a child I was taught that God is in everything. I thought that this concept was so simple that even someone like me could understand it. Now that I am getting old, they want me to literally see God in vegetables. For the last five years, every year there is an aubergine somewhere that, when you slice it, it has the word Allah running through it. I am sure if you slice it the other way you can see your own husband's face and if you move it sideways you can read something obscene. There is always a cloud shaped like Muhammad. I know some people see Yassoo on a cross or his mother in a pretty dress in every seasonal fruit. Why do people need that kind of evidence? Isn't there always a flood or an earthquake or a child run over by a speeding car driven by another child to remind us that God exists?'

Alice Bhatti is looking at the baby, not really paying much attention to Hina Alvi's rant about miracles. 'What have you heard?' she asks her, because she doesn't really know what is going on in the outside world. She has let people kiss her hands but refused to let them touch her feet.

'I have heard all kinds of stupid things. I have heard that Alice appears at people's bedsides in the middle of the night when she is not even on duty, when she is not even in the hospital, when she is probably fast asleep in her bed. I have heard that when she is on duty, bedpans disappear and reappear cleaned and polished. I have heard that IVs self-adjust, I have heard strangers turn up offering A-negative, free of cost. I have heard that Dr Pereira is thinking of starting his old band again. And making gospel music. All I want to say is, stop with the miracles and stick to your day job. This miracle business is strictly a seasonal thing. You have seen those ice-candy vendors who come out in July? Do you ever see them any other month of the year?'

Alice Bhatti has actually been yearning to go back to her boring job. Because she has already started getting returns; people who are cured one day come back the next day with a new malaise. She already knows that her miracles are turning out to be her curse, like a prophet who brings the dead back to life, and then those brought back complain that they've come back to the same old life. It is turning out to be like the time spent with her fellow inmates in the Borstal, whose loneliness she tried to cure with aspirins and long talks about the wonders of human anatomy and jokes about doctors. They always came back the next morning looking even more lost.

'Do you think you are doing God's work?' Hina Alvi asks her. 'Because I know that God's work is done not through prayers and not through kissing hands. You have to get your hands dirty.'

The baby has gone to sleep. He feels weightless in Alice Bhatti's arms. She presses him against her stomach.

'He makes us sick. He cures. I am only doing my duty.'

'Look, what you did there was OK, not your fault. These people will get bored very soon and find another messiah, somebody who cures their cancer but in the process also doubles their money. So the real miracle would be if we don't leave this child to become rat food.'

'I was thinking of taking him home with me.' Alice Bhatti

has been thinking about a baby, but not this baby, since she found out about her pregnancy. But in this moment it sounds like the right thing to say, and having said it, it seems like the right thing to do, the only thing to do.

'You were thinking of taking him home? Is that why you haven't gone home for three nights? Is that why you have been sleeping in Noor's bunk? Do you even have a home any more? Or have you somehow made your husband disappear? Now that would be a miracle.'

The baby stirs in his sleep and punches the air in slow motion with his tiny clenched fists. 'You know what it has been like. It's impossible to walk out of that gate,' says Alice.

'You can't really just pick up a baby and take it home,' Hina Alvi is officious now, all procedures and paperwork. Alice Bhatti can see that she has given it some thought. 'You need to apply, fill out forms, your husband needs to sign up.'

'Can you keep him for a few days? I mean, I'll take him when all this is over.' Alice Bhatti is not sure if this is the right time to tell her that this baby has a sibling on the way.

'Me? Sure. If you want him to die of neglect. I can change nappies and vaccinate him but I wouldn't know how to feed him. Actually, I wouldn't even know how to pick him up in my arms. So if you want to come with me, we can take him home.'

TWENTY-SIX

NOOR IS HAVING DINNER with important men in a dream when he wakes up to find himself surrounded by four guns and Teddy Butt in a very bad mood. In his dream, the important men are wearing suits, they arrive in single file carrying brief-cases, then sit and eat with silver cutlery, starched white napkins on their laps. Wearing a white coat and a surgeon's cap, Noor himself sits at the head of the table carving a roast chicken the size of a small sheep. The important men are talking about important stuff. Although Noor can only pick out a few words, like *mission statement, evaluation* and *holistic*, because it is English they are speaking, he knows that they are talking about something important.

A boot hits Noor in his ribs and he looks at the man seated on his right, then to his left, as if not expecting such bad table manners from gentlemen of this calibre. When he opens his eyes, he sees three guns on a food trolley and the fourth one, a small black snub-nosed thing, in Teddy's hand. Teddy holds it not from its grip but along his palm, like they do in those bullet-bending futuristic movies.

'Where is she?' Teddy asks in a shrill whisper. His boot is still tentatively prodding Noor's side, as if the answer to his question might be hidden in his ribcage. Noor is used to Teddy's untimely visits, mostly with requests for drugs that were banned years ago, but Teddy has never stopped by at this hour of the night, not with four guns, not when Zainab is fast asleep. Noor rubs his eyes, stifles a yawn and concludes that Teddy hasn't dropped in at two in the morning for a casual chat. Zainab's breathing rattles in the background, a local train, chugging away, starting and stopping, not bound to any timetable. The night creatures chirp outside. Number 44 groans and other patients cough and curse him in their sleep. It's a chorus of the damned. Noor notices that Teddy has carefully drawn the curtain around Zainab's bed and now they are in their own private little room.

Earlier in the night, Teddy had also woken up after a dream. He had come home early from a five-day trip in the interior after not finding not-Abu Zar. He waited for Alice for a while. He stood in the window and thought that him being home would be a nice surprise for her when she came back from work. He went in the kitchen and rearranged the utensils; there was nothing to eat in the fridge. He thought maybe he should go out and get some vegetables and cook some food for her. But if she didn't find him home on her arrival, then there would be no surprise for her, so he decided to hang around.

He went to the bedroom and noticed that her wardrobe door was half open. He looked into it, and there was nothing except a dark blue silk nightie that she wore in bed. He rummaged through the drawers and found nothing, no socks or panties. He opened his own side of the cupboard. None of his clothes or what remained of not-Abu Zar's posters had been touched. Again he opened her side of the wardrobe. The blue nightie was the only evidence of the fact that he once had a wife. In the lower drawer he found a rolled-up poster. He took it out and unfolded it. It was a picture of Jesus Christ. He felt sudden panic, as if somebody had been hiding a stash of heroin in his apartment without his knowledge. He looked at His flowing hair, pink-hued eyes, lips slightly open, the halo around his head drawn in rainbow colours. He went to the kitchen and drank a glass of water, then put the poster under the pillow and lay down on the bed, hoping it would calm his nerves. Why had she taken all her stuff? Where had she gone? The place where he could look was the Sacred. The only person he could ask was that lapdog of hers, Noor. But why had she left? And why had she left behind a poster of her prophet?

He drifted into sleep and saw a rain-soaked street, its drains bubbling, and a man who looked like Jesus Christ riding a bike through the knee-deep water, trailing a twenty-foot-long bamboo pole on the carrier. The man got off his bicycle, took his bamboo pole, bent over a manhole and pushed the pole back and forth in an attempt to unclog it. A few children ran past, splashing water on him and taunting him by shouting Yassoo Choohra, Yassoo Choohra. The man looked up at the children and smiled.

Teddy didn't know how long he had slept for, but when he woke up, he saw his face resting on the poster that had slipped out from under the pillow. He found himself cheek to cheek with Yassoo, his mournful eyes staring at Teddy. He felt a wave of panic and rushed to the Sacred.

'You are a snake in my sleeve, you son of a bitch.' Teddy rattles off insults with passion but without any sense of timing, mixing them up as they come along. He is doing something that he has seen other people do. *Shut up.* Noor wants to tell him to shut up, because not only does he have no idea what Teddy is talking about, but he is worried that Zainab will wake up. He gets up, pulling on his shalwar and thinking that he should somehow convince Teddy to step outside and then talk. He doesn't get the chance to make any suggestions about a change of venue for their conversation. Teddy puts the gun to his head, presses it against his temple and asks: 'Where is she?'

'Who?' Stifling a yawn, Noor says it in a voice that sounds like, I don't like you barging in here like this, the visiting hours are long over, arms are not allowed on hospital premises without the written permission of the Chief Medical Officer. And why have you brought four guns anyway? Is there a loot sale on somewhere?

193

Teddy takes Noor's right hand, puts the barrel of his pistol between his two fingers and twists them like those demented schoolteachers who think that by inserting and twisting a pencil between the fingers of a sleepy student they can make him recall the exact date of an obscure historical event. Noor's face twists in a suppressed scream; he points to Zainab and waves his free hand, frantically trying to say *Don't wake her up.* He brings his mouth closer to Teddy's ear and whispers, 'Alice is not on duty. I haven't seen her all day.' Teddy looks satisfied with the answer. Noor is about to turn away when he gets an unexpected Junior-Mr-Faisalabad-powered punch in his stomach and doubles over. He sees Zainab smile in her sleep. He is in pain but can't scream. He doesn't want her to wake up and find her only son surrounded by so many guns and being thrashed by his old friend.

Zainab sits up in her bed, her eyes still closed, and starts to hum a song. In any other situation this would have amused Noor, he might have hummed along, and in the morning they both might have laughed at this, made jokes about an old woman who sings in her sleep. But Noor knows that Zainab is delirious. Her fever has probably shot up. He needs to take her temperature to find out. But Teddy is standing between him and Zainab, loading and unloading his other guns as if demonstrating them to a potential customer. A cat with one of its ears covered in a smudge of blood, which in turn is covered by a swarm of houseflies, shoots from under the bed, dashes into the corridor and looks back at them as if saying, Couldn't you have found another place to play your little game?

'I know you are related to her, you know where she is. Where are you people hiding her?' Teddy puts his pistol on the food trolley, picks up a stainless-steel automatic that looks like a high-end surgical instrument, moves the safety catch on it and puts it to Noor's neck. Noor can't figure out the logic of this. Is there a different gun for every question? What will Teddy ask when he picks up that thing that looks like a Kalashnikov's nasty old uncle? And why am I being associated with the Bhatti clan?

'But I am not related to her,' he says in a startled voice, a slightly aggressive statement of what he thinks is a well-known fact. If a few months of sharing a cell, which you shared with twenty other people as well, makes you family, then he is probably related to a few hundred women who had ended up in the Borstal after stealing a Rado watch or fornicating with their neighbour or attempting to kill their husband.

'She herself told me,' says Teddy, shaking his head like someone who is sick of living in a world where people lie needlessly, where people just make up stuff to confuse other people.

'She tells many things to many people, it doesn't mean—' A sharp jab from the stainless-steel muzzle cuts his explanation short. His lower lip feels soggy and on fire at the same time, and a loose tooth almost pierces his philosophising tongue.

Zainab stirs in her sleep and Noor looks around and again counts three guns on the food trolley.

He has often thought of asking Zainab what people see in their dreams if they can't see. Do you just hear voices? He can't believe that he has never asked her. He decides that he must ask her tomorrow, then realises that people with guns to their head must make these kinds of pledges all the time.

'But you know I am a Musalman, masha'Allah,' says Noor and is surprised at what he has just said. He has never used this expression before. He has heard Dr Pereira say it quite frequently. It started as an attempt to make his older patients feel at home, but now it has become an integral part of his inventory of good manners. *The Sacred has a severe shortage of doctors, there is no way of telling whether the medicines we use are real or fake, we can't even get the janitors to turn up for work, but masha'Allah people still have confidence in us, seven thousand patients walk in through that gate every week.*

Teddy looks puzzled. His gun-wielding hand goes limp, and

for a few moments he looks like the same Teddy Noor has spent many afternoons with, trading tips about bodybuilding and debating why, if girls like bodybuilders in the movies, how come they don't like them in real life? For a moment Noor feels that his denial backed up by his pride in being a Musalman has made Teddy reconsider his assumptions. But Teddy is not about to give up. He has spent enough time in the investigation centres to know that telling a Musalman from a not-Musalman is easy enough; it only involves pulling someone's shalwar down, parting their dhoti or unzipping their pants.

Teddy Butt waves his gun towards Noor's shalwar. 'Show me. Prove it.'

Noor wants to shout out his defiance. No. No. It seems it doesn't matter whether you are in that hellhole called Borstal or this hellhole called the Sacred. They like to play the same games. In the Borstal, every crime, real or imaginary, every mistake, accidental or deliberate, ended in a punishment that involved Noor taking off his shalwar.

Noor wants to tell Teddy that he doesn't do it any more. Not in front of his mother. So what if she can't see him naked. He is seventeen years old and she is his mother and *he* can see *her*. He was twelve and Zainab still insisted on changing his clothes with her own hands as it gave her a measure of his growing body, but the day he got his first erection he refused to let her change his clothes again. Now she reaches out sometimes and feels the fuzz on his face with the tips of her fingers and sighs.

He looks at Zainab, who has slipped back into deep sleep now, her mouth slightly open, a fly hovering over her nose. He wants to go and shoo it away.

He shakes his head in an emphatic no.

The jab that brings his left eyeball out of its socket is a gun slap, the side of the gun hits his temple, something pops and there is an intense pressure in his forehead as if his eyeball is straining to leave the socket behind. As he drops his shalwar, he has an intense desire to look in a mirror. His right eye is shedding tears, his left eyeball has popped out of its proper place. But he doesn't feel pain any more. He just doesn't want a shot fired here. That would not only wake Zainab but also really scare her. Loud bangs give her headaches that last for days.

Noor wants to move his hand to push his eyeball back in its socket but decides against it because that might remind Teddy that there is a trigger on this gun and probably a few dozen bullets in it, waiting for the slightest movement of his finger.

Noor starts to educate himself. Watch the finger on the trigger, forget about all the crap about the man behind the gun, all the nonsense about steady nerves; what he might say or how you might answer is all redundant. Because that slight movement of the finger can terminate the most persuasive argument in the world.

Teddy starts putting his guns in a bag like a plumber finishing his job. Then in a casual voice he asks Noor, 'Do you love her?'

If somebody had asked this question during the day, without the presence of a gun, Noor would have laughed it off, he would have used the word 'co-worker', mentioned their camaraderie; he would have definitely invoked team spirit and family atmosphere. After all, he is Dr Pereira's protégé; he has learnt all the good manners and ultra-polite, pointless bullshit. He might even have said she was just like his elder sister. But now with an eyeball dangling out of its socket, his lip broken and a tooth lodged in his tongue, he knows that Teddy has asked the only relevant question: Noor knows that he loves her, whatever that means. It's often said that love turns some people into martyrs and others into poets and philosophers. Obviously it turns many into downright liars and criminals.

'You are asking the wrong question,' he says calmly, as if he is taking the medical history of a stupid patient who doesn't know what to ask his doctor. 'What you should be asking is, does she love me?'

Teddy listens to him quietly, as if trying to decide whether what Noor has said might mean something else. 'And last I saw her, she had a baby. A boy. Shouldn't you be worried about that baby?'

'Baby?' says Teddy.

'A very cute baby. Everyone's saying it's a miracle. You guys need to communicate more.'

Teddy moves towards Zainab and pulls the pillow from under her head. Zainab sits upright for a moment looking straight ahead and then falls back on the bed and starts to snore. Noor has had enough; he lunges towards Teddy. But Teddy has drawn his pistol and moved its safety catch. He wraps the pillow around his left forearm and presses the gun into the pillow. For a moment he shuts his eyes and his face muscles clench in anticipation of pain, like a junkie a moment before the needle enters his flesh. The sound of the gunshot is strangely muffled, like someone coughing into a pillow. But suddenly the room is full of white little feathers flying everywhere. Some have blood on them.

TWENTY-SEVEN

'Should we give him a name? I hate it when people call him "dead baby",' says Alice Bhatti, sitting in the passenger seat of Hina Alvi's tiny car. Hina Alvi is an awkward driver. She doesn't drive so much as she carries out a running feud with her car, banging her fist on the dashboard, changing gears abruptly and promising to teach it a lesson when it stalls. It's strange to see her outside the Sacred. Suddenly she is in a world where she doesn't have total control, where she cannot expect each one of her wishes to be carried out. Her face is softer, even her hair looks a bit limp and real. She drives hunched over the steering wheel, and curses every time a vehicle passes her on the wrong side.

'Can we call him Little Yassoo while we think of a proper name and do the paperwork?' asks Alice.

'Is that a joke? Little Jesus? Does this world need another baby prophet? Do you want him to die young and single and misunderstood for eternity?'

'I had a neighbour who was called Jesus Bhatti,' says Alice. The car bumps over a speed breaker and the baby begins to cry.

'See, even he doesn't like it. I think just Little is fine with me.'

Alice picks up Little from her lap, puts his head on her shoulder and presses him against her chest. His shaved head tickles her cheek. They travel in silence. Little falls asleep in Alice's arms. She looks towards Hina Alvi and wonders if she should thank her for offering to put her and Little up, but then decides that it might be a bit early.

＊   ＊   ＊

199

Sister Hina Alvi opens the double lock on the door of her second-floor flat; the air inside is stale, as if trapped for a long time. Burgundy-coloured frayed velvet curtains are drawn, and even when Hina Alvi flicks on a light, the room stays semi-dark. She takes Alice Bhatti straight to a bedroom, as if she doesn't want her to see the rest of the apartment. The bedroom is small but has a double bed on which Hina Alvi has already prepared a little nest for the baby, complete with a pink baby blanket and rows of plastic parrots on a mobile positioned over the pillow.

'Nestlé formula is in the fridge, nappies in the cupboard. I am going to sleep for a while. If you need anything, just knock on my bedroom door,' says Hina Alvi before walking out of the room. Alice feels that Hina Alvi is already regretting her decision to invite her to stay.

As Hina Alvi shuts the door behind her, Alice sees a Bible Study Centre calendar from the year before hanging on the inside of it. This is probably her idea of making me feel at home, Alice thinks. Alice does feel at home and drifts off into a deep sleep with her hand on Little's stomach. When she comes to, it takes her a while to orient herself. Little has wet his nappy; she changes it, cleans the drool on his face, comes out into the living area and goes straight to a window to draw the curtain.

'I don't like to open the curtains. I have some really nosy neighbours.' Hina Alvi's voice catches her by surprise.

Alice Bhatti looks back. It takes her a moment to locate Sister Hina Alvi, and when her eyes adjust to the darkness, she sees her kneeling in front of an open cupboard. First she thinks that Hina Alvi is looking for something in the cupboard, then she realises that she is still on her knees, hands folded at her chest, and she seems to be whispering something vaguely familiar. 'Are you OK?' Alice asks. When she doesn't get a response from Hina Alvi, she rushes towards her, suspecting that she has either pulled a muscle or is having a stroke. She stops when she is just behind her. In the cupboard, right in front of Hina Alvi, is an altar, a simple affair, plaster-of-Paris Yassoo figurine on a tin tray, some withered marigolds and a tea candle.

Alice Bhatti freezes; she feels as if she has walked in on a very private act, that she is witnessing something she is not supposed to, but she is afraid to move back now. Backtracking would mean that she had meant to spy on Hina Alvi, and now that she has discovered her secret, she wants to walk away with it. Next she does what she thinks is the only logical thing to do: she starts to go down on her knees behind Hina Alvi, but as soon as she bows her head and folds her hands, she hears Hina Alvi say, '. . . and the glory be yours, now and for ever', more of a sigh than a prayer. Hina Alvi gets up, blows out the candle and shuts the cupboard. Alice Bhatti finds herself praying to a Formica panel.

'No reason to get excited. I am the same senior sister you have known all along,' Hina Alvi says, taking her dupatta off her head and sitting on a chair at the small round dining table.

'Do people at the hospital know?' Alice Bhatti is not excited, just flabbergasted. She has always felt ambivalent about faith-based camaraderie, she has never bought into we-are-all-His-sheep-type sentiments. In fact she feels a bit let down. Is Hina Alvi helping her because she considers her a sister in faith? What is Hina Alvi's faith anyway? What kind of woman goes around insisting that everyone address her as Ms Alvi, a name only slightly less Musla than Muhammad, and then goes home and prays to a Yassoo hidden away in a wardrobe?

'What is there for them to know? Why do they need this knowledge?' Hina Alvi's voice is low, as if she is talking to herself. 'Will it improve the conditions in the hospital? Will it save some-body's life?'

'It's your personal choice and I know that you are not the first one. And who can blame people if they choose to hide their religion? All I am saying is that you have done a good job of it. I never suspected—'

Alice Bhatti is cut off sharply by Hina Alvi. 'What would you have suspected? Is this some kind of illness that a trained nurse like you should have detected?'

Alice Bhatti keeps quiet and desperately wishes that Little would wake up and start to cry so that she can get out of this awkward situation. She wants to be understanding, she *is* understanding, but she also knows that whatever she says will come across as some sort of inquisition.

'I slept with Mr Alvi. I was married to him, hence the name. I pray to Lord Yassoo because I was born a Christian.'

'You took his name?' Alice Bhatti asks in the hope that they'll talk about her marriage. Maybe she'll tell her something more about Mr Alvi. Why can't they just be two colleagues talking about their bad marriages instead of suspecting each other of bad faith?

'What's wrong with taking your husband's name? Everyone does it. And if you think I should have gone back to my maiden name after my divorce, then you try changing your name on your ID card and see if you can do it in one lifetime.'

Alice Bhatti feels that this conversation has already gone too far. 'Yes, I know. That's why I never thought of changing my name. Do you want me to make some tea? Is there anything else around the house that I can help you with?'

'Oh, stop trying to be a considerate house guest. It's so irritating. That's why I never have people over. Either they are rude and want to be waited on and leave filthy cups and plates behind. Or there are others who just want to take over your house and rearrange the furniture.' Hina Alvi is staring at her as if trying to decide whether she can trust this girl with her kitchen or her life story.

'I am only trying to help,' Alice says and turns to go back to her room. She is already wondering how she can escape this place without offending Hina Alvi any further. She is also wondering who are worse: Catholics, or Catholics pretending to be not Catholics?

'Hannah. That was my name. Hannah,' Hina Alvi says, slightly lost, as if she has just remembered a word that she hasn't used for a while.

'I guessed that much. Easy enough.'

'Massey. Hannah Massey.'

'Bishop Massey's daughter?'

'You are quite naïve, even for a Sacred nurse. No wonder the whole city thinks you are some sort of idiot-saint. Do you actually believe Bishop Massey's daughter, any bishop's daughter for that matter, would be slaving away at the Sacred? She can buy a hospital in Houston if she wants. Actually she runs a bed and breakfast in Houston.' Hina Alvi laughs. 'Imagine. Madame Massey always had her breakfast served to her in her bed and now she runs a bed and breakfast. They are distant relatives but still very embarrassed at their poor cousin who went and married a Muslim. If I was a bishop's daughter, I would probably not change my name either.'

'I am no bishop's daughter, not even related to a common priest. But it never occurred to me to change my name.'

'Well I like the name Alvi. And changing back to Massey might give someone the idea that here is a Musalman abandoning her faith. And you know how much they disapprove of that. Listen, I am a fifty-one-year-old single woman. That is a whole religion in itself, with its own rituals. It has its own damnation and rewards. I don't think I need to shout Lord Yassoo's name on street corners to prove who I am. Can you make some tea now? Two tea bags for me, please.'

Next morning, over breakfast, Hina Alvi is relaxed. With her washed hair draped in a towel, she helps Alice to bathe Little, who can't seem to make up his mind whether he likes being immersed in warm water or not. One moment he giggles, the next moment he begins to cry his lungs out.

It's after Hina Alvi has made breakfast of toast and fried

eggs and Alice has made two cups of tea that Alice musters up the courage to talk about her pregnancy. Hina Alvi isn't surprised, and if she has any sarcastic insights to share about contraceptives and nurses, she keeps them to herself. Her advice is measured and to the point. Alice needs to tell Teddy immediately. The only thing marriage is good for is children. Men change after they have children; they don't necessarily become better human beings but bearable human beings. Sometimes they become responsible and grow up, even bums like Teddy have the potential. Alice must not give him the impression that she is planning to leave him, even if she is planning to leave him.

'You go, make him a meal and wait for him to come home. Then sit down at the table with him and tell him with a smile. Tell him he's going to be a father. They like the sound of that. And if he continues to be an absentee dad, then we'll kick him out.'

Alice Bhatti is not sure if this is such a good idea. She has just cleared out her wardrobe, she doesn't want to lug her stuff back to Al-Aman and pretend nothing has happened. And what would she do with Little? She can't leave him with Hina Alvi.

'I'll take him with me to the Sacred. I have got enough slaves there to take good care of him.' Hina Alvi is precise with her instructions. 'And when you are done, come back to work. We will both wait for you there.'

TWENTY-EIGHT

INSPECTOR MALANGI BRAKES HARD to avoid running over a spotted dog that jumps from the pavement and starts to limp leisurely across the road. The car stalls. He has been planning to get his battered Toyota overhauled soon or replace its engine (or get a new chassis and a new body as well, but he has been wondering whether if he replaces both it would still be the same car). He restarts the car but before he can move forward, the traffic light turns red. Inspector Malangi hears the knock on his car window and rolls it down to shoo away a boy who, in his thick jacket, is clearly overdressed for the weather as well as this kind of work; he is offering him a trip to Mecca in lieu of five rupees. Since when did beggars start wearing Klashni jackets at traffic signals? Inspector Malangi wonders. He has just given and received his farewell presents at the G Squad headquarters. His short speech had ended with a plea to 'forgive and forget but remember me in your prayers'.

He is feeling generous, like people do when embarking on a new life, and his hand automatically reaches for his wallet as he prepares a short lecture about the curse of begging and the dignity of work. The boy opens his jacket, flashes a rusty-looking Mauser, then bends down, puts his neck through the window and whispers, 'Hands on the steering wheel.' The traffic signal starts its countdown: 90, 89, 88 . . .

Inspector Malangi almost pities this boy who, with a gun tucked inside his jacket, thinks that he has got the situation under control. If Malangi presses the accelerator down to the floor, he'll probably find the boy's decapitated head in his lap, leaving a writhing, headless body on the road. But he knows that boys this age don't understand the velocity of life. There was a time when he would have done something like that just to teach the boy a lesson, but he has left that life behind. He wants to spend his retirement working on his children's maths, a subject in which they have consistently underperformed, despite private tuition. After thirty-six years of public service, the only thing Inspector Malangi has learned is that the next generation needs to do better at maths than you.

'Take out your wallet and put it on the dashboard.' The boy in the Klashni jacket looks sideways as he barks his orders. A newspaper hawker, an old man in a tracksuit, hurries towards Inspector Malangi's car waving a copy of *The Daily Ummah*, but then sees the robbery in progress and swiftly crosses the lane using the newspaper to fan himself and continues to hawk his paper on the other side of the road.

Inspector Malangi feels a pang of nostalgia for the life he has left behind just this afternoon. The days and nights that he spent hunting them down, talking to them late into the night, testing their supple young bodies to the limit. He'll miss these boys. This one looks quite jittery and nervous, someone new at this, someone still not sure whether what he is doing can be a long-term career option or just a one-off for tidying up his monthly budget. Inspector Malangi looks past the boy in the Klashni jacket, and, as he expected, he sees another boy on a motorbike, poised to take off, revving the engine, looking at the traffic building up behind them, then looking at the traffic light, where the red-digit countdown continues in slow motion. A baseball cap is pulled over his face, and Inspector Malangi has that veteran policeman's premonition that he has seen this boy before. But boys this age all look the same; fashion victims with no individuality.

For a moment Inspector Malangi thinks that it's ironic that he is being waylaid by boy robbers on the very day that he has quit the G Squad, hung up his uniform, returned his government-issue Beretta and started his life as a law-abiding civilian, the kind of harmless, responsible citizen they show in life-insurance advertisements. He looks at the lone traffic policeman standing on the roadside, cooling himself under the shade of a tree. Inspector Malangi realises that there's nothing ironic about his situation. There are probably a few hundred people being held at gunpoint across the country right now; what is so special about him? Boy robbers can't look at your face and tell that only two hours ago you were a feared cop, heading an elite police squad in the city. And isn't that a relief, because if they knew who they had got at gunpoint, what ideas might they get in their young, hot heads?

Inspector Malangi has spent his last afternoon at work tying up loose ends: two prisoners are transferred to judicial custody, another one is told to walk. He runs fearing a bullet in the back of his neck, but Inspector Malangi just stands there waiting for him to turn the corner, then returns to his office and starts clearing out his desk. He is going through his drawer when Teddy shows up looking lost, like a pet whose owner has suddenly decided to move house and has no plans to take him along. Inspector Malangi remembers that here is one more person who needs to be sorted. He can't tell Teddy to just walk out, that he is free to go. Where will he go? Other members of the G Squad have their careers; they can take care of themselves. This boy needs his help. Teddy's left arm is in a cast and perched in a sling around his neck. Inspector Malangi observes his plastered arm mournfully but doesn't ask him how he got hurt. With his career over, all curiosity about human affairs has drained out of him. Who cares why people shoot each other or themselves. There is always a reason. A good reason. Or a bad reason.

Here is yet another man who is not sure any more if he is a man or not, Malangi thinks. A woman can do that to you, especially a woman you have loved. It is unpleasant to talk about these things, especially on your last working day, but

Inspector Malangi feels he can't just walk out of this life without passing on the knowledge he has acquired in thirty-six years of working and loving.

'Sit down,' he says, and then resumes clearing out his drawers and starts talking with his head buried in the desk. 'Do you know what a woman in love is like? You probably knew it once but now can't remember. Have you ever seen a mad filly? When a filly goes mad, there is not much you can do. The best rider can try and mount it and it'll still kick up a storm. You can chain it to its bones but it'll still run away in the middle of the night. That is a woman in love for you. What do you do when everything fails? They need to be put down. For their own good. There is no other way.' He produces a velvet pouch from the bottom drawer and begins to untie the shiny silver wire securing it.

Teddy's arm in the cast has developed a really bad itch. He desperately wishes he could scratch it just once. He also wants to ask Inspector Malangi how he knows, about him and Alice, but then decides against it. You don't ask the head of the G Squad about his sources. And then it occurs to Teddy that if a common ward boy in the Sacred knows, then probably the whole city knows.

'Yours is only a domestic situation. Things always blow up around the house. The gas cylinder, a leaky oven, a cupboard can fall, someone slips out of a window. It happens every day.'

'We are not living together any more,' says Teddy, his gaze fixed on the velvet pouch with expectant eyes, as if Inspector Malangi is about to produce a solution to his life's problems, or at least give him an expensive watch as a farewell present. Inspector Malangi produces two solid gold bracelets from the pouch and caresses them gently, as if trying to remember the texture of the soft wrists these bracelets might once have adorned.

'Where is she now?' he says, stretching out his hand so that Teddy can see the bracelets closely. 'Dead. Rage of youth.

Is there a single day in my life that I don't remember her? Yes, there are days when I actually don't. But here,' he knocks his forehead with his knuckle, 'she's always here. And what was her punishment? A bullet in the head, two seconds of flashback and now she doesn't even remember that she was the most beautiful woman that G Squad ever put handcuffs on. And what do I get? A lifetime of heartache, a career destroyed, children who keep failing in maths. A wife who keeps taunting me that I am not man enough for her. But you don't have to suffer what I suffered. Let them share our suffering a little bit.'

Inspector Malangi pauses for a moment, not sure if Teddy is following him. 'Come with me.' He puts the gold bracelets back in the pouch, ties the silver wire, takes out a bunch of keys and starts walking. Teddy follows him to the maal khana. Inspector Malangi flicks the light switch on; the storeroom is still semi-dark, full of shadows and strong, pungent smells.

'Let me show you something,' Inspector Malangi says, removing a bedsheet from a wooden coffin with a glass cover. In the dimly lit room Teddy can see a mummy, the kind they show in tourist advertisements for Egypt. The mummy has the rosy cheeks of a young mountain girl and the mournful eyes of an old woman who has seen all her offspring die in her lifetime. 'It's a fake, of course. Only seventy years old, but a true artist manufactured it in his backyard and then was trying to pass it off as booty from Balochistan, some minor pharaoh's runaway cousin who ended up here. A British museum almost bought it.' He pulls the sheet back on the coffin. 'Do you get my point? They are fakes even when they are dead. These women, I tell you, they continue to peddle these fantasies from their coffins. You can't trust them even when their hearts stop beating.'

Teddy is not really sure what a fake Egyptian mummy has to do with him and Alice, but suddenly he feels an acute sense of loss. He feels he was promised an authenticated five-thousand-year-old love from the very depths of some pyramid. What he got was a fake from someone's backyard in Balochistan.

'Take whatever you need,' Inspector Malangi tells Teddy, his hand sweeping the room. Teddy has been here before, but only to pick up a weapon that can't be traced back to the G Squad. Standing in the shadow, he wonders what he could possibly do with two tonnes of hashish piled to the ceiling, or crates of DVDs or boxes of fake Indian currency or rocket launchers without any rockets.

'Do you love her?' Inspector Malangi asks in a neutral tone, as if asking Teddy what he had for breakfast.

Teddy thinks it's a trick question and shuts his eyes. 'This is something that I have been asking myself.'

'I think the very fact that you have been asking yourself this question – that's your answer. And if you love her, you'll never forget her. That's the nature of love. If you love somebody you'll remember them no matter what, even after you have screwed every whore of every nationality that washes up on these shores.'

Teddy nods in agreement. The smell of hashish is making him dizzy and he remembers Alice's smooth chin nuzzling his neck.

'And don't you want her to remember you? Let's say you put a bullet through her, will she remember you after that? She won't remember anything. She definitely won't remember you. You are a young man, you have a lot of life ahead of you. Do you want to spend that life in oblivion, forgotten by the only person you loved and the only one you are guaranteed never to forget?'

'You are right, I was angry. I was very angry.' Teddy points to the cast on his arm. 'But now I am not angry. I don't want revenge, I only want justice. Fair is fair. I just want to make sure that if I can't have her, then nobody should be able to have her. Is that not fair?'

'She has already been had,' Malangi interrupts him. 'It's

better not to think about these things. It'll only drive you crazy. Even saints don't make babies without having a bit of fun first. Forget about that. Stop pitying yourself. Stop pitying her. Remember it's about love. You need to give her something she'll never forget. Never.' He points towards a glass cupboard with a double lock. The label above the cupboard reads *Hazardous Material*. Inspector Malangi goes to the cupboard, unlocks it and stands next to it like a chemist showing off his life's work.

He takes out a glass bottle, then puts it back and looks around for a piece of cloth. He wraps it around his hand and unscrews the bottle carefully. He pours a drop on to the wooden shelf in the cupboard. A hissing sound, smoke rises from the spot where the liquid drop fell and in an instant it burns a hole through an inch and a half of solid wood.

'Try this and she'll always remember you. This is the only thing that'll hurt as much as love hurts.'

Carefully they put the bottle in a small gunnysack and Inspector Malangi walks Teddy to the outer gate. 'You also need work, because this place is going to the dogs. There is this old family, nice people, they need a driver cum bodyguard type person. Work is a bit boring but the money is good. They also have some business pending with your wife. They'll protect you. You'll get to see the world.' He leads him to a gleaming Surf surrounded by four guards in black uniform. There is no number on the registration plate, just some words in bold red. 'Try it out. I hope you people get along,' says Inspector Malangi, introducing Teddy to the guards. 'And keep that stuff away from your body, make sure it doesn't spill. It's as precious as gold.'

The boy goes through Inspector Malangi's wallet carefully, as if he is interested in something besides the couple of thousand-rupee notes in it. Then it seems he has found what he was looking for. He turns his head towards the boy on the motorbike and nods. The boy pulls back his baseball cap and revs his bike in response. Inspector Malangi has seen this little exchange a million times before. It means, our job here is done, let's get the hell out of here.

It's only when the bullet pierces his neck that Inspector Malangi realises what that job was. He grips his neck with one hand and before pressing down on the accelerator looks out at the boy on the motorbike. In an instant he realises that the boy is not-Abu Zar. He has already put his gun back in his jacket and is not even looking towards him. The car lurches forward, Inspector Malangi slumps down on the steering wheel, the car swerves and hits the traffic signal at the precise moment it turns green, and blocks two traffic lanes behind it. An impatient horn sounds behind him. Another one honks. Soon it becomes a chorus of angry, protesting car horns. An ambulance is stuck in the traffic and its siren begins to wail. As he bleeds to a quick death, Inspector Malangi has the same thing on his mind as that on the lips of all the impatient drivers stuck behind his car: when will our nation learn some road manners?

TWENTY-NINE

ALICE BHATTI WAITS TILL two a.m. for Teddy to return home, then calmly walks into the kitchen, picks up the plate of food that she had prepared for him and covered with a white paper napkin and chucks it in the garbage bin. She immediately regrets it. She feels guilty, like she always does when good food, any food for that matter, goes to waste. Yassoo's flesh, she remembers Joseph Bhatti admonishing her. You are throwing away His flesh in the garbage bin, and although her father mostly used this line to force her to eat whatever concoction he had rustled up, whenever she sees food being thrown away, she feels Yassoo's body is being soiled. And although she has drifted far away from Yassoo, the idea of throwing food away still repels her. She can often be seen taking leftover plates of hospital food outside in the compound and handing it over to those camped out under the Old Doctor. Now she is angry with herself because she has done something she strongly disapproves of. She is angry with Hina Alvi. Who takes marital advice from someone who was divorced thrice? She is angry at Teddy. She doesn't mind him being away. Men should go away so that they can come back and then go away again. Their comings and goings make a home a home. She would like to know where he is, though, and when he is coming back. So that she doesn't have to make food for him that goes to waste and then sit here and wonder whether spinach and potato curry really equals Yassoo's flesh.

There is nothing unusual about his absence, but it galls her because for once she actually has things to tell him. She knows that when he does come back from work, he comes back in the early hours of the morning, sometimes with hair covered in sand and sometimes boots caked in mud. He is usually so exhausted it seems he has been wrestling with desert monsters. Or wading through marshes. On these days he usually returns on a big motorbike, the kind that traffic police sergeants drive, complete with a siren, but he has never talked about any work with traffic police. Or sometimes he returns in a fancy car with Emirates registration plates. One day he came home in a Bedford truck, full of refrigerator cartons. Someone usually comes and takes the vehicle away the next day. Alice always hoped that some day he'd offer to drop her to work, but he was always asleep when she left for work and the vehicle would be gone by the time she came back.

She goes to bed and sleeps fitfully, dreaming of a lone horse galloping on a motorway as a sixteen-wheeler trailer with a bright orange container on top speeds towards it. A fat mosquito trying to enter her ear startles her out of her dream. She feels nauseous with anxiety and goes to the bathroom and retches into the sink. She comes back to bed and a fluffed-up second pillow mocks her. She drags herself to the window and peers down at the spot where he parks his return vehicles. As she expected, the spot is empty, and two dogs are trying to eat each other's faces. She can't tell if they are fighting or trying to get to know each other better.

In a fit of resentment she decides to change and go to the Sacred. If he comes home now he'll find her all dressed up to go to work. Ah, you are back. *I was leaving for work.* Or he'll find her already gone. She puts in extra effort with her uniform, applies some mascara, and as the sky turns muddy, half promising a sunrise, she leaves Al-Aman. She leaves her bag open and clothes strewn around the room. She is not sure what this is meant to convey: that she has come back but may leave again, at short notice if she needs to. She also leaves her side of the bed unmade as some kind of protest against his absence.

In the bus, she is the only passenger in the women's section, and the driver looks at her as if he understands the predicament of people like her who can't sleep all night because they have to start early.

The driver puts on a tape, and what Joseph Bhatti used to call the Musla anthem starts to play. There is no music, just a bunch of men shouting at the top of their voices demanding to be teleported to Mecca.

It's still dark when she reaches the Sacred. She can hear the medico-legal John Malick singing in his office. She goes straight to Zainab in the general ward and, as she had expected, finds Noor dozing in a chair next to his mother's bed. His left eye is covered in a bandage. Zainab is barely breathing. Alice bends over to take her pulse, and as soon as she touches her wrist, Noor wakes up with a groan and then jumps out of his chair. 'When did you come? Where have you been? That husband of yours has been looking for you.'

'He should have looked at home first. What happened to your eye?'

'First tell me what you have been telling Teddy.'

'What do you mean? I'll have to meet him before I can tell him anything. Your eye looks in really bad shape.'

'You should have seen it without the bandage. I had a cartoon eyeball. He thinks there is something between us.'

'What does that mean?'

'He thinks we are lovers.'

Alice starts to laugh, and then can't stop laughing. She can't remember the last time she laughed like this. Noor puts his finger on his lips and signals towards Zainab. 'But we are. We are,' she whispers. She feels that there is another Teddy that she has never known. Jealous Teddy. Going-around-trying-to-find-about-her-life Teddy. She likes this Teddy.

Where is Teddy?

There is only one place that she can go and look, and although she has the name of the outfit and some idea that it's police work he does, she has no idea where this place is. Noor is the only person she can ask; he also has no clue, but goes away and comes back within five minutes with an address, the number of the bus that goes there and an offer to accompany her, but then he looks at Zainab and sits on her bedside. 'It's the seventh week,' he mutters.

'I'll be back and we'll give her a sponge bath. That'll revive her,' says Alice.

The sensible little boy that he is, he doesn't ask her why she wants to visit the G Squad offices so early in the morning. 'I wouldn't go in if I didn't know anyone who works there. Someone you really know. The person who gave me the address told me, don't think of going there, they eat little babies and don't even burp, and it's all legal.'

Alice Bhatti stands outside the G Squad centre and tries to look purposeful. The centre is a series of interconnected townhouses; there is no sign saying G Squad, or anything else for that matter. She isn't sure if she'll find the Teddy she is looking for here. There are a couple of other women camped outside the centre. One has improvised a tent with a sheet and seems to be running a one-woman protest camp. *Give Me My Son or Take Me In*, says a placard reclining against a suitcase that she is using as a pillow. Across the road from the main gate a man wearing a police shirt and striped pyjama bottoms naps in his chair, one hand holding a walkie-talkie that crackles occasionally as if someone is barking incomprehensible orders to an invisible army. In the other hand he holds a rusted gun that hasn't seen any action since it left the armoury in the previous millennium. Alice watches as his shoulder dips and the gun starts to slip out of his hand; he jerks and catches it, with his eyes still closed, then puts it in his lap. The metal gate is boot-polish black and a furlong long and it doesn't seem it'll open for anyone. The walls are topped with shards of broken glass and coils of razor wire. Searchlights mounted on the corners of the centre are still on, but the watchtower is empty. A teapot and two cups sit on a small table, probably meant to indicate, we have got many people to man this watchtower, some of them were just here, they have just had tea, they are still around, you still want to try something funny?

Alice Bhatti isn't sure if she can actually knock at this impregnable door; she isn't sure if someone will actually open it, and if somebody does open it what will she ask then? *Do you have an officer called Teddy Butt who works here? I am his wife. Do you have a prisoner called Teddy Butt here? I am his wife. I am married to someone who doesn't really work here but he does work for some people who work in this place.*

She feels a cold shiver in her nape, the kind you feel when someone is following you secretly, when someone is staring at your back and doesn't want you to know. She turns around and sees that the guard in police shirt and pyjamas has woken up. He is holding a small round mirror in one hand and clipping his moustache carefully with a tiny pair of scissors.

The gate opens and a Surf emerges and makes a slow turn in the other direction. For a moment Alice catches a glimpse of an arm in a cast, cradling a small gunnysack as if carrying something precious. And then she sees the familiar Devil of the Desert registration plate and starts walking towards the bus stop with quick steps.

She looks at the bus conductors, who yell and sing and hawk their destinations, thump the sides of their buses, scream at the drivers to change the music, address everyone according to their age as if it wasn't a bustling bus station but a large family gathering. Alice looks at them with complaining eyes, blaming them for enticing her here in the first place and now not taking the routes she might have liked to take.

She turns into China Street and stops in front of the first shop, which displays dentures the size of a small sofa with bright pink gums and promises of painless extractions and 'new, natural, artificial dentures while you wait'. An old Chinese man sucking on an ice candy comes out of the shop and bares his

217

teeth. Alice Bhatti moves along quickly till she crosses a small square and enters what seems to be a medicine bazaar. She sees rows and rows of clinics with huge billboards announcing cures for an impossibly long list of sexual dysfunctions. A giant cut-out of a bodybuilder announcing physical and spiritual revival in a seven-day crash course hovers over a street corner; she feels a lump in her throat. Men scurrying in the street seem upset at her presence in this particular part of the city, as if she has caught them with their pants down; they cross to the other side of the road to avoid her. They look in the other direction, pretend she isn't there. She finds it a bit uncanny. Her experience of walking in bazaars, travelling in buses, going to shops has taught her that whatever their status in life, whatever they are selling her, whatever they might need from her, they always have a reason to stare at her, size her up and then zero in on her breasts. They look upwards, downwards, they look sideways, they scratch their balls or pretend to be interested in what she is saying, but their gaze always returns to her breasts. Sometimes they thrust their hands in their pockets and count their coins with such concentration it seems they are saying their rosary. There was a teacher in her nursing school who would gaze at her chest unashamedly, then look towards the ceiling, put his forefinger in his ear and poke his ear in a circular fashion with such rigour that *her* ears hurt. She thought of telling him that if looking at her breasts caused him earache, he should probably try and not look.

It seems to her that the unspoken language that is used by men and women on the street to communicate doesn't exist in this bazaar. She feels as embarrassed as the men do. It should probably be called I-was-born-with-a-small-one-but-I-have-been-saving-money street. She hurries along, passes a fast-food joint that promises authentic Arabic parathas, sees a billboard quoting Rumi's couplet to sell steel-reinforced concrete. A sturdy man with a white beard showers her with prayers for healthy children at the top of his voice and stretches out his cap. His sincere efforts impress her, and she drops in a two-rupee coin and starts walking faster.

She tries to remember something about Teddy's job, the name of his boss. If she could remember the name of that inspector with the walrus moustache, the one who patted her head and gave her a digital Quran in a velvet wrapper and said no modern home is complete without it. She wishes she could remember a title, work timings, pension plan, a salary, and she realises she doesn't know any of these things. She remembers Teddy's long days in the gym, evenings watching National Geographic, his nightmares when he mutters in his sleep and says: 'We are going for a walk, we both need fresh air, don't worry, don't look back, they don't like it when you look back.' And then wakes up and shudders and looks at her as if it's all her fault.

She is familiar with the routine by now. At first there are hints at a one-on-one meeting with the new police chief, a lot of repeated ironing of clothes in anticipation. But after dressing up properly, he disappears in a Hilux that turns up to pick him up and returns him in the morning covered in dust, his hands bruised, as if he has been fighting wild dogs all night. He breaks his six raw eggs into a glass, gulps them down, makes a face as if he has just shot himself and then falls into bed. The first couple of times she removed his shoes and tried to unbuckle his trousers, but every time she touched him, he curled up into a ball and whimpered, as if the people in his dream were trying to break his bones.

But since he lost that boy and brought home his posters, he has hardly ever been home.

So who is this man Teddy Butt? She wanders through the markets as if she is hoping to find an answer advertised in a shop window and will get it after haggling it down to a reasonable price. She goes through Empress Market, where Pathans sell tomatoes and baby hawks in the same shop, women with bangles up to their elbows peddle pink chicks perched on baskets full of guaranteed desi eggs, a blind man brandishes money plants in used Chivas Regal bottles that don't require earth to grow in, and a Burmese-looking man sells a plastic device that carves onions, carrots and turnips into roses. Why would anyone want an onion cut up like a rose? she wonders.

What kind of woman marries a man who cries over melting glaciers and comes back from his job with sand in his hair? She looks at a cage full of chickens trying to climb over each other as one of them is caught and its throat gets slit to the soundtrack of looped God-is-great playing on a cassette player.

She turns away and starts walking back towards the bus stop. The cackle of the caged chickens and the soundtrack of their death follows her for some distance. She catches a bus bound for the Sacred, as the conductor is giving a last thump on its side and shouting at the driver to move on. She knows that she should do all her waiting at the Sacred.

A motorcycle stops next to her bus. She thinks she recognises the boy but is not sure where she has seen him. She moves towards the window to get a better look when another boy wearing a long coat comes from behind and stands next to a car with his head in the window. The boy on the motorbike watches him impatiently, then looks up towards the sky, and she realises that it's the boy on the poster. She tries to get off the bus in a hurry, the traffic signal turns green and the bus lurches forward but stops again. Alice watches the commotion at the traffic signal; around her a chorus of impatient horns is performing a crescendo.

THIRTY

ZAINAB'S MOUTH IS AGAPE, her eyes are open but Noor knows that she is gone. A fly sits on her lower lip, then goes inside her mouth and comes out. Noor doesn't have the strength to shoo it away. His good eye is dry; the one under the bandage throbs as if his eyeball wants to spring out of its socket again.

Soon after her arrival at the Borstal, Alice Bhatti gave Noor a plastic syringe to play with, without the needle of course. For months it was the only toy he had; he used it as a water pistol, pretend weapon and pen. He also injected many magical fluids in Zainab's arm to cure her blindness. One day he caught a butterfly that had wandered in through the bars. It was a big one, and covered half of his palm. Its yellow and black tiger stripes glowed brightly He had a brilliant idea. What if he made butterfly juice with it? He rolled the butterfly's wings and inserted it into the cylinder. He imagined that when he squeezed it, he would get a liquid the colour of gold with black stripes, and if he squirted that on to Zainab's eyes, she would get her eyesight back. When he thrust the plastic plunger in the syringe, what he got was mud-brown goo. He never played with that syringe again.

He pulls the sheet over Zainab's face and walks out. He has always wondered how he would feel, what he would do, where he would go first. Now he knows. He needs to go to the medico-legal's office to get a death certificate, then inform the mortuary and book the funeral bus. He isn't really sure why he needs a death certificate, but he starts to walk down the steps leading to the compound with a clarity of purpose, knowing that it is the only thing he needs right now.

He sees Alice Bhatti under the Old Doctor and waves towards her. He doesn't know why he is waving. Is he saying hullo to her? No, he is saying: Hullo, Alice, my mother is dead. But Alice is not looking at him; her eyes are fixed above his head, above the rooftop. Then he realises that all the other patients under the Old Doctor are also looking at the horizon. He turns around to follow their gaze and bumps into someone. He is curious to see the face of the man he has bumped into. The only thing he remembers is that the man's arm is in a cast and he is carrying a small gunnysack.

Teddy Butt barely manages to stop the bottle falling from his hand. 'Are you blind?' He curses the boy who bumps into him and then rushes past without apologising. He can see Alice Bhatti under the Old Doctor. She stands in her white coat, oblivious to her surroundings, looking up into the sky. Teddy moves forward and stumbles again. This time, it's the legless beggar woman on the skateboard who grabs his right leg. 'God has blessed you with such a beautiful wife, buy me some Xanax. The nights are becoming longer.' As Teddy rummages through his pocket for some change, he wonders why everyone is looking up at the sky.

EPILOGUE

An Open Letter to the Congregation for the Causes of Saints
The Vatican
From Joseph Bhatti
French Colony

Our Holy Mother appeared on the fourth of September last year above the roof of the Out Patient Department of the Sacred Heart Hospital for All Ailments after the gates of the hospital had been shut because it couldn't take in any more patients. The residents and workers at the hospital didn't recognise the Holy Virgin in the beginning as her face was covered in a veil and the infant she carried was making a ruckus. The onlookers were most fascinated by a beam of light that fell on the OPD and bathed it in a milky glow. It was the ward boy, a long-term resident of the Sacred, Noor, son of Zainab, who pointed out that the sky was clear and there was no moon. And then above the roof people saw a silver throne hovering, held aloft by a flock of peacocks on which sat a likeness of our Holy Mother.

And the likeness of our Holy Mother beckoned my only daughter Alice Joseph Bhatti to join her on the throne.

My daughter did not suffer the pain that her estranged husband meant to cause her by pouring half a litre of sulphuric acid on her angelic face. Instead she ascended to Heaven with our Holy Mother. The throne that had arrived to take her away was already there, that's the reason none of the people surrounding her noticed her tormentor as he approached her unscrewing the acid bottle and professing his eternal love for her. They were all looking up at the horizon, fascinated by the spectacle of our Holy Mother on her throne.

As is common in such cases, people didn't recognise the heavenly signs in the beginning and instead first focused on small unusual things, little discrepancies, minor malfunctions. An X-ray machine rolled through the corridors of the ortho ward, came to a stop on the edge of the stairs, then extended its mechanical arm and started whizzing as if it was being controlled by an invisible force and taking photographs for posterity. A patient with an oxygen mask in ICU ripped it out and stood up and started complaining that the smell of roses was making him dizzy. An IV drip in the general ward turned to milk. The skewed wooden cross at the entrance of the Sacred, which had not been repaired or painted in years in the hope that it would make people forget that the Sacred was a Catholic establishment, straightened itself and started to glow amber.

The first witnesses were the residents of Charya Ward. All twelve of them swore that they saw a likeness of Sister Alice Bhatti dressed like our Holy Mother in a blue head-scarf, a halo around her head, ascending on a throne held aloft by a flock of peacocks. Their testimony was dismissed by the local Diocese Committee to Investigate the Miracle on the grounds that they all belonged to the Muslim faith and were long-term residents of the psychiatric ward. The very simple fact that they were a fractious bunch, and no two of them had ever agreed on anything, was ignored by the Committee. Also ignored was the historical precedent observed in the apparition of our Lady of Fatima, where the testimony of a thirteen-year-old Muslim boy was considered sufficient despite the well-known fact that thirteen-year-old boys, Muslim or not, dream of nothing but beautiful women and can conjure them up when none exist. The medico-legal officer Dr John Malick also witnessed the apparition and kneeled down and sang the praise of our Lord Yassoo and then of our Holy Mother. His testimony was deemed inadmissible on the grounds that, although born and raised a Catholic, he had official inquiries pending against him that accused him of being drunk on duty, accepting illegal bribes to issue fake injury certificates and running a private practice that dealt solely in written-to-order sick notes.

There were several witnesses who saw a flock of kites, their beaks upturned, flying sluggishly around the throne. They flew so gracefully, they seemed to mock the air that carried them. The Committee concluded immediately that a holy apparition accompanied by scavenging birds like kites must be either the work of the devil or a deliberate attempt to bring an already beleaguered Catholic Church into disrepute. Or at best, they said this was some Choohra folklore emanating from French Colony that was being projected as the work of the Holy Spirit.

Can anybody with an iota of common sense and a grain of love for our Holy Mother suggest that it's my daughter Alice Bhatti's fault that there were no doves or white pigeons, which the committee always expects to see at such occasions?

The same committee that took less than nine months to bestow sainthood on a Polish nun in our neighbouring country, despite overwhelming evidence from the local community that she was nothing but a stingy old witch who revelled in the suffering of dark-skinned, malnourished children, didn't even bother to investigate the sublime acts associated with my daughter Alice Bhatti. There is justifiable anger in the Choohra community that this case was either never sent to the Congregation for the Causes of Saints, or, if it was sent, then crucial evidence was misrepresented or deliberately misplaced.

225

The attitude of the National Diocese was not very different either. The same fathers who encourage the celebration of a man-made and very commonplace statue stuck in a cave that might or might not have shed some tears seventy-three years ago undermined Alice Bhatti's case for sainthood by ignoring various other testimonies that bore witness to the miraculous and blessed nature of that evening.

Perhaps the Divine Will knows the working of the devious minds that trade in our Holy Mother's name, turn God's house into a centre for commerce of the souls and plot their next land grab or scheme to get more money out of the Vatican's wealthy friends by portraying their native followers as illiterate wretches. How else can you explain that on the morning after that blessed night, out of a clear blue sky, without warning, without any thunder and not a cloud on the horizon, lightning struck the Old Doctor – a two-hundred-year-old peepul tree that had survived three hurricanes and generations of Sacred patients who chopped bits off it for firewood. Sister Alice Bhatti had taken many a serene lunch break under its shadow. Such was the impact of the lightning that the tree split into two, smoke emanated from it for days and never a leaf grew on it ever again.

Freak weather phenomenon was all the Committee had to say about it, as if it wasn't a committee to validate the claims of a holy apparition but a club of amateur meteorologists.

It's self-evident that the Committee's negative verdict was the result of the same prejudices that the local diocese has shown towards what they prefer to call lower castes. They claim to be Yassoo's children, but at heart they remain devotees of the Hindu goddess Kali, always judging people by their ancestry rather than their devotion to our Lord Yassoo and what they do for Yassoo's children.

It was asked in their meetings, although the Committee never put it on record, that if it really was our Holy Mother revealing herself, then why wouldn't she reveal herself to a Catholic from a good churchgoing family and of good education, instead of a junior nurse of questionable character?

And they did make a big deal of her character.

The Committee was quick to pounce on the biographical details and reproduced a number of rumours, as the unfortunate expression goes here, as the gospel truth. They accused her of fornicating with a godless communist in her student days. In another example of their callous approach, they called her a penis-slasher and a Xanax thief. As a grieving father, I suffered the additional trauma of having to read these allegations. They said that she had walked out on her loving husband and was living in sin with another woman, a senior nurse, and that the two of them planned to raise a bastard child as husband and wife. It's unfortunate because this filth presented as the Committee's findings – mere rumours, unsubstantiated allegations and lewd innuendoes that are the fate of any working lady in this place – have become a matter of canonical record. Can we blame the poor fathers in our French Colony when they prefer not to send their girls to work?

The Committee of course thought that it clinched the argument by claiming that Alice Bhatti had spent two years in the Borstal jail after a conviction on charges of 'disorderly behaviour with intent to murder'. First of all this is factually incorrect: she was sentenced to eighteen months but she spent only fourteen months there and her sentence was reduced for good behaviour and exemplary moral character. And also, how can spending time in jail automatically be a proof of someone's guilt? Did our Lord Yassoo not spend two nights in the Sanhedrin's prison? As the Committee was writing its verdict with a pen dipped in the poison of prejudice, weren't there hundreds of thousands of our Lord Yassoo's followers languishing in prisons all over the world for saying His name or circulating a photocopied page from the Holy Bible, or just for believing in their hearts that Yassoo was the son of God? Try shouting that out in a public square in this place and you'll be lucky if you only end up in a jail and are not lynched on the spot.

There was a piece of photographic evidence that the Committee claims it lost; they claim they saw it, but, since they weren't sure of its authenticity, it was sent to the Colorado Institute of Authentification of Pictures and Symbols and was lost in the mail. According to the Committee's notes, 'It's a blurred picture but you can see a peacock, its wings stretched upwards, and framed in it was a head shot of Alice Bhatti as if she was dressed for a fancy-dress party.'

What were they thinking? Do they think that our poorly paid nurses with twelve-hour, six-day shifts, with a one-and-a-half-hour commute on each side have the time to go to fancy-dress parties? In peacock costumes?

I, Joseph Bhatti, father of Alice Joseph Bhatti, retired janitor for the Municipal Corporation, resident of French Colony, have been compelled to make this petition because Bishop Massey wrote in a side note that the peacock motif was a clever ploy to appeal to the European members of the Committee who make up the Congregation for the Causes of Saints, to give a touch of the exotic to this rather implausible fable and play upon the members' preconceived notion of our country.

In their so-called investigation, the Committee didn't take into consideration the biographical detail, which has been substantiated from multiple sources, that when Alice was twelve, I, her father Joseph Bhatti, rescued a baby peacock from the sewer and gifted it to her soon after her mother had been taken by Him. In my line of work I have rescued dead and almost alive human foetuses, hens, kittens, piglets, jewellery boxes and more puppies than I care to remember. It was said in the report that Alice Bhatti had claimed that she was brought up by a peacock mother. I am sure she said no such thing. It was a peacock, a male peacock, a dumb pet, and it had no hand in her upbringing and no part in the miracle of that night. The peacock could have easily become someone's meal. I am sure the members of the Committee have never been in a situation where they have contemplated eating a fancy pet. This was food for our people, not exotica. I saved it from becoming someone's dinner. And as far as her upbringing is concerned, I take full responsibility.

And what about the other witnesses, those who have nothing to do with the Sacred, or the Church, and those who hardly knew Alice Bhatti? There were at least eight witnesses who swore they saw a Toyota Surf floating two feet above the ground with its hazard lights on just before the likeness of our Holy Mother appeared on the roof of the OPD.

And what about the miraculous recovery experienced by that fat legless wretch who hobbled around the hospital with a skateboard stuck between her arse cheeks begging for Xanax? The lame shall walk, we were promised. And here the lame were skateboarding up and down a ramp so steep that even our ambulances find it hard to negotiate it.

As Our Lady of Alice Bhatti's peacock throne began to ascend and the kites became still in the air, their wings folded in respect, the same legless wretch came down the ramp skateboarding like a demon, standing on the board with her arms spread as if she had inherited the factory that manufactures Xanax.

As mentioned earlier in this submission, in our

neighbouring country a Caucasian nun starves poor people to death and is declared a saint. Here our poor Alice Bhatti cures the incurable and is declared a common criminal. Although she herself never claimed to have any miraculous powers, she always said, 'It's Him who cures. I just stitch up what has been cut open by life.'

All of the seventeen people who saw the apparition couldn't bear to watch the face of the apparition on the throne because it was so luminous, like the sun on a very hot day. It was only the mad skater who claimed that a gust of wind blew in her direction and unveiled the face for a moment and that She looked like a ghoul. The Committee pounced on the word – some suggested that they actually inserted it in the text of the report – and concluded that a holy apparition couldn't look like a ghoul. Does the word ghoul or its synonyms not appear in the Old Testament? Is the word forbidden? If you ask me, half our clergy look like ghouls.

The Committee also noted that if Alice Bhatti was considered so exalted at the Sacred after the miracle of the dead baby, why did she breathe her last at another, Musla hospital? First thing is, martyrs usually don't die amongst their own. (Lots of Musla martyrs do, but that is beyond the scope of this submission.) The second explanation is that the Sacred doesn't have an Acid Burns Unit, and it was Dr Pereira who put her in the ambulance and rushed her to another hospital, where her mortal body breathed her last. This was another one of Dr Pereira's futile mercy missions. As far as I am concerned, she had ascended to the heavens before that first drop of acid touched her face.

So the question remains, what did people see that night? Did they see only our Holy Mother? Or did they see Alice Joseph Bhatti – it pains me to remind you, my daughter Alice Bhatti – ascend with her to the heavens?

There is only one thing left to do, and that is to tell the complete story of Alice Bhatti, her birth and suffering and marriage and miracles associated with her, and then leave it to the people to decide whether she deserves to be recognised as Our Lady of Alice Bhatti. It's being done in the hope that common people hopefully don't share the prejudices of those who in the name of our Holy Lord have set up bloodsucking business ventures.

And since Sister Alice Bhatti's story can't be told without telling the story of her time at the Sacred, why not start the story when Alice Bhatti came to the Sacred, looking for a job?